"Kevin! Thank goodness you're all right," Julie whispered

"You scared the devil out of me. I've never had a patient faint before."

"Faint? Men don't faint!" Suddenly freed of her intimate hold, he grabbed the armrests to keep from tumbling onto his head.

"Then you passed out. Swooned. Had a case of the vapors. Whatever you choose."

Kevin was mortified and retaliated. "Get this damn chair right side up."

Julie stood defiantly above him, leaving him in an awkward and vulnerable position. "Not until I say so, Mr. Royce. It's too soon for you to be charging around. Next time you faint, I might not be around to catch you, and you could hurt yourself."

She left the room, and Kevin wondered, after this marvelous display, how the hell he was ever going to face Julie Bennett again.

ABOUT THE AUTHOR

Blind Faith is Maureen Bronson's first solo effort. She previously coauthored three other Harlequin novels. Maureen has set her story in Tolt, Washington, a charming town not far from her home, Seattle, where she lives with her husband. The couple recently celebrated their twentieth wedding anniversary. They have three children.

Books by Maureen Bronson

HARLEQUIN SUPERROMANCE
149–TENDER VERDICT

HARLEQUIN HISTORICALS
32–DELTA PEARL
96–RAGTIME DAWN

Blind Faith

MAUREEN BRONSON

Harlequin Books

TORONTO • NEW YORK • LONDON
AMSTERDAM • PARIS • SYDNEY • HAMBURG
STOCKHOLM • ATHENS • TOKYO • MILAN
MADRID • WARSAW • BUDAPEST • AUCKLAND

Published April 1992

ISBN 0-373-70496-8

BLIND FAITH

CHAPTER ONE

KEVIN ROYCE CURSED silently and rubbed his tender jaw. The throbbing pain eased for only a second before it once more roared to life, causing the whole side of his face to ache. Miserable, he took a deep breath and then a sip of steaming coffee, hoping the heat would work a miracle. It didn't, and he looked up from his desk to see Carlos Romero, his partner in Maximum Security Systems, smiling at him.

"No sympathy from me." Carlos waved his hand as if dismissing Kevin's agony. "If you'd kept your last appointment with the dentist, you wouldn't be in this fix."

"Remind me to be as compassionate the next time one of your mutts bites you," Kevin grumbled.

"When that happens, it's an accident." Carlos laughed unsympathetically. "You brought this toothache on yourself."

"Once a drill sergeant, always a drill sergeant."

"That's right," Carlos agreed.

Kevin leaned back in his chair and propped his feet on his cluttered desk. "The first time I saw you I thought I'd found El Diablo living in San Diego disguised as a Marine Corps drill instructor."

"I was good, wasn't I?" Carlos said with no attempt to hide his pleasure. "It's not easy to take a pampered little boy like you were and in just a few weeks turn him into a man who can defend himself."

"I don't think I'd survive your loving concern again," Kevin observed, shaking his head.

"I've got news for you, kid. In thirty minutes you're about to meet *the* master driller."

Kevin ran his fingers through his hair and groaned at both the pun and the stab of pain in his jaw. Three weeks ago he had returned to civilian life, packing his uniform away after twenty years in the Marine Corps, and made his way back to his hometown of Tolt, Washington to join Carlos. From the moment of his discharge, his damn tooth hadn't stopped throbbing.

"Quit frowning," Carlos told him. "Dr. Bennett's easy on the eyes, sweet to the ears, and her touch is as gentle as a summer breeze. If you scowl at her the way you are at me, she'll refuse to look in your mouth."

"Are you in love with her, or do you get a finder's fee every time you send a patient through her doors?" Kevin asked.

"Actually, I had to bribe her to give you another appointment. After canceling two, you're lucky she hasn't blackballed you."

Trying to get his mind off this morning's seven o'clock appointment with Julie Bennett, Kevin asked, "How many pups did Ariel have?"

"Four beautiful babies," Carlos bragged. "Their delivery took all night and I think I'm more exhausted than she is. The only reason I'm here now, and not in bed, is curiosity. I wanted to see if you're finally miserable enough to get that tooth yanked out."

"Thanks, but I'll do without the surgery. A few pills to kill the pain and I'll be on my way."

"Sure. If it takes a fairy tale to get you to the doc's, go right on believing that."

The office door swung open and Kevin's brother George sauntered in.

"Doctor? Somebody sick?" George asked, apparently catching the tail end of Carlos's remark. He shrugged out of his slicker and straightened the navy-blue shirt of his uniform, which identified him as a member of Tolt's police force.

"Drink this coffee and you will be." Carlos grimaced at the bitter brew in his mug. "Your baby brother makes it so strong it shrivels your tonsils."

Kevin was in no mood for his partner's banter. "It's guaranteed to keep me awake through the night shift and that's all I care about. I'm not a caffeine gourmet like you, Carlos."

George walked over to the coffeemaker and poured himself a mugful. "Tastes good to me." Every morning since Kevin had returned to his hometown, George had made it a ritual to stop by the security office on his way to work.

"Well, Chief, catch any bad guys last night or did we scare them all away?" Carlos asked the same question each day; it was a private joke between the men. George was Tolt's chief of police, and Carlos liked to tease him, maintaining Maximum Security was eliminating all his business in discouraging burglaries with its guard dogs and alarms.

Glancing at his watch, Kevin saw it was still early, but decided to leave. He felt his temper might get the better of him if one more crack were made about his appointment. He didn't know which bothered him most, his tooth, Carlos's razzing or the thought of that first whiff of the nauseating medicinal odor that permeated every dentist's office.

"Still raining?" Kevin asked George.

"It's slowing down. The weatherman says it'll quit soon. Leaving?"

"Yeah, I thought I'd get a head start on my day," Kevin answered nervously.

"Why so jumpy?" When Kevin didn't reply but just pulled on his jacket, George persisted. "Where're you off to this early?"

"To earn another purple heart," Carlos said. "Your brother wasn't nearly this terrified during his full tour in Nam. I keep trying to tell him Dr. Bennett isn't the enemy. Maybe you can convince him, George."

"Julie Bennett?" George pronounced her name as if he were chewing each syllable.

Kevin frowned. "Yeah, why?"

"She's a hard one," George said fiercely.

The pounding in Kevin's jaw suddenly intensified tenfold. "Hard? But Carlos said she was gentle."

"I'm not talking about her skill as a dentist. I've never set foot in her office and I never will. The only time we met was when she came bursting into the station, accusing one of my deputies of harassment."

His brother's vehemence surprised Kevin. "Harassment? That's pretty vague."

"Sexual harassment, she called it. Claimed my deputy said he'd tear up her speeding ticket if she'd spend the night with him. But my deputy swears it was the other way around, and Julie Bennett made the offer."

"Whom did you believe?" Kevin inquired. It didn't make sense that a woman, new to a small town like Tolt, would risk ruining her reputation and career by making a false charge.

"Butler's the best man I have on the force," George replied defensively. "Why should I take the word of some newcomer over his? He said she was only bellowing because he was going to report her bribe and she was trying to cover her tracks."

"Hogwash," Carlos commented. "Unadulterated hogwash. Julie Bennett is a lady and that's spelled with capital letters."

George flushed. "It was a judgment call, and I was justified in backing Butler," he retorted angrily.

Kevin knew that both George and Carlos were strong-willed, opinionated men and neither one would give an inch, so rather than stick around to umpire their argument, he left the office to drive across town.

He felt no urge to push the speed limit and enjoyed a leisurely tour of the deserted streets. When he had left Tolt, there had only been one traffic light in the tiny town and little to capture the attention of a rambunctious eighteen-year-old. But both Tolt and Kevin Royce had changed in twenty years.

He meandered through the back streets, noting the subtle signs of prosperity alongside minimal growth. Tolt's population had expanded, the business district keeping pace with the community's increasing demands, but it was still considered a sleepy town in comparison to many other cities in western Washington.

The explosion of growth in Seattle and many other communities around Puget Sound had changed the region so much that many of his old landmarks were missing. In fact, when he had landed at Sea-Tac International Airport after a four-year absence, he'd gotten lost in the maze of freeways, disoriented by the new housing developments and irritated by the crunch of midday traffic. But sixty minutes north-east of Seattle, his sense of dislocation had vanished when he'd spotted the rust-colored water tower on the outskirts of Tolt.

This morning Kevin was content to creep through the main business section, luxuriating in the pleasure of being home to stay. His attitude toward the rural community had been transformed, and rather than praying for its development as he had in high school, he hoped Seattle's urban sprawl would never spread this far.

He pulled into the clinic's empty parking lot, and his thoughts were yanked back to more urgent matters—his appointment and the woman who would be poking in his mouth. How could two men he admired have such divergent opinions of the same person? Was Julie Bennett a Madonna, as Carlos claimed, or a tramp, as George seemed to believe? There was only one way to solve the puzzle, and, much as he dreaded it, he would have to find out for himself.

He slammed the van door and walked across the damp asphalt to stand under the eaves by the main entrance. If he waited here, he wouldn't be able to avoid Dr. Bennett the moment she showed up for work, and it would be impossible to manufacture an excuse for driving away.

JULIE BENNETT cautioned herself to slow down as she neared the hospital zone and her clinic. She found it difficult to keep her foot off the gas, for she drove like she did everything, fast. There just didn't seem to be enough time in one day to accomplish all that needed to be done. This morning she'd tried to leave her apartment a half hour early, but her efforts had been sabotaged by a phone call from her mother in Florida. Now she wouldn't have time to review her patients' files over a cup of coffee during the quiet moments before her staff arrived.

Mentally readjusting her work schedule, she knew she would have no chart on her first patient, only a record of broken appointments. Julie wondered if Kevin Royce would keep this one. If he didn't, she was determined he'd pay for the hour, anyway. It was her policy to charge patients who canceled more than once without twenty-four hours' notice, and she had already cut him enough slack. In fact, if Kevin was anything like his pompous, pigheaded brother, she should charge him double.

Julie's office was in a clinic, one of eight multiplex buildings next to Tolt General Hospital. The medical-dental cooperative that had built the complex had intentionally chosen a site adjacent to the hospital, but had made sure the clinics were set back far enough from the road to retain their privacy. The long driveway was landscaped with trimmed laurel hedges and rhododendrons, making it difficult to see the offices from either the street or the hospital.

Rounding the last curve, her attention was caught by the blue lights of a police cruiser blocking the entrance to her building. She couldn't park in her nor-

mal slot and wedged her sedan into another. She rolled
down her window and heard the crackling of the
cruiser's radio. She jumped out of her car and jogged
up to the officer who had his back to her. If someone
was hurt, at least she could administer first aid until
the paramedics arrived.

"What's going on?" she asked the policeman in
front of her, who, she belatedly realized, was in a frozen stance, legs apart, arms extended and eyes trained
straight ahead. When he didn't answer, Julie looked
closer and saw he was aiming his gun at two men who
were sprawled on the wet sidewalk. Trying to grasp
what was going on, she rapidly surveyed the area and
noticed another officer to her left, aiming his weapon
in the same direction.

"Back away, lady," the first officer ordered.

Retreating a step, she stared at the men on the
ground. The small, scruffy one was obviously getting
the worst of the bargain. He was pinned down by a
much larger, stronger fellow who clearly wasn't intimidated by the revolvers pointed at him. Indeed, he
appeared to be having the time of his life, and she had
no doubt who the good guy was.

The flashing blue lights bounced off the victor's
dark hair, making it appear ebony, accenting a fiercely
handsome face and turning his perfect white teeth even
whiter when he smiled. His smile impressed her; he
was in fact saluting her with a marvelous grin.

She knew immediately who he was—the determined set of the square jaw and the Royce arrogance
were too familiar.

"Step away, lady," the officer repeated.

"Can you cuff this creep? Then we'll all be safe," Kevin suggested to the officers.

When he stood and hauled the suspect to his feet, Julie noticed a sack of prescription drugs spilled across the pavement. Obviously, Kevin had somehow interrupted a burglary of the pharmacy that was located two doors down from her clinic. If her mother hadn't called, she would have been alone in the building when the thief paid his visit.

Julie watched as the closest officer holstered his gun, walked over to manacle Kevin's prize and recited the man's constitutional rights. Shivering, she looked up for a moment and noticed that the rain and clouds had drifted north, allowing the first glimmers of morning light to warm the sky. Struck by Kevin's stature as he assisted the deputy, he appeared larger than life in the same way that the Cascade Mountains surrounding Tolt seemed taller, sharper and more regal when the sun first crested behind them. It was an appropriate analogy, she realized. Kevin was a mountain of a man with immense shoulders, an expansive chest and a narrow waist that tapered into streamlined hips.

Her assessment appeared to go unnoticed, but she felt guilty for ogling. He was more than just pleasant to look at and her eyes were magnetically drawn back to him. Shamefaced, she forced herself to speak casually. "Mr. Royce?" she said.

At her query, Kevin lifted his head and studied her. The lady who had been obscured by shadows was now bathed in the rosy sunrise, a flattering backdrop that softened her serious expression. Her beautiful russet-colored hair, sprinkled with raindrops, was pulled back at the nape of her neck. If they hadn't been strangers, he would have suggested she let her hair hang loose to frame her features.

"I feel compelled," he said, winking, "to reply, 'Dr. Livingstone?'"

Julie smiled. "Actually, Mr. Royce, it's Dr. Bennett."

Carlos hadn't exaggerated, at least not the part about Julie Bennett being easy on the eye and sweet to the ear. "Call me Kevin."

"We finally meet," she replied, her tone gently chastising as she extended her hand. "Or have you found another excuse for canceling?" Julie nodded toward the prisoner who was being prodded into the patrol car.

Now that his surge of adrenaline was subsiding, Kevin's jaw was starting to hurt again. Nevertheless he eagerly latched on to this latest excuse for postponing his appointment. "Sorry. I have to go down to the station to make a statement."

The second officer, who was standing next to Kevin, checked his watch. "That won't be necessary, Mr. Royce. Take a few minutes to answer some preliminary questions and we'll finish the complete report later."

"Good," Julie said, rummaging in her purse for her keys. "I'll be waiting for you, Kevin."

"Wait, Dr. Bennett!" The young officer stepped protectively in front of her. "Let me check your office. Then I'll speak to Mr. Royce."

"Thank you," Julie said, suddenly nervous. There might indeed be an accomplice lurking in one of the empty rooms, but she wished Kevin were escorting her instead of this baby-faced kid.

Her fear proved to be unfounded and it took only a few minutes to quickly inventory her supplies and determine that the thief had not tampered with her part of the building. Julie relaxed and tried to pump the deputy for details about Kevin Royce's part in catching the burglar, but the young man adroitly sidestepped her questions. Eventually she was left alone to speculate. She decided that before her new patient left her office this morning, she would drag every detail out of him.

When he finally appeared in her reception room, Kevin Royce was a different man. The smiling, confident hero had vanished, replaced by an apprehensive, glowering hulk who looked as friendly as a trapped badger. His eyes darted from side to side, searching the office as if he were in a hostile environment.

Trying to put him at ease, Julie nodded toward the window and said, "Despite everything, it's turned out to be a fine morning."

"Has it?"

Only two words, but venom saturated them. If she hadn't seen him so relaxed and amiable just minutes ago, she would have taken his animosity personally. Why had he changed so dramatically? Had one of the police officers said something to upset him?

"I'd love to stand here and exchange pleasantries, but I've other patients arriving soon. Shall we?" she asked, pointing to the hall.

Kevin didn't respond and Julie stepped behind him, subtly prodding him out of the waiting room. He allowed her to nudge him past the receptionist's desk and her private office, but halted abruptly in the doorway of the examining room. She took his elbow gently to guide him to the empty chair, but it didn't work—Kevin was rooted to the threshold.

"Mr. Royce, please move aside. If you don't, I can't get around you and into the room."

"Good."

"Don't you want me to examine you?"

"No."

His blunt reply startled her. "Then why are you here?"

He didn't answer.

The longer he stood in her way, the shorter his sentences became. Suddenly Julie recognized his behavior. The man was nearly tongue-tied with fear! Articulate, talkative people were known to become speechless when confronted by the reclining chair, the console of drills and all the other dental paraphernalia.

"I won't hurt you, I promise," she said calmly. "I can fix your tooth without any pain, but you need to sit down first."

Kevin tried to believe her, but gaining control of his terror wasn't easy. While he'd been in the Marine Corps, red alerts, incoming mortars and strafing artillery had never unnerved him as much as a visit to the dentist. "Come on, Royce. Move out," he muttered under his breath and stepped forward.

Julie resisted the urge to pat his arm and tell him he was a brave boy. Smiling, she waited patiently for him to sit down. When he finally leaned back in the chair, she clamped a paper bib around his thick, muscled neck and wondered where the hero of the hour had gone.

To still his panic, Julie sat down on her stool, put her hand upon his shoulder and locked her eyes with his. "Tell me how you caught the burglar this morning."

Kevin, grateful for the reprieve, eagerly snatched the opportunity to delay the examination. "I was here early, waiting for you, and noticed a light flickering around in the pharmacy. Anyone authorized to be in there wouldn't use a flashlight, so I called the police on my car phone."

"But you didn't wait for them." She hid her smile and waited for his answer. Kevin sounded as if he were making a report, his tone of voice formal and distant, his words precise.

"No. I decided to scout the exterior just to see how the guy managed to bypass the security system and get inside undetected."

"Why?" If she'd spotted an apparent robbery in progress, she wouldn't have budged from her locked car.

"Professional curiosity," Kevin admitted. "I own a company that installs security systems."

"What did you discover?" Julie found his dangerous pursuit intriguing.

As he spoke, Kevin relaxed visibly. "There was a ladder propped up on the end gable of the building. It took only a second to see that the wire to the klaxon had been snipped. A minute later I found where the thief had entered. He knew enough to smash the window rather than open it and break the magnetic connections of the alarm."

"And?" she prompted. What she really wanted to know was how Kevin had ended up wrestling with the burglar.

"Well, the cops hadn't come yet, so I waited until the guy was sneaking out and tripped him. Nothing fancy about it."

"Sounds pretty heroic to me," Julie said, smiling at his modesty. It was amazing that George Royce's brother could be so humble.

"Bull. I was just too cowardly to go in after him."

"You mean too smart." Julie sensed that he was downplaying his shrewd capture.

Her comment made Kevin laugh, but the moment he did so, his jaw burst into searing pain. It was so intense that he grimaced despite his concentrated attempt to hide it.

"Pretty bad?" she asked.

"A twinge now and then."

"To quote you, 'bull.' The side of your face is swollen. Open up, Mr. Royce," she said in a coaxing tone of voice.

"Kevin, remember? It makes me feel less like a patient."

"Then call me Julie, if it helps."

As she delicately probed in his mouth, she continued talking to him in a soothing tone. "You have beautiful teeth. When was the last time you visited a dentist?"

"Ahh . . ." Kevin gurgled, trying to speak with the mirror wedged against his tongue. Julie Bennett was the prettiest dentist he'd ever known, but she had the same irritating habit all of them shared. She asked questions when it was impossible to answer intelligibly.

"Why, you've never had your wisdom teeth removed!"

Reaching up, Kevin grabbed her wrist and pulled her hand away from his face. "Take those pretty little fingers out of my mouth, or I'll end up biting them off."

Julie laughed at the good-natured threat. "I think we'd better discuss your past dental care before we go any further."

"Insignificant. The last time I was in one of these chairs was twenty years ago."

"You mean you haven't seen a dentist since high school?" Her voice rose, expressing her shock.

"Close. Boot camp. Some old navy goat who went to school with the Marquis de Sade got a hold of me and that cured me for life. I haven't been back since."

"You sound proud of that." Kevin seemed to be bragging, but Julie found such neglect appalling. Nature had blessed him with remarkably handsome teeth, and it was a sin that he had not protected his gift with frequent checkups. "Let's get started on a full set of X rays."

After Julie had finished, she left him alone in the room. Kevin squirmed in the chair, waiting for her verdict. All through the series of X rays he had felt her disapproval and, for some strange reason, Julie's opinion mattered. Positive that all he needed was a few pills, Kevin was unprepared for the worried frown that crinkled her forehead when she returned.

"Well, Mr. Royce, I must give you your due. You're virtually immune to pain."

"I can generally handle minor discomfort," Kevin replied carefully. Feeling the throbbing in his jaw, he knew he damn well wasn't immune.

"As well as being too brave for your own good, you're not too quick about picking up on sarcasm. I wasn't paying you a compliment."

"Oh," Kevin muttered.

"By ignoring what your body was telling you, you've endangered your health. See this," Julie said, insisting he look at his X rays.

"What do I look for?"

"Here," she said and pointed to a dark spot on one film. "This shows the abscess surrounding your upper right wisdom tooth, which is impacted. The infection is eroding the bone and it won't be much longer before it breaks through to your sinuses."

Instantly Kevin felt light-headed at her graphic description, terrified of what she was going to say next. His stomach began lurching wildly until he could feel beads of perspiration dotting his forehead.

"The best oral surgeon in Tolt is Otto Hartmann," Julie said, continuing to study the series of X rays. "If I call him, he'll wedge you in right away. Could you leave work early if he can see you this afternoon?"

Intellectually Kevin couldn't argue with her, but emotionally the words, "oral surgeon," intensified his phobia. "I'll think about it," he told her. "And you don't need to bother calling your friend. I can dial a phone."

"After your infection is cleared up, Dr. Hartmann will be able to remove that tooth. He'll give you an anesthetic and you'll wake up wondering when he's going to start."

"All you dentists say the same thing."

"That's because it's true. Now, Kevin," she said, turning back to the films, "after you've tended to your wisdom tooth, you're going to need further work done on these two molars."

"I'm too busy to bother with all this nonsense. Surely this can wait a while?"

Julie could feel herself edging closer to exasperation with Kevin's flippant attitude. She decided to quit pampering him. A grown man who was brave enough to capture a felon could face the truth. "If I'm going to treat you, we'll have to overcome your childish fear. You must learn to trust me or I won't be able to help you."

At her accusation, Kevin looked as hurt as if she'd slapped him. "Wonderful chairside manner, Dr. Bennett."

"Please forgive me." Sighing, Julie took another tack. Kevin Royce was the most trying patient she'd treated since dental school. Four-year-olds were co-operative in comparison to this man. "Kevin, you can't stand the pain indefinitely. This isn't a matter of choice. This is an emergency. You must let Dr. Hartmann remove that tooth."

"Can't you just give me a few pills and then we'll talk about it?" he asked, struggling to keep the panic out of his voice.

"No, it can't wait. In good conscience, I must advise you that Dr. Hartmann should operate as soon as the infection's under control."

When Kevin didn't respond, Julie found her irritation beginning to override her professional detachment. Fighting to keep her tone of voice friendly and neutral, she continued, "If general anesthesia frightens you or the word surgeon is what has you stumped, I could give you a few healthy shots of Novocain, and pull the tooth right here. I'm qualified to do the work, but most patients are more comfortable and experience less bruising if they let an oral surgeon do the extractions."

When he still didn't answer, Julie turned to him and saw that all the color had drained from his face; his breath was coming in short, shallow gasps and his pupils were dilated. As Kevin's head slumped forward onto his chest, she silently reprimanded herself for not recognizing the depth of his terror. While she had been busy rationalizing his need to see the oral surgeon, Kevin had fainted.

Her training had prepared her for just such an emergency, but until this second it had only been theory. The textbooks claimed that generally a patient only stayed unconscious for a minute or two if he or she was just anxious, but healthy. Taking his pulse, she found it steady and strong; Kevin Royce certainly appeared fit.

"Come on, Kevin," she said and gently shook him. "Wake up. Kevin, wake up."

Glancing at her watch, she stared at the second hand sweeping around the dial. She knew that he wasn't in any danger, but it seemed as if he'd been out for ten minutes, not two. Julie grabbed a clean towel and squirted it with cool water. She wiped his forehead and cheeks, talking to him the entire time.

"You're all right, Kevin. I won't hurt you."

He wasn't responding, and her inner alarm bells screeched at her to do something more. Fighting off panic, she reasoned that what he needed was to have his head lower than his body. The only way she could accomplish that was to tilt the chair backward. Using the hydraulic pedal, Julie started to elevate his legs about twelve inches higher than his head, wincing as the old chair creaked. She took her foot off the pedal, but the chair kept on tipping back until Kevin was almost standing on his head.

It was too much of a slant and the worn bolts snapped. Kevin's inert body started to slide off the slick vinyl. Julie made a frantic grab for him, but his weight foiled her attempt; she threw her arms around his shoulders to save him from tumbling to the floor.

Before Kevin opened his eyes he was pleasantly aware of an intoxicating scent and a soft warmth surrounding him. Confused, he blinked and found he was staring into a pair of startled blue eyes. Was he dreaming? If this was a dream it was the first time he'd ever been held by an apparition that looked and smelled and felt so real. He clutched his fantasy, afraid of losing it too soon.

"Kevin! Thank goodness you're all right," Julie whispered, uncomfortably aware that her chest was shoved against his, her arms wrapped around his massive shoulders.

Even though he was crumpled in a heap at one end of the chair, Kevin made no attempt to move, but smiled mischievously. "Your bedside manner has improved, Dr. Bennett."

"You scared the devil out of me," she said. She relaxed her grip and sighed loudly in relief. "I'm a good dentist and my patients don't usually faint. You're my first victim."

"Faint? Men don't faint!" Suddenly freed of her intimate hold, he grabbed the armrests to keep from tumbling onto his head.

"Then you passed out. Swooned. Had a case of the vapors. Whatever you choose."

Kevin was mortified and retaliated. "Get this damn chair right side up."

"I can't. You broke it."

"Then give me a hand."

Julie stood defiantly above him, leaving him in an awkward and vulnerable position. "Not until I've written out your prescription and you've promised me you'll make that appointment with the surgeon I recommended, Mr. Royce. Until I say so, lie there and don't move a muscle. Besides, it's too soon for you to be charging around. Next time you faint I might not be around to catch you and you could hurt yourself."

She left and Kevin pivoted his weight in the chair until he was sitting on the tilted back, his feet firmly grounded and his head cupped in his hands. He swallowed a drill-field expletive. How the hell was he ever going to face Julie Bennett again?

CHAPTER TWO

BY MID-MORNING Julie's head was pounding as ruth-
lessly as a pair of cymbals in a college marching band
and she felt as if she had been working for two straight
days. On top of the excitement of the burglary and
Kevin Royce's fainting spell, her hygienist had called
in sick, forcing Julie to reschedule several appointments. Then an emergency, a child with a broken
tooth, had further disrupted the already fractured
timetable.

Feeling pulled in ten directions, she took advantage
of a brief respite between patients and headed to the
other end of the building to relax over a cup of coffee. Her friend, Theresa Post, was sitting at the table
when Julie entered the lunchroom and sank onto a
chair.

When she'd moved into her office last year, Julie
had become friendly with Theresa, a nurse for the
general practitioner next door. The clinic complex was
unique in that four separate offices shared a back
hallway along with a lunchroom and laundry facili-
ties. Though the building had been designed nearly
twenty years ago, as the antiquated alarm system and
Julie's equipment attested, it was still an efficient, ec-
onomical and sensible arrangement, which allowed the
different staffs to mingle and socialize.

"I thought once I was out of dental school life would be a cinch. This morning makes those years look like an extended vacation," Julie said, groaning and rubbing her neck.

"Want to match war stories?" Theresa commiserated.

"Is yours about a dimpled sixteen-year-old boy?" Julie shook two headache capsules into her hand and downed them with a gulp.

Theresa grinned wearily. "I have a theory," she said, burying her fingers in her short black hair and massaging her temples. "Each child should have two mothers. One to raise them from birth to twelve. Another, maybe a prison matron, to take over until they're twenty. It's either that or enlist Mark in the service, but they won't take him until he graduates. If the army wanted him, he'd have khaki on those little buns so fast—"

"Come on," Julie protested, "Mark's a good kid."

"You think so? How about convincing his vice-principal?"

"He was kicked out again?"

"The word is 'suspended.' If Mark keeps it up they're going to suspend him from the gym rafters."

Julie laughed. "What did he do? Talk the kids into going on strike against the school lunches again?"

"No, the fleet of pizza trucks didn't block the bus zone, he didn't publicly correct any of his teachers, and he didn't even get caught throwing ice cream on the ceilings."

"Sounds like a good week to me," Julie said. "Better than average."

"Not quite. He was running a poker game in the boys' locker room."

"Gambling on school property is serious," Julie said, trying to keep from smiling. "How much did he win?"

"Win? Mark's into his classmates for twenty-five dollars," Theresa said, smirking. "It serves him right."

Julie sat up straighter. "You aren't going to bail him out and pay his IOU's, are you?"

Theresa dropped her gaze and studied the tabletop. "I already did. I know, I know," she said, holding up a hand to halt Julie's lecture, "but if I didn't help him, his friends wouldn't speak to him."

"So?"

"So I made him promise to mow the lawn all summer."

"Just like you made him promise to rebuild the fence after he crashed his buddy's motorcycle through it? Seems to me I saw you hammering the slats back up, not Mark."

"This time I really mean it," Theresa said firmly.

From Theresa's manner, Julie knew she had pushed enough. "How was your date last night?" she asked, switching topics.

"His idea of a good time was to take me to the laundromat and treat me to a can of pop and a candy bar from the vending machine after he was done matching his socks."

"You're not serious. No one is that bad," Julie said, laughing.

"You don't believe me? Let my cousin introduce you to a few of her husband's friends. If they quit scratching long enough to shake your hand, we declare a local holiday. Enough about my scintillating social life. I heard you almost interrupted a robbery this morning," Theresa said, getting up and refilling both their coffee cups. "Scuttlebutt has it Kevin Royce saved the day and visited you afterward."

"Do you know him?" Julie hoped so. Maybe Theresa could tell her something about Kevin, who seemed to be the antithesis of his brother.

"Not personally, but I've heard lots of stories." Theresa's brown eyes sparkled playfully, hinting she had all kinds of gossip to share.

"I thought we made a deal we weren't going to gossip anymore," Julie said.

"All right," Theresa said and sighed loudly. "I'll only tell you what I've seen with these two eyes. Fact one. He's single and handsome."

"I know that much."

"You noticed? Dr. Julie Bennett actually took her blinders off and noticed a hunk?"

"I look at men, I just don't drool like some women I know," Julie teased, pointedly cocking her head in Theresa's direction. "Besides, it was impossible to ignore how big Mr. Royce is when he broke an exam chair."

"How did he manage that?"

"Fainted."

Julie summarized the story and had to slap Theresa on the back after she started to laugh and choked on her coffee. Once she was able to speak again, Theresa said, "Sounds like you were a little hard on him."

"No, I wasn't. He was ready to deny how dangerous his infection was. Denial seems to be a common Royce trait."

"Don't condemn Kevin just because he has the misfortune of sharing George's last name." Rising and putting her cup into the sink, Theresa turned and leaned against the counter. "Cain and Abel were brothers, too, remember?"

"Okay, okay. Next time I see him, and I doubt very seriously that it will ever happen, I'll be nice." Julie paused, glanced at her watch and continued. "I'm shorthanded today and have to get back. Don't let Mark wiggle out of mowing the lawn."

"You mean the way you're wiggling out of this conversation? Don't you want to stick around and hear the rest of the facts about Kevin Royce?"

"Later." Julie crossed the room to Theresa's side and added her mug to the collection building in the sink. As Julie started down the short hallway, she heard Theresa calling out, "He was a hero in Vietnam."

Curiosity about Theresa's comment was promptly replaced by more immediate concerns the moment Julie picked up her next patient's chart. The young woman was developmentally disabled and had a difficult time understanding instructions, making her appointments a test of patience and diplomacy. Julie was taking her time while she leafed through the records when a muffled groan of frustration from one of the examination rooms pierced her concentration. She leaned in to investigate the sound.

She recognized a familiar, long-legged, massive form sprawled on the floor. Kevin was crouching beneath her dental chair but, because of his size, there wasn't much room to maneuver. The chair and cabinet, as well as her rolling stool and the instrument tray, took up what little space there was in the tiny room.

"What are you doing?" Julie cried in disbelief.

The crescent wrench slipped off the nut again and Kevin bit his lip to keep from cursing. "How anyone can work all day in such cramped conditions is beyond me," he said, trying to look up at her. He banged his head on the chair and stretched out flat on his back in exasperation.

"You haven't answered my question."

"I'm trying to fix this thing," Kevin told her. "I don't want you bouncing your next patient on his head, just because you won't pay for decent equipment." Why did he find it so annoying that Julie had small offices with only basic equipment? He spent hours cooped up in that cubbyhole of a monitoring room at Maximum Security Systems with office equipment that was a mismatched, motley accumulation scavenged from a surplus store. This layout of Julie's, with its floor-to-ceiling windows, was spacious compared to their fireproof, windowless room. When he and Carlos had more business, which meant more funds, they would upgrade the office furniture and hire personnel to stare at those computers. Until then they were each making do, alternating duty on the night shift.

"I'm sure you noticed that the room is vacant, Mr. Royce," Julie explained slowly. "That's because the repairman hasn't arrived yet. And if you don't like my equipment, I'll be glad to double your bill and apply the difference to a down payment on a new chair."

While Julie was speaking, Kevin had slithered back under the chair. He turned the wrench one more time and felt the rusted bolt break free. "Cancel the repairman, Dr. Bennett," he said and started on the next bolt.

"But not your appointment with Dr. Hartmann." Julie left the room grinning. Ordinarily she wouldn't have taunted a patient that way, but Kevin Royce had earned a nip or two of revenge.

"Not in my lifetime," Kevin said quietly, confident that the prescription he had filled would be enough to stave off further treatment.

He reasoned his way out of the appointment by telling himself Julie had been exaggerating his problem. Besides, he didn't have dental insurance to cover the bill. The high price of insurance was one of the few negatives of being self-employed, but he considered it a small sacrifice for the freedom of being his own boss.

Finished with his repairs, Kevin squirmed out from under the chair and looked at the outdated equipment Julie had inherited from the former owner. It was obvious she was in the same predicament as Maximum Security. They were both trying to win over the population of Tolt and establish their careers on a shoestring budget. Carlos had spent six months building their operation before Kevin retired from the corps, and they had expected that their new company would have to drum up business, inspiring trust in the community before they were accepted. He wondered how long Julie had been here and guessed only a year or two at the most. George had sneered that she was a newcomer to Tolt, but his brother considered anyone an immigrant if they had not graduated from the local high school.

The comparison set Kevin thinking. He was baffled by George's story about Julie Bennett. It just didn't make sense that she would jeopardize everything, the years of school and her financial investment in Tolt to avoid a silly speeding ticket. The truth had to lie somewhere between George's distorted version of Julie and her conservative mien. Either Julie Bennett had a split personality or George was the poorest judge of character Kevin had ever known.

Mulling over the situation again, he waited for the next room to empty, toolbox in hand. If one chair was creaky and dangerous, they all were, since they were of the same vintage. Julie passed him without lifting her eyes. She had her arm wrapped around a pudgy girl's shoulders and he was struck by her caring manner.

He entered the second examining room and tested the chair. Deciding it needed to be secured better, he set to work. He hoped that by making the repairs he would show Julie he was sorry about his earlier behavior without sacrificing his pride or risking the whip of her quick tongue. It had always been like that for him—action was far easier than words.

Julie was busy with her next patient, waiting for the set of impressions to harden, and Theresa's last comment, "He was a hero in Vietnam", echoed in her head. She wondered what Kevin had done to earn the Marine Corps' respect and realized she could speculate forever. Whatever it was, he must have been extremely young at the time, because he wasn't over forty now and the war had ended almost twenty years ago.

She jerked her attention back to her patient and forgot about Kevin Royce until later, when she caught a glimpse of him out of the corner of her eye as she walked past room # 3. There he was, hunched over his toolbox, intent on his task.

Silhouetted against the windows, he was captivating. Julie secretly catalogued his crisp profile: proud forehead, bold, straight nose, ample lips and square-cut jaw. Madison Avenue admen would sell their mothers to get their hands on a man who looked as good as Kevin Royce did at this moment. Virile, rugged, capable, yet still vulnerable. Julie decided he would look equally handsome and seductive in a tuxedo or overalls.

He felt her gaze, it was almost tangible, and knew it was Julie before he even looked up. Some women had ice in their eyes, others revealed only a deadening indifference, but Julie's blue eyes radiated an energy that reflected her emotions.

Kevin cocked his head. "Had a few spare minutes and thought I'd mend this baby, too," he said, patting the worn chair.

"Thank you, but that wasn't necessary."

"I wanted to do it." Holding up a washer, he said, "I'm almost finished with this beast. Two down and one more to go."

"What's wrong with them?" she asked, wondering if she should order new chairs. Her budget could barely withstand such a major expenditure, but the safety of her patients had to come first.

"Come here," he said, pointing at the base, "and I'll show you."

She crouched close to him and studied the rusty pile of sheared bolts on the floor. "How did they get like that?"

"Years of mopping these vinyl floors and letting the water pool around them. You should consider remodeling and putting in sturdy carpet."

"Tell my banker," Julie said.

"I think we must deal with the same Scrooge. Mine insists I pay off my first loan before I get another dime."

Head to head, Julie inhaled his light after-shave and examined his tanned features. There wasn't anything weak or ordinary about this man. "That's right," she said, remembering his comments about his company. "You run your own business, too. Maximum Security Systems."

From what she had learned over the past year, she could testify that starting a new business was risky, and it still scared the devil out of her. Anyone willing to take such a gamble had to be either crazy or courageous. Julie hadn't made up her mind which she was; probably a bit of both.

"How's the pain? Did you pick up both of the prescriptions I called in?" It was an unnecessary question. She could tell from the clarity of his eyes he hadn't taken the pain pills, anyway.

"I picked up the antibiotic, but the other's unnecessary."

"I hope so, but it'll be at least twenty-four hours before there's any improvement."

"So the druggist explained."

His stubbornness was astounding, but there was no point in trying to change his mind. "Will the chairs be safe enough when you're finished?"

"As good as new ones."

Julie ran her hand down the outmoded shape and sighed. "Not quite, but thanks for your help. And don't forget to call Dr. Hartmann. Give him a chance to prove he can help you."

From his position Kevin had a spectacular view of her legs as she retreated. Julie's calves curved gracefully to her ankles. She looked as great from behind and below as she did from the front and above. Angles. It was all a matter of angles, and Julie Bennett's physical geometry was perfect.

When he finished with the chair in the third examining room, he closed up his toolbox and headed for the van. Before he reached it someone called his name. "Mr. Royce? Kevin, isn't it?"

"Yes?"

A stocky man crossed the parking lot and extended his hand. "Ted Underwood. I manage this clinic cooperative. Wanted to thank you for this morning."

"Forget it." Kevin tossed his gear into the truck. "But you'd better update your security, or I can guarantee it'll happen again."

"Precisely why I'm standing here," Mr. Underwood explained. "How about analyzing our needs and submitting a bid?"

Grinning, Kevin nodded. "Happy to. I'll need you to walk me through so I can count doors, windows and other vulnerable accesses."

"Do you have the time right now?"

"Sure do," Kevin said. "Just let me grab my clipboard."

They started at the complex farthest from the van. It was the first of the eight multiplex buildings, and by the time Ted Underwood and Kevin reached Julie's office, Kevin had nearly finished his evaluation. Since each building was basically the same, it wasn't going to take much time to complete the estimate.

"Hello, Ted," Julie said pleasantly as she looked up from a patient, but did a double take when she saw Kevin. "Back again so soon, Mr. Royce?"

"You've adopted me but don't know it yet, Dr. Bennett."

"I thought you hated dentists," she said, noting the easygoing way he leaned against the door frame and the crinkle of suppressed laughter around his eyes.

"Only when I'm a patient."

"Then there's a chance we won't always be enemies, after all?" She tried to sound flippant, not wanting Kevin to know how important his answer was.

"Are you a gambling woman?"

"Occasionally."

"Then it's a top-heavy chance, Dr. Bennett."

Julie caught his wink and couldn't help but grin as he strode from the room. "Odds that good?" she said to his retreating figure.

Kevin didn't turn around but simply stuck his thumb high in the air—clearly a sign of his supreme confidence. She had never known a man whose body language was so revealing. Returning her attention to her patient, Julie whistled gaily under her breath.

"Do you ever mix business with pleasure?"

"What?" For a second Julie thought her patient had asked the question, but realized Kevin had stuck his head back into the room. "It depends on the pleasure and which business I'm mixing it with," she answered lightly.

"Great," he said. "I'll call sometime."

JULIE WAS SURPRISED at herself for encouraging Kevin and even more amazed that he was interested in her, but after a week of waiting to hear from him, her initial astonishment turned to anger. She told herself that she had been temporarily deluded by his brash masculinity and self-confidence when he was actually nothing but an annoying, squeamish patient.

Yet despite her stern admonition to put Kevin out of her mind, Julie found herself surrendering to her curiosity and pumped Theresa for more information about him. She felt a twinge of conscience at breaking her own rule about not gossiping, but she couldn't resist, so was disappointed when she discovered Theresa knew very little. All her friend could say was that Kevin's brother George had offered him a job on the police force, which he had refused.

The following morning, after finishing with one of her preschool patients, Julie removed her rubber gloves and took the phone call her receptionist had put on hold. "Otto Hartmann, Julie. Your referral, Kevin Royce, was a no-show for surgery this morning. We called his office, but they said he was out in the field. I thought maybe you knew where he was since I heard his firm is rewiring your place."

"I guess the stories I've heard about the Tolt grapevine are true."

"Blame it on Ted Underwood. He can't stop saying enough good things about Kevin Royce."

"Hope Mr. Royce's security system is more reliable than he is," Julie observed.

"He kept his consultation appointment and I agree with your recommendation. His tooth's in bad shape."

"Now, if we could just convince Mr. Royce."

"If you happen to see him, tell him he can't waste time playing games," the oral surgeon went on.

Julie sighed and explained that Kevin wasn't just nervous around dentists, but became frozen and panic-stricken the moment he opened the office door.

"As long as your antibiotic temporarily alleviates Kevin's discomfort, I'm worried that he'll ignore the tooth altogether," Otto told her. "If you find him, send him over and I'll have a man-to-man chat with him, stressing the urgency of his problem. Then we'll book an appointment for the next day while he's still more frightened of me than of his imagination."

"Thanks, Otto," Julie said, knowing how hard it was to juggle a calendar at the last minute. She'd hung up and started toward her office when her receptionist called after her.

"If Dr. Hartmann is looking for Mr. Royce," the young woman said, "I saw a van marked Maximum Security parked next door."

"How long before I have a break between patients?"

"Not until lunch."

Julie's temper simmered throughout the morning, alternating between understanding and anger. It had taken three attempts to finally get Kevin through her front door, and she wasn't about to let him pull his shenanigans on her colleague. Assistants, nurses, anesthesiologists, all had to be paid, regardless of whether or not the patient showed, but this was a factor that Kevin had apparently not taken into account.

At noon, Julie didn't simply go looking for Kevin, she went hunting and found her quarry in the basement, splicing wires.

"Mr. Royce," she called loudly and firmly.

He pivoted and smiled when he recognized her. "What an unexpected pleasure, Dr. Bennett."

Ignoring how good he looked in his jeans, his rolled-up sleeves exposing muscular forearms, she said, "I'm surprised you're working after your surgery this morning."

He glanced at the calendar on his watch and blanched. "Damn, I forgot."

"Just like you forgot your first two appointments with me?"

"It's the truth."

"Why do I find that implausible?" She didn't come right out and accuse him of purposely ignoring the appointments, but the tone of her voice made her implication clear, she hoped.

"Get off my case, lady. I've been busy getting these buildings wired so all of you white-coated jawsmiths and sawbones can go home nights and know your offices are safe."

Julie almost laughed at his words. The man definitely had a command of the language, but she wasn't exactly tongue-tied, either. "Listen, you retired embassy bellhop, don't try to feed me a line about how you're sacrificing your health to protect me. It doesn't wash. Now you *may* have honestly forgotten, but I think we both know why you did."

Kevin glared at her. "Your compassion is touching, Dr. Bennett."

"It vanishes when it slams up against stupidity."

"And I don't respond well to nagging. In fact, I become downright obnoxious," he said, almost visibly digging his heels in.

"Do you respond to whining?"

"Nope."

"Tears? Would they soften your crusty nature?" She tried not to smile, but the comic turn their argument was taking had defused her temper.

"Blackmail doesn't work, either."

"How about if we sit down and talk rationally?"

Kevin unhooked his tool belt and placed it on the concrete floor. His black lunch pail was in the corner and he retrieved it, holding it aloft as if to inspect its contents. "Why not? Time to knock off for lunch, anyway."

"Enough in there for two?" She sat down on a crate next to him and gulped when he opened the lid. "What in the world do you call that?"

"Pickled herring, stale crackers and a banana."

Julie picked up the brown piece of fruit by its withered stem and dangled it in front of him. "No, this used to be a banana, but now it qualifies as compost."

"It didn't look so bad at four o'clock this morning," he apologized. "How about a hamburger? My treat."

"Considering the option of sharing your garbage pail," she said, chuckling, "a greasy burger sounds wonderful."

Kevin snapped the lid shut and, without looking, tossed the offending lunch over his shoulder. "Your pleasure, your choice," he said, gallantly offering his arm.

They'd made it no farther than the parking lot before Ted Underwood spoiled their plans. "Kevin," Ted hollered, "we have a problem!"

"What do you do, Ted, hide in the shrubbery and wait for me?" Kevin inquired.

"Sorry, but every time Theresa Post answers her phone it disconnects and your computer demands she punch in her code."

Rubbing his chin, Kevin asked, "Is she the only one in her office that happens to?"

"Yeah, that's what's so weird."

"Not really. Certain female voices have a pitch that the computer falsely interprets as a code tone."

Ted shook his head. "Can you fix it right away? Theresa's on the phone a great deal. You know, calling in prescriptions, checking on patients."

"No problem. I'll just have to go back to the office and change a chip in our main terminal." Kevin looked at Julie and shrugged helplessly. "Can I have a rain check, J.B.?"

"Certainly. I really didn't have a lot of time for a long lunch, anyway." Surprised at the nickname—no one except Kevin had ever called her by one—she decided that "J.B." was nice, personal without being nauseating.

"Catch you later," he said and ran back into the basement to collect his tools.

It wasn't until she returned to her office that Julie realized she and Kevin had never settled a thing. They had bantered, argued and teased, but had not discussed his urgent need to see Otto Hartmann. Kevin had guided the conversation away from her subject. He was as elusive as a moonbeam, a master at making her forget her objective.

Sitting down at her desk, Julie was perplexed. Why did she involuntarily choose words like "elusive" and "moonbeam" to describe Kevin? They were way too poetic to be applied to a man she barely knew. Certainly, they were not the kind of words she would apply to his brother George.

CHAPTER THREE

THE RINGING of the telephone shattered Julie's pleasant dream. Refusing to open her eyes, she groped blindly around the nightstand until she found the receiver. "Hello," she croaked sleepily.

"Good morning, J.B. It's Kevin Royce. Would you like to cash in your rain check tonight?"

"You sound as chipper as a rooster at dawn and just as aggravating." She pried her eyes open to glance at the alarm clock and groaned. "Do you know what time it is?"

"Oops, five-thirty. I'm sorry. I forgot to check."

He sounded appropriately contrite and Julie immediately forgave him. "Are you always this annoyingly cheerful in the morning?" she mumbled, trying to stifle a yawn.

"With my schedule, this is early evening. At least for today," he explained. "I just finished an all-night stint in the monitoring room and it's time to relax."

Sitting up in bed, she quickly calculated how many hours he worked in a day and yawned again at the thought. "How can you stay up all night, work today on the clinics and even think of going out tonight? Are you a masochist?" She stood up and walked toward the kitchen, trailing a long cord behind her. She set the telephone down on the counter and punched the button on the coffeemaker, overriding the automatic setting.

"Afraid I'll fall asleep with my face in a plate of spaghetti?"

She tried to laugh but found it impossible this early. "We're eating Italian, I take it," she said as she stuck her mug under the coffee maker.

"Is Angelo's all right with you?"

"Wonderful." She was indifferent to food in the morning and didn't even want to think about it.

"Don't worry," he said, "I'll grab a nap before I pick you up at seven."

"Will you be at the clinic today, prowling in the basement again?" She tried to sound appropriately indifferent about his schedule, but knew she was secretly hoping to catch a glimpse of him.

"I finished late yesterday after you left. Ted wanted the system operating by this weekend."

"Then seven tonight," she said.

After she hung up the receiver, she realized she felt perkier than she normally did after her third dose of caffeine. Turning on some lively music and stretching out the morning kinks, Julie wondered how Kevin had found her unlisted number. Perhaps he enjoyed special privileges granted to someone in the security field. The thought was unnerving. How much else had he uncovered about her personal life? The balance in her checking account? Where she was born and the date? Which university she had attended? The interest on her bank loans?

There were very few ways Kevin could have found her phone number, and only one seemed likely. George Royce. She would have given her phone number to

Kevin if he had asked, so it galled her to think that George might have been the one to hand it out to his baby brother without even considering that she might object, or that such meddling was a violation of professional ethics.

The thought was enough to spoil her entire day, but Julie refused to give George Royce that much power over her. It was a beautiful morning; bright red tulips, canary-yellow forsythia and pink-throated azaleas were blooming right outside her window, and she sat down to soak in the spring radiance, determined to enjoy every minute. Besides, what did it matter how Kevin had found her telephone number? But however hard she tried to push George out of her mind, every time she relaxed her guard a tickle of irritation crept back in.

At Maximum Security, Kevin had put the phone back in its cradle and was sipping his coffee. Imitating Humphrey Bogart, he saluted the receiver and said, "Here's looking at you, kid."

"Still seeing Ingrid Bergman in the shadows?" George asked from behind him.

Switching roles as he turned his head, Kevin aped Gomer Pyle. "Gol-l-l-y, Sarge, you shouldn't sneak up on a guy like that."

George just shook his head. "It's a wonder you never spent any time in the stockade with that talent of yours."

"The week of detention in my sophomore year taught me high school principals don't have a very good sense of humor, and I figured my officers wouldn't be any more amused."

"You were a nervy little kid," George said and smiled. "It sure is good to have you back home." He squeezed Kevin's shoulders affectionately as he walked by.

"Everything all right?" Kevin was worried. The lines and smudges around George's eyes and the slump in his shoulders made him look twenty years older than himself, rather than eight.

"Just tired. We had another false alarm at Nickerson Electronics last night. They've got to do something about it. My men aren't taking the calls seriously anymore," George replied. "Last night was the third night this month we were sent on a wild-goose chase, and it's only the second week in May."

"Exactly what do they do over at Nickerson?" Kevin inquired. "All I know is that they own one of the most sophisticated security systems available, and that Carlos supplies their guards with trained dogs."

"Nickerson Electronics is a major defense subcontractor for the federal government," George told him. "Right up your alley. Their contract requires them to take every reasonable precaution," he went on. "Bud Nickerson, the owner, claims no one breached the system, but every siren in the plant was wailing. What do you think?"

"Why ask me? Call up the people who installed the system. Have them check for bugs in the monitors or maybe a computer malfunction."

"Can't." George eased himself stiffly and carefully into a chair. "The company folded a few months back."

"Who the devil's watching the shop now?" Kevin was appalled at the idea of Nickerson's sensitive information being rendered vulnerable by a lack of maintenance.

"Bud decided to handle things in-house, since computers are what they're experts at."

"Who's in charge? Bud?"

"No. He's hired and fired a couple of guys in the past few months, and his latest packed up and left this morning. I told Bud to hire you to straighten things out."

Kevin let his chair spring forward. "Thanks, but I'm not qualified to come in and repair a complex program that I'm not familiar with."

"Fertilizer, and you know it."

"George, it takes too much time to fumble with another man's work, check it out, test the system."

"Do you mean that you're too busy to accept the job if Bud offers it to you?" George asked in audible disbelief.

"No."

"Then what's the problem? Nickerson Electronics has more than enough revenue to pay you anything you ask. The company's reputation is at stake, and Bud wants to see you today."

"Sounds like an imperial summons. What did you say about me to get his attention?"

"Nothing much. I just told him you were a wizard with computers and had the highest security clearance issued by your former employer."

Kevin rolled his eyes. "Fabulous. Didn't you consider you might sound like a prejudiced relative?"

"Gripe, gripe, gripe. Is that all the thanks I get? Just meet with Nickerson and then decide if you can handle it." George got up and left without saying anything more.

As Kevin collected the papers in front of him his eyes fell on Julie's home and office phone numbers. Ted Underwood had provided a complete list for Kevin's files of all the clinic co-op members in case an emergency arose. Reminded of his date with her, Kevin smiled. It seemed lately that every time he closed his eyes, he saw her laughing blue eyes, long cinnamon hair and half-parted, velvet lips. Still smiling, Kevin picked up the phone to set up an appointment with Bud at Nickerson Electronics.

IT WAS NEARLY SIX O'CLOCK by the time Kevin finally left the electronics plant. He had inspected the perimeter of each structure, first checking every contact point for signs of tampering or of any condition that might be causing the system to trip, setting off the false alarms, but each unit seemed to be in perfect working order. Next he had scrolled through the computer files, looking for a programming error that might activate the alarms. Nothing obvious had jumped out at him. If anyone had tampered with the program, they had been bright enough to cover their trail. After promising Bud he'd be back first thing in the morning, Kevin hurried home in his van.

Racing into his apartment, he didn't even check for calls on his answering machine. There was only enough time to jump into the shower and dress or he would be late picking up Julie. The force of the cool water turned on full blast stung his skin, pins and needles banishing his fatigue.

He toweled dry and looked into the mirror. His hair, after a month, was starting to grow out, and he was finally beginning to look like a civilian. This was his first date since his return home, and he fumbled nervously with his tie, feeling like a teenager dressing for dinner before the prom. He had taken his date to Angelo's on that long-ago night, too.

Angelo's—so many happy occasions had been celebrated at that restaurant! His parents had observed each of their wedding anniversaries and birthdays with a family dinner there, and George had proposed to Denise in a back booth of the dimly lit main dining room. The restaurant held some bittersweet memories, as well. After Kevin and George's parents had been killed, Angelo had comforted his two "adopted" sons with meals at his private table, tucked into a corner of the fragrant, hectic kitchen.

But dwelling on the past wouldn't get him to Julie's on time, and Kevin increased his pace. One final hesitation to check the crease of his pressed trousers and the knot in his tie, and he was out the door.

JULIE SPUN in front of the mirror and enjoyed the way her flared linen skirt swayed. When she had first bought the teal-colored sweater and skirt she had shuddered at the price, but now she was happy she had splurged. She didn't have many opportunities to wear anything other than conservative work clothes or jogging shoes and shorts, and this was one of her few really nice outfits.

As she was dabbing perfume behind her earlobes, the doorbell rang and Julie took one last look into the mirror. All week long her thoughts had kept returning to Kevin, vacillating between distraction with him and irritation with herself. What unbidden emotion would seize her tonight when she faced him?

"Hi!" she said cheerfully as she flung the door open, expecting to see the solid bulk of his body. When she stared into empty space, she quickly adjusted her gaze and found Theresa planted on her doormat.

"Little overdressed for our tennis game, aren't you?" she asked, twirling her racket in her hands.

"Oh, no, I forgot all about it."

"Gee, I wouldn't have guessed."

"Clever girl," Julie said and motioned Theresa inside. "I'm sorry. I accepted a dinner invitation from Kevin. When he called me this morning, I wasn't awake enough to remember I'd promised you to play tonight."

"Good, because I'd hate to think you'd turned Paul Bunyan down in favor of letting me clobber you again on the court," Theresa said.

"And you wonder where Mark gets his smart mouth?" Julie commented. "He's merely an understudy."

"Forget the insults. I'm only interested in the sordid details. Tell me everything."

"There's nothing to tell. It's our first date." Julie tried to sound as nonchalant as possible.

"What's he have over my cousin? Other than a job and his own hair, of course." Ever since they had become friends, Theresa had been trying to play matchmaker between Julie and her own unending supply of unattached male relatives. After months of badgering, Julie had finally agreed to have dinner with one of Theresa's cousins. The evening had been such an absolute disaster that Julie would never agree to another blind date.

"Goodbye, Theresa." Julie gently pulled her friend toward the door.

"Call me when you get home, if it isn't too late. I want a full report." Theresa started to leave and saw Kevin coming up the walk. "Your logger is here, and does he look great! If you get tired of him, he can park his shoes under my bed anytime he wants."

"Behave yourself." Julie laughed in spite of herself.

Kevin noticed Theresa, but his attention was riveted on Julie. She looked elegant and sophisticated tonight, much more approachable than she did in her white lab coat. As he stepped closer he could see her eyes were smiling mischievously, and was intrigued by the touch of impishness in her expression.

"Hello, Julie. Hi, Theresa. On your way to play tennis?"

"Tennis has become my favorite hobby since the health club hired that gorgeous instructor."

Kevin laughed. "How long have you been playing?"

"Long enough to know that cute men running around in shorts are good aerobic exercise for this old heart. I'm late. Have a good time, you two."

Kevin somehow suspected Theresa had made a comment about him and searched Julie's blue eyes for a clue. Their happy glint reassured him that her friend's assessment must have been fairly positive. "You look lovely, Julie. Whatever you call that color, it's perfect for you."

Graciously accepting compliments had never been easy, and she had to force herself to say, "Thank you."

"Are you ready, J.B.? I'm starving," he said, pulling her out the door.

ANGELO'S was a subdued din of bustling waiters and hungry patrons, but Julie and Kevin were immediately escorted to a secluded table next to a window. Several times in the past year Julie had dropped by this restaurant but had always had to wait at least an hour for service.

"When did you make our reservations?" she asked, unfolding the ivory linen napkin in her lap.

"This morning."

"Amazing. Whom did you bribe?"

"Angelo's a friend. After our parents died, he helped George keep me under control."

"I had no idea, Kevin," she said.

Kevin heard the compassion in her voice and realized she wanted to know more but was too polite to pry. He appreciated her tactfulness. "I was fifteen when my father's plane plowed into the side of a mountain," he went on. "They were on their way back from celebrating their twenty-fifth wedding anniversary in San Francisco."

"My father died when I was thirteen, so I can imagine how difficult it must have been to lose both your parents. I'm sorry."

"It was hard at first, but George took good care of me," he replied. "I owe my brother a lot."

Julie smiled and nodded, afraid that if she said another word, Kevin would notice she didn't share his opinion of George.

"Enough of my childhood. I'm more interested in you," Kevin said.

"Nothing too exciting. I was born and raised in West Seattle and graduated from the University of Washington. After I finished college, one of my professors told me about a dentist he knew in Tolt who wanted to retire. The terms were reasonable, so I bought the practice and here I am."

"You make it sound so easy. What about the struggle to get through school? Why did a beautiful young woman like yourself decide to torture people for a living?"

"Kevin," Julie said and stopped for a moment to take a sip of water and gauge her words. "You and I need to establish a few ground rules before we go any further. I'm proud of what I do. The service I provide to this community is a vital one, and I don't hurt people. If you had been to see a dentist in the past twenty years, you'd realize we've improved our techniques just a bit."

"You mean dentist bashing is out?"

She saw the rebellious glint in his eyes and her irritation vanished. "You leave my profession alone, and I won't repeat the rumors I've heard about Marines being seagoing bellhops." She saw his jaw twitch at the insult and knew she had scored a point.

"Fair enough. Any other rules?" He didn't know a thing about her personal life, but couldn't imagine a woman as lovely and intelligent as she was sitting home for lack of dates.

"Just be honest with me," she said softly.

"Do you always ask people to be honest with you, or do I enjoy special privileges?" He could tell Julie's request was merely a preface; she was visibly edgy, biting the corner of her bottom lip.

"Does your occupation give you access to the phone company's records? Or possibly George's files?"

Before Kevin could respond to her odd question, a waiter took their order for cocktails.

"George has the right to see the phone company's records if he has a case that requires it, but I don't have any reason to poke around in them," Kevin said once the waiter had left. "Why?"

"So your brother just had to pull a few strings to get my number?" Julie suggested as blandly as she could manage.

"George had nothing to do with my asking you on a date."

"How else could you have found my private number?"

Kevin could feel his jaw clenching and took a gulp of beer to douse his anger. "Do you always make wholesale accusations? Did it ever cross your suspicious little mind that my company requires the address and phone number, both personal and business, of every customer who subscribes to my service? Ted Underwood was kind enough to supply them."

Mortified, Julie squeezed her eyes shut to block out Kevin's stony expression. "Kevin, I'm sorry. No, it hadn't entered my—what did you say?—'suspicious little mind.'"

"Here, try one of these stuffed fresh figs." He picked one up from the antipasto tray the waiter had delivered and handed it to her. "They're the best."

"Are you suggesting I put something other than my foot in my mouth?"

"Let's just say we're even now. After we order, why don't we talk about a safe subject? How about the weather?"

While Julie studied the menu she realized she would have to tread gently when it came to Kevin's brother. An only child, she had never shared a bedroom with a sister or fought with a pesky younger brother. She envied Kevin his intense loyalty to George. From now on she would have to be careful of what she said, for Kevin had made it quite clear his brother was not an acceptable target for random potshots. And, much as she detested George, she admired Kevin's devotion. There was nothing more abhorrent than betrayal within a family. The bitterness she still felt toward her stepfather for losing all her college money still surfaced if Julie thought about it for any longer than a heartbeat.

"Why did you set up shop in Tolt?" Kevin inquired. "I'm sure there were plenty of other opportunities for a woman with your skills." He mentally patted himself on the back for making a positive comment on her profession.

"Tolt's a pretty town. It's bound to grow and the price was reasonable. Logical, dollars and cents types of reasons. Why did you come back?"

"All sentimental ones. This is where I was raised, and George and his wife, Denise, are here. I've lived all over, but, as the saying goes, there's no place like home. My own backyard is only a few minutes from skiing, fishing, sailing, or backpacking, and I can still drive to Seattle in an hour." Kevin shook his head. "I sound like a real estate agent with an overpriced house to peddle."

"It's nice to hear someone who loves his home boast about it," she said, smiling. "You missed it, didn't you?"

He studied her face and wondered what family background had created such a striking profile. Julie had a perfect mouth with smooth, kissable lips, a classic nose, and a pair of blue eyes that were full of unshared secrets. "I thought we were going to talk about you?"

"My life hasn't been nearly as exciting as yours."

"Stick with me, kid, and I'll change that," he said in his best Bogey voice.

"How are you at Donald Duck?"

"Passable," he said in an excellent imitation.

His ability to mimic famous voices made Julie laugh, and the rest of the dinner continued on a light-hearted note. She couldn't remember ever having a more pleasant evening. They made each other laugh, but it was a gentle form of humorous repartee; everything was perfect as long as they didn't discuss Kevin's family.

"If you had a free Sunday and the weather was nice, how would you spend the day?" Kevin asked suddenly.

Twirling a long strand of angel hair pasta around her fork, Julie didn't need any time to think of her first choice. "I would hop in my car and start driving. I like to explore back roads and follow them just to see what

I can find. Ever been to Lebam? Concrete? Mossy-rock?"

"Not for years. What do you do when you get to these exotic destinations?" he teased. Kevin was intrigued by Julie's fascination with the whistle-stop towns of western Washington.

"Poke around junk stores, check the local paper for garage sales and auctions."

"Why?"

"Because I like dusty little shops and quiet country roads," she said and added a generous measure of cream to her coffee.

"I had you pegged as the type who liked lounging in the sun with a good book or prowling through a mall."

The waiter discreetly left their check and Julie was sorry to have the evening end so soon. "I hate lying in the sun. It drives me bonzo because it's a total waste of time. I also detest malls. I want to be outside doing something, meeting new people, discovering unfashionable places."

Kevin handed the young man his credit card and the waiter glanced at the name imprinted on the plastic. "Pardon me, Mr. Royce. Dinner is on the house."

"What?" Kevin was sure he hadn't heard correctly.

"Compliments of Angelo," the young man insisted.

"Oh, no," Kevin said, putting the card back into the waiter's hand. "Tell him I appreciate the gesture, but I'm paying."

The credit card was set down again and the waiter said, "Thank you for dining with us, Mr. Royce."

He walked away before Kevin could object. "Excuse me, please, Julie. I have to go straighten this out with Angelo. This must be his way of welcoming me home. He's probably trying to make me feel guilty for not bringing you back to meet him before we were seated."

She waited at the table, and before Kevin returned, the waiter asked if she would like her coffee refilled.

"Mr. Royce is lucky to have Angelo for a friend," the young man said as he began clearing the table.

His undisguised sarcasm surprised her. "Do you know Mr. Royce?" she asked.

"Not personally. I was told that he has dinner here nearly every night."

He walked away with the loaded tray, and Julie's suspicions began to simmer anew. Did Kevin really think she was dumb enough to believe that their "complimentary" meal was an error? She had no trouble envisioning George abusing an old friendship, and apparently Kevin followed in his brother's footsteps.

Kevin reappeared and stood at her side. "Angelo's left for the evening. I'll sort this out tomorrow."

"How naive do you think I am?" Julie inquired while she pulled her wallet out of her handbag. "It's plain to me that if your name is Royce, you don't have to pay. That was acceptable when you were fifteen, but now it's despicable, and I want no part of it." Without counting the contents, Julie emptied her wallet and slapped down the money. "This should cover the bill."

"For heaven's sake," Kevin implored her, "put that away! I'll take care of it tomorrow."

"Consider it my treat."

She whipped around and was marching across the crowded dining room before Kevin could grab her arm. He was stalled behind an elderly couple and had no choice but to wait while the lady negotiated her walker through the aisle. By the time he made it to the front door, Julie was halfway across the parking lot. "Julie! Wait!"

She either didn't hear him or was ignoring him. Whatever the reason, he wasn't about to stand out on the street, hollering after her. Amazed at how fast she could clip along in her high heels, he jumped into his van and caught up with her at the intersection.

"This is ridiculous. You arrived with me and I'm taking you home," he told her, leaning out of the passenger window while he tried to steer.

Julie acted as if she were deaf and Kevin invisible.

"I'm not going to let you walk," he said.

"And who gave you the authority to tell people what they can or can't do? Your brother? Are you making a citizen's arrest?"

Kevin stepped on the gas and pulled onto the side of the road, where there was a wide shoulder. He watched her start to turn around, then stop and face him. Standing with her purse clenched in front of her as if she were holding a dangerous weapon, she waited for him to reach her.

"Can you honestly say you didn't know a thing about that little arrangement?" she demanded furiously. "How stupid do you think I am?"

He picked a handful of small rocks and began pitching them across the street into an empty lot. "Actually," he said casually, "I staged that scene for your benefit. All those people were just actors, the restaurant doesn't really exist, and Angelo is my code name." He brushed the dirt off his hands.

His explanation was so calmly stated and so ridiculous that Julie started to laugh. It was clear that, insulting though her accusations had been, Kevin wouldn't allow himself to be drawn into an argument. She admired his sense of humor and self-control. "Is it all a cover for the spaceship you're building for NASA?"

"How did you find out?" Kevin asked. "They weren't supposed to tell you."

She thought about the three-mile trek to her apartment. If he was gracious enough not to leave her stranded, the least she could do was accept his offer. "High heels and hiking don't mix," she said and opened the van door.

Kevin started driving before he spoke again. "I know what you're thinking, but you're all wrong. You think that George accepts free meals from an old friend, abuses his position of authority, and I jumped on the bandwagon."

Julie rubbed her feet together, and the only sound to be heard was the faint swish of her hose sliding back and forth.

"Well?" Kevin demanded.

"The thought did occur to me," she admitted quietly.

"That's just great, Julie. If you think my brother is a cheat, what category does that put me in?"

"I don't know," she said and wrapped her arms around herself. Even though it was mid-May, the night was chilly and she felt cold. "Was it his idea for you to open Maximum Security? Did he guarantee success?"

He pulled up at a stop sign and glanced over at her. Darkness obscured her face but he understood what she was implying. "You're assuming George accepts gratuities from people, which we both know is illegal. And you think people will be afraid to use any security business except mine, because he's my brother."

"The facts all point in that direction," Julie said hesitantly.

"Just like the facts pointed to your trying to get out of paying a traffic violation by offering Butler your body."

She gasped. "Where did you hear that filthy lie?"

"Everyone in town knows about it."

"People are saying that about me?" she whispered.

Kevin could hear the horror in her voice and regretted repeating the slander. He leaned across the span between the seats and touched her arm, but she shrank away from him.

"You and your brother are both alike. You're both cheats, only you're not as smart as George. He doesn't get caught."

CHAPTER FOUR

'I'M LEAVING,'' Julie told her receptionist the following afternoon. "I'll be back in time for my three o'clock."

She had tried to forget the fiasco of her date with Kevin, but it was impossible. Last night Theresa had accused her of always assuming the worst about him, and her conscience still plagued her today. Had she condemned him without solid proof?

Angelo was the only person with an answer, and she used her delayed lunch hour to pay him a visit. When she opened the heavy wooden door, she paused to let her eyes adjust to the dim lighting before she walked across the restaurant's deserted vestibule. A short, stout man with silvery-gray hair was busy on the telephone, taking reservations.

"A table for one?" he asked as soon as he was free.

"I'm not here for lunch," Julie said. "I was hoping I might speak with Angelo."

"I'm ashamed of myself," he said. "A beautiful woman knows my name and I can't greet her properly."

Julie smiled at his old-world chivalry and introduced herself. She watched his face for a flicker of recognition as he returned the greeting and, when she didn't see one, she continued. "I had dinner here with Kevin Royce last night."

"You have a complaint? Your food was bad? I'm so sorry, Miss Bennett."

"No, everything was delicious. Our waiter was polite and kind. Too kind. That was the problem," Julie explained.

"A complaint because the service was excellent?"

She heard the disbelief in his voice. "Not really. The problem came when we tried to pay for the meal. I don't understand why the waiter refused to let Kevin pay for our dinners."

"Unusual, I agree. Please have a seat while I see if anyone in the back can explain."

"Thank you."

It was just minutes before he returned. "Would you be kind enough to join me in a small snack?"

"Angelo," Julie said and placed her hand on his arm, "I didn't come here to wheedle a free meal out of you. Really, all I care about is finding out why Kevin wasn't allowed to pay for our meal."

"Humor an old man, Miss Bennett. Eating alone isn't good for the digestion."

"You make it impossible to say no," she said, smiling. Angelo made her feel as if she were doing him a favor by accepting his hospitality.

"Wonderful."

After they were seated, he said, "There's a logical explanation for last night's misunderstanding. Your waiter was new, it was his first night, and I had given him instructions that Mr. Royce wasn't expected to pay for his meals. He didn't recognize Kevin, only the last name on the credit card. A simple case of mistaken identity because I forgot that there are two Mr. Royces in town again.''

Julie was surprised that Angelo openly admitted that George accepted gratuities. Her opinion of George Royce had been poor before Angelo's explanation, but now she despised the police chief for abusing an old friend's generosity. She could tell there was more that Angelo wasn't saying, but out of respect, Julie asked no more questions. Instead, she listened attentively to Angelo reminisce about Kevin's high school years, his days of glory as a football hero and his agility on the basketball court. Angelo was clearly the product of a bygone era. Now she understood why Kevin was so fond of him.

"The pizza was excellent and so was the company," she said when they finished.

"Please, my dear, come back to visit, eat some more pizza, make me smile. Besides, my cooking will put some meat on your bones, so Kevin can find you in the dark."

"You're outrageous," Julie told him, laughing.

"One of the rewards of surviving this long is that people overlook eccentricities." Angelo patted her hand. "Julie, a bit of advice. Look farther than the end of your lovely nose for the truth. Sometimes it hides in the shadows."

All the way back to her office Julie puzzled over Angelo's cryptic comment. It didn't make a particle of sense, but there was one fact that was painfully obvious—she owed Kevin Royce an apology.

But, urgent though her need was to clear her conscience, Julie couldn't escape until she finished with her last patient at seven o'clock. Two days a week,

Tuesday and Wednesday, she offered early-evening appointments to accommodate people who couldn't leave their jobs during the traditional workday. It had been a good marketing strategy, enticing new clients into her office, and substantially increasing her practice.

Relaxing at the front desk, she thought about how she might make amends to Kevin. Even though her pride was still smarting at his repeating the malicious lie about her, she had been the first to jump to false conclusions. Kevin was no more guilty of accepting a bribe than she had been of offering one.

As she rifled through the charts and found his, she scribbled down his address on a slip of paper. He had used his files to contact her and she had immediately assumed the worst. Now here she was, employing exactly the same tactics to locate him. The similarities between their actions were too great for her to brush them aside, and she realized that her prejudice against George had come back to haunt her again.

Hurrying out the door, it occurred to her that she would probably miss Kevin. He had said that he handled the monitoring station on alternate nights, and she knew all too well that he had been free last night. Still, she was obligated to try. If she waited until tomorrow, she was afraid she would lose her courage.

But first, a quick stop. Goodies from her favorite delicatessen would be an appropriate peace offering. After she'd filled a large wicker basket with enough cold cuts and salads to excuse both slander and libel, she headed for Kevin's apartment.

He lived in the middle of a huge complex of anonymous units. They all looked identical, and if she wasn't careful, she would be knocking on the wrong door. The large numbers on the front of each building assured her that she wasn't the only person concerned about getting lost in the jungle of beige siding and tidy asphalt.

Finally she found his apartment. "Please be home," she said under her breath as she knocked on the door. If he slammed it in her face, she'd hate to admit how disappointed she would be, but knew she would have earned it.

After what seemed like minutes, the door opened. "Julie!" Kevin exclaimed. "What in the world—?"

"A bribe, so you'll accept my apology." The word had just popped out, and Julie wondered if he would misunderstand and think she was being sarcastic. "I jumped to false conclusions without any proof."

"Come in. Please." He stepped aside and gestured for her to enter.

Julie glanced around the small living room and saw that he only had two pieces of furniture, a nondescript couch and a large, well-worn recliner. It was obvious Kevin had not invested much effort in decorating his apartment, but he had several interesting statues and carved figurines on a bookshelf against the wall.

Handing Kevin the basket, she walked across the room to inspect the largest piece. It was a bust of a young Asian woman. Her ebony hair was pulled back from her delicate porcelain features and a tight mandarin collar fitted around her long, graceful neck. The elaborate design of her robe was intricately painted and Julie ran her finger across the raised pattern.

"I found her in Hong Kong," Kevin said.

"She's lovely." Julie lifted her eyes and looked directly at him for the first time since he had opened the door. "Hong Kong has always sounded so glamorous. What was it really like?"

"Crowded, expensive, humid and incredible." He couldn't describe the romance of Hong Kong, the beauty of the harbor as the sun faded and lights began to dot the flotilla of boats bobbing side by side, the excitement of finding a tiny shop filled with treasures hidden down a crowded, twisting street.

She pointed at the basket. "Aren't you curious about your surprise?"

"Yes, but I need to apologize to you, as well. I shouldn't have repeated what I damn well knew was a lie and I had no right to humiliate you." Kevin toyed with some loose change in his pocket and continued. "If you'll give me another chance, I'd like to get to know you better, Julie."

"I'd like that, too."

Kevin was amazed at how easy it was to be honest with her. Julie Bennett was a bright, attractive, sensitive woman, and he was grateful their first two encounters had not sabotaged what he hoped might become a special relationship.

"Do I still deserve a present?" he said with a devilish grin.

"I think so," she said and helped Kevin unpack the food.

"Let's sit by the fire," he suggested after he poured them each a glass of Chablis.

Julie sat down on the carpet next to him. "I didn't know if you'd be home. Thank goodness you were."

"For the next few days I have banker's hours while Carlos covers my night shift. I'm going to be busy with a complicated job."

"Carlos?"

"Yes, Carlos Romero."

"I know him," she said.

"He's my partner. We were in the Marines together. I started out hating him because he was my drill instructor in boot camp and ended up opening a business with the guy."

He explained how Carlos had been discharged six months earlier and had done most of the preliminary work on establishing Maximum Security Systems. Julie paid close attention to what he was saying about his plans for the business. His goals were ambitious. Many people wandered through life without any clear objectives, accepting what fell at their feet, but not Kevin. He knew what he wanted and was willing to work hard to get it.

Shifting her eyes away from the fire, she studied his solid build. There wasn't an ounce of fat on his body, and his short-sleeved knit shirt was pulled taut across his back. Kevin Royce was every woman's dream. What would it feel like to run her hands across his back, tracing the outline of each muscle? She imagined removing his shirt, and realized it didn't matter whether his chest was smooth and sleek or covered with dark curls.

Julie was so engrossed that she jumped when he moved unexpectedly and jerked her back to reality. He reached across the small gap between them and touched her hair. She tipped her head back, luxuriating in the way he was coiling it around his fingers.

Lately she had been wondering if she should have it cut in a shorter, more contemporary style, but had always liked it long. From the way Kevin was toying with it, he did, too. When he moved his fingers to her shoulders and gently kneaded the rigid muscles, she sighed softly.

"Angelo called me just before you arrived," he said, continuing his massage. "He told me all about your visit and warned me to treat you right. You must have made quite an impression on that Italian rascal."

"He's a character, all right, and a diehard fan of yours."

"If I tell you what else he said, besides raving on about you, will you try to listen with an open mind?"

The strained tone of Kevin's voice alerted Julie that he was going to mention George. "I'll do my best," she said, wishing she had never heard the man's name. That policeman was bound and determined, even when he wasn't around, to ruin any chance she might have of getting to know his younger brother.

"George doesn't pay for his meals because he can't afford to," Kevin said.

"But—"

He interrupted her by placing his fingertips upon her lips. "My brother makes a good living and shouldn't have to sponge off his friends. But Angelo said George really doesn't have the money, and he was adamant that he couldn't say why."

She could tell that Kevin was upset, but decided the best thing to do was to simply listen without saying a word.

Dropping his fingers from her lips and starting to rub her neck again, he continued. "I don't understand what's going on. It's not as if George has a large family to raise. He and Denise have never had children. And he's lived in the house that Mom and Dad left us all these years, so the only payments he has to make are the property taxes and insurance premiums. Where in the hell is all his money going?"

"Medical bills?" Julie suggested.

"They haven't been sick," Kevin said. Standing up, he paced back and forth in front of the fireplace, each stride demonstrating his angry turmoil. "Even when I was overseas, I called him at least once a month. George would have said something if there was a problem."

"Then," she said, joining Kevin in front of the fire, "why don't you just ask him? Don't accuse him of anything, but ask him nicely to explain."

"It's about all I can do." He cushioned one of her slender, long-fingered hands between his own. "Enough about George. I need to be positive you don't believe I had anything to do with the misunderstanding at Angelo's."

"I wouldn't be here if I did." Julie looked up and touched his cheek, feeling a trace of stubble. "Let's forget last night ever happened."

"Bless a woman with a feeble memory. But there's one thing I need to say before we bury the past," he said seriously. "I want you to hear it from me first."

Julie's heart began to pound. This was the type of line that was a common opening statement from married men. Surely Kevin wasn't married! "Go on," she said as calmly as she could manage.

"When I was twenty-three I married a Dutch girl. I was stationed in The Netherlands as an embassy guard in The Hague and I fell in love with a secretary there."

She stepped back, trying to break free of Kevin's hold, but he wouldn't release her. "Please, Kevin," she said as her composure threatened to crumble.

"What's wrong? Are you so old-fashioned you won't date a divorced man?"

"Divorced? You're sure?" She knew the question sounded moronic but Julie didn't care.

"About as positive as I can be," he said and scratched his head. "If not, my ex-wife and her husband have a major problem. She's happily married to a naval officer and has three children."

"Kevin Royce," Julie said and jammed her hands on her hips, "can't you make a simple, declarative statement? Wouldn't it have been easier just to tell me you're divorced with no children?"

"I guess so, but it seems a little blunt. I didn't just blurt it out because I know what it's like to go out with women who outline every disaster in their personal life on a first date. It always sounds like they're whining." He added another log to the fire, then sat down on the floor again and patted the space next to him. "Did you think I had a family hiding in the broom closet?"

Feeling guilty for having nearly condemned him once again without any real provocation, she sat down close to him, one knee touching his. "I don't believe in blind faith."

"So I've gathered."

"This is starting to feel like a therapy session. Do you have any more skeletons to dig up and dissect?"

Kevin held his hands up in submission. "Not me. Clean as the driven snow."

"Somehow I doubt that," Julie said, relief overpowering her. "You want me to believe you stayed in the barracks every night, polishing your shoes and brass belt buckles the entire time you were in the Marines? Does my head look hollow?"

"Well," he said and laughed, "I did leave the base once or twice, but I'd rather hear about your escapades in college than bore you with my humdrum tales."

"How about the first time I pulled a tooth? It was one of the most exciting days of my life."

He fought the unpleasant clenching of his stomach at the mention of teeth. "No, thanks. I have a better idea. Let's quit discussing both your past and mine." Kevin scooted behind Julie and wrapped his arms around her waist, easing her back against his chest. He liked the feel of her firm body wedged against his and the sweet scent of her hair that sparkled with burnished highlights.

"All I care about is this moment and how much I want to kiss you," he said, resting his chin on her shoulder, his lips close to her ear.

His warm, moist breath caressed her neck and Julie felt goose bumps cover her arms. It was an innocent spot for a man to kiss a woman, but as his lips nuzzled her skin Julie's reaction was far from chaste. She tilted her head and swept her hair aside in an unspoken bid for Kevin to continue his delightful nibbling.

Before she knew what was happening, Julie found herself pivoted around. The firelight flickered in his dusky eyes and he wore a satisfied grin. She watched him part his lips and moistened hers in anticipation.

His mouth covered hers with a forcefulness that frightened her for a moment. Kevin wasn't just kissing her; Julie knew he already wanted to make love to her. It was too soon for her to consider such a step, but she didn't want to let him go, either—not yet. Curling her arms around his neck and drawing him closer, she rubbed her hands across his back, delighting in the strength of the hard muscles.

He nudged her lips apart and circled the tip of her tongue with his. Slipping one hand from beneath her back, he trailed his fingers up and down her rib cage, ever closer to the swell of her breast. She knew she should sit up and put an end to the increasingly intimate contact, but was enthralled by the way he made her feel. Each nerve in her body screamed for his touch.

"Would you care to adjourn to the other room?" Kevin inquired, straightening.

"A tempting offer," she said, pulling his hand away, "but impossible."

"Impossible or improbable?" Kevin bent his head to take a gentle bite of her neck.

"No chance this side of heaven or hell." She wiggled out of his grasp and tried to get to her feet as gracefully as she could, but a painful yank on her hair stopped her. "Ouch!" she cried.

"Your hair is tangled around the button of my shirt," he explained as he tried to free the twisted strand.

He finally resorted to wriggling out of the shirt and handing it to Julie. When he stood up, her eyes followed him, and she couldn't help staring at the magnificent image he presented. A small sprinkle of brown hair was centered on his chest and narrowed to a thin trace at the waist of his jeans. She had seen posters of men in similar poses, but none of those models had had the presence of Kevin Royce.

Gritting her teeth, she ripped her hair off the button, scrambled to her feet and mutely handed Kevin his shirt. If she didn't leave now, Julie knew she would be tempted to accept his invitation. And that would be a catastrophe.

CHAPTER FIVE

JULIE SLOWLY SLIPPED her hands down through the Styrofoam pellets and connected with cool, smooth porcelain. The box had been delivered to her office early in the afternoon but she hadn't found a spare moment until now to open it. It had no return address, Fragile was boldly printed on each side and Confidential was scrawled across the front.

She gripped the object and pulled it out of the box. Rising out of the sea of white packing was Kevin's statue. The Asian lady she had admired last night was even more breathtaking in direct sunlight. Astonished by his generosity, she took the edge of her jacket and wiped away the last shreds of Styrofoam before she searched in the box for the teak platform. Taped to the piece of beveled wood was a note.

Dear Julie,
You seemed to admire her last night and I wanted to repay your thoughtfulness. Please accept her as proof of my sincerity and affection. One lovely lady deserves the other.
Kevin

She traced her finger lightly across the neatly printed message and savored the moment, committing every wondrous sensation to memory. Then she looked up Maximum Security's telephone number. Julie didn't expect to reach Kevin, but at least she could leave a message.

"Just tell Kevin Royce that Julie Bennett called and thanked him. He'll understand," she said to the young man who answered.

Julie looked at the statue and studied it once more. The figure's regal head was proudly held high; she had a serene expression in her beautiful, almond-shaped eyes and wore a slight smile on her lips. The statue looked as if she were savoring a cherished secret, and Julie couldn't help but smile at the happiness she sensed. It was amazing what a talented artist could do with simple clay and paint.

Although she was hoping for a phone call, Julie assumed she wouldn't see Kevin again for several days. So when she walked out of the clinic and noticed his van parked two slots away from her car she felt an involuntary rush of excitement.

Kevin watched a spontaneous smile light Julie's face when he caught her eye. She couldn't hide her emotions any more than he could perform a ballet solo, and he grinned at the image. He couldn't successfully guide a woman through a waltz without flattening her toes.

"Kevin," Julie said when he climbed out of his van and walked up to her, "I don't quite know how to thank you. I feel almost guilty that you parted with something you value so much."

"Believe me," he said, lightly brushing his hand across her cheek, "you should have her. When I found her, I knew I wasn't buying her for myself. I was just keeping her for a little while until she found a home."

She started to thank him again, but he put a finger against her lips. "Are you hungry?" he inquired, breaking the serious mood. "I have to be back at work in just over an hour, but I wanted to see you."

"Absolutely." Kevin's query felt like an invitation to a college study date and Julie was flattered that he had taken the time to spend his one free hour with her. She hitched up her skirt and climbed into the van.

Kevin pushed the gearshift into Reverse and made an elaborate show of backing out of the parking spot to hide his response to the brief glimpse he'd had of Julie's slim, stockinged legs. Her skirt was straight and moderately short and, when she had been struggling to get into the van, he'd caught a flash of long, curved thighs. Damn it, he wanted more than an hour with her, he wanted the entire night.

"Do you like good old-fashioned hamburgers and thick chocolate shakes with a side order of crispy onion rings?" Kevin asked, pulling onto the arterial. "This place isn't fancy, but their burgers are the best."

He looked at her with such hope she wouldn't have said no even if she'd been a staunch vegetarian. "Only if I can have a chocolate malt."

Close to the edge of the freeway but hidden behind a gas station with a busy grocery mart was an old-fashioned drive-in. Hanging from poles at each parking stall were illuminated menus with phones to call in your order so that your food could be delivered to the car. It looked like something out of the 1950s, not a reproduction but an original.

"I've been up and down this road a dozen times," Julie exclaimed in amazement, "and I've never noticed this place!"

"It's an anachronism. The owners don't need to advertise because the local people keep them busy. All the high school kids congregate here on weekends."

The hour they had to eat and visit wasn't nearly long enough, and Julie was disappointed when they had to leave. "Too bad you have to go back to work."

"If it wasn't absolutely necessary, believe me, I wouldn't," Kevin replied, visibly frustrated.

LATE THAT NIGHT Kevin's frustration escalated when he received a phone call at his office from Bud Nickerson. There had been another false alarm. "I don't understand it," Bud said to Kevin. "There's no sign of forced entry and the system's working."

"But that's impossible. If the system were working, it wouldn't be tripping." Kevin was exhausted, and his inability to diagnose the problem in Nickerson Electronics' computer was adding to his exasperation.

"I know it doesn't make any sense. I even stayed late to see what happens when I'm not around," Bud explained. "No one knew I was still in the building when the alarm went off. I checked it out myself. The system is working the way it's supposed to."

"I don't know what to say, Bud. There has to be a malfunction somewhere."

"That's obvious, but how long before we find it? Days? Weeks? This is getting ridiculous."

He knew Bud wasn't accusing him of incompetence, but Kevin was beginning to doubt himself. "So far every program I've checked has been clean. There's no sign of a virus or tampering."

"I'm disconnecting the system and doubling the guards and dogs. At least they're reliable."

"That'll be expensive," Kevin warned.

"What do you think it'll cost me to lose my government contracts because I can't secure my buildings? I want both you and Carlos in my office first thing tomorrow morning."

At the end of his shift, Kevin was promptly relieved by a man Carlos had hired and trained just over a month ago. He headed home to shower and change clothes before heading back to the office to meet Carlos.

Kevin explained to his partner why Bud was deactivating the system. "Nickerson Electronics does more than create software for the defense department. They're assembling computers that could be used to design and develop sophisticated military weapons."

Carlos blanched, his olive complexion taking on an ashen hue. Kevin nodded. "Bud has every reason to be nervous."

"You don't think..."

"I don't think anything, yet. But I'm damn well going to find out. While I'm searching through those computer programs, you need to train the rest of Bud's people to work with the dogs."

Carlos beamed. "Two days is all I need to have a full crew outfitted and in place."

"How about six o'clock tonight? Bud refuses to use the system again."

"That means I'll have to be there tonight myself. Who'll handle the monitoring room?"

"Who else?" Kevin returned dryly, gesturing as he spoke.

"We need to hire three more people, Kevin. One for the night shift, another for the office and a relief for both days and nights in the monitoring room."

"Can we afford it?"

Picking a piece of lint off his slacks, Carlos said, "We can't afford not to. Otherwise, we'll have to start turning work down."

"I'll call an employment agency and set up interviews for late this afternoon. We don't have time to screen people ourselves." Kevin picked up the phone and was halfway through dialing when the other line rang, so he picked it up and responded.

"Good morning, Kevin. This is Julie. How would you like to go to a party tomorrow night?"

Her voice still sounded sleepy, and he had a provocative image of her lying in bed, her tousled, sunstreaked hair fanned across the pillow, soft, sculpted shoulders bare and the covers slipped down to reveal just the top of a luscious, kissable breast.

"Kevin? Are you there?"

"You have my undivided attention." He wondered what she would say if he told her just how focused his attention was.

"Theresa invited us to her fortieth birthday party on Saturday night. Rather than crying about her age, she's throwing herself the kind of party she's always wanted and never had. Isn't that great?"

"Too good to miss."

"How about Carlos? Theresa would love to meet him." Although Julie had only met Kevin's partner once when he had come in for a routine cleaning of his teeth, she distinctly remembered that he was a handsome man in his mid-forties. She had described him to Theresa as being something between an aristocratic South American diplomat and a handsome, streetwise hoodlum, and Theresa had been nagging her to introduce them since she'd learned he was Kevin's business partner.

"Hey, Romero! A friend of Julie's named Theresa Post has invited you to a party. I know it's hard to imagine that an attractive woman would be interested in you, but it takes all kinds."

Carlos cuffed Kevin on the back of the head and snatched the receiver out of his hand. "I would love to come, Julie. Please thank Theresa for including me," he said and handed the phone back to Kevin.

After giving Kevin the address and time, Julie added, "Theresa doesn't want any gifts. Don't work too hard and I'll see you Saturday night."

He opened his mouth wide to whoop in delight and a sharp stab galloped to his ear. Obviously, the infection in his tooth was making itself felt again. Beginning as a vague twinge now and again, by Friday afternoon his tooth was waging a full-scale attack. He had finished the antibiotic Julie had prescribed and assumed he could stall rescheduling his appointment with Dr. Hartmann until it was more convenient—like sometime in the next decade. But right now his damn tooth felt like an active volcano with a cork stuffed in it, and he knew he couldn't wait for it to calm down on its own. There was no ignoring the pain this time.

Julie was on the phone checking back on a patient who had had major work completed the day before when her receptionist pushed a note across her desk; Kevin Royce had walked in as an emergency.

"Kevin, let's go to my office," she suggested, joining him in the waiting room. She took his elbow and prodded him across the hallway. She didn't dare put him into an examining room, for he was visibly petrified, sitting on the edge of his chair and rubbing his hands back and forth across his knees while he stared straight ahead. He looked up at her and she immediately wanted to wrap her arms around him to reassure him.

"Problems with your wisdom tooth again?" she inquired.

"You know I've been busy. I just haven't had the time to see that friend of yours."

"Dr. Hartmann?"

"Yeah. I really was planning on making another appointment."

"As soon as work slows down. Right?"

"Exactly." He brightened at her understanding and tried to force himself to relax. "Could you give me another prescription?"

"Kevin, this is the last time. I can't allow you to jeopardize your health by giving you an unending supply of antibiotics. It wouldn't be ethical on my part."

"I deserve the lecture. I know what you're saying is true, but..." How could he explain his terror? He wanted Julie to think he was a man, not a quivering mass of gelatin without enough courage to walk into an oral surgeon's office.

She could see how mortified he was and searched for a way to put him at ease. "Would it help if you knew I'm terrified of bugs? When I was growing up, I spent every summer with my cousins in eastern Washington. The oldest boy loved to torment me by putting any kind of creepy crawly he could find under my pillow. To this day I can't get into bed without checking the sheets first."

"But at least you have a logical reason," he said. "I don't have any excuse."

Julie crossed the room and stroked his hair. "Somewhere, buried underneath this thick skull, there's a negative association. Maybe a dentist frightened you as a child or hurt you."

He captured her hand and kissed her fingers. "Nice try, but it doesn't wash. The adult in me knows better."

"I also know that my cousin isn't around, boobytrapping my bed with grasshoppers, but it doesn't stop me from checking every night."

"I don't want to sound abrupt, but if you really want to make me feel better, please write up that prescription. This little hunk of ivory is demanding immediate action."

AFTER KEVIN HAD LEFT and the office was locked up, Julie headed straight for the boutique where she had spotted a gorgeous, washable silk suit. She wanted a new summer outfit to wear to Theresa's party and justified the small splurge as a reward for paying off one more of her college loans. Checking the length of the skirt in the three-way mirror, she stared at her reflection and knew she had been right. The deep apricot silk felt luscious against her skin, the color was perfect, and the softly flowing jacket, slim skirt and simple shell were flattering. Julie couldn't wait to show Theresa her new outfit.

"Wow," Theresa said after Julie walked out of the bedroom. "Pretty sexy, Dr. Bennett."

"Do you really think it's okay?"

"If you don't light his fire, send him in Monday morning for a checkup. We couldn't let a man that ill wander the streets by himself."

Julie laughed. "I'll change and help you in the kitchen."

Carefully folding up her new clothes, she thought how much fun she and Theresa had when they were together. Even with all her problems with Mark, Theresa never lost her sense of humor. Julie rejoined her friend in the kitchen, and soon the two women were having a great time, laughing and gossiping while they fixed trays of appetizers for the upcoming party.

"I want to know what the surprise is," Julie said. "I promise I won't tell a soul, and besides, I deserve a reward for services above and beyond the call of friendship."

"That wouldn't be fair." Theresa shook her head. "I—"

"See you later, Mom," Mark interrupted, grabbing a carrot as he walked by.

Theresa slammed down the vegetable peeler and caught Mark by the arm before he got off the back porch. "You're not going anywhere. You promised me you'd mow the lawn tonight."

"I will, tomorrow," Mark said. "They're waiting for me at the school to help decorate for the dance to-morrow night. I can't let them down."

"Be back by eight," Theresa told him.

Julie was tempted to scold Theresa for giving in to Mark so easily, but didn't. She knew how Theresa blamed herself for Mark's irresponsible attitude and wouldn't add to her friend's guilt. At least Theresa was trying to cope with single parenting, unlike Julie's mother, who hadn't even made an attempt. When Julie's father had died, her mother had replaced him in six months with a less than ideal man, the first in a succession of revolving-door stepfathers. The second one had invested her college money at the racetrack, and Julie could still remember the overpowering sense of betrayal she had experienced when her mother tried to justify his behavior. After that, Julie had quit trying to build a relationship with her stepfathers and begun plotting a constructive way to escape.

But all that had been years ago. Whether she liked it or not, her mother couldn't survive without a man, and Julie had at least learned to understand her mother's dependency. She had also vowed that she would never fall into that trap herself.

"Are you silent because you disapprove?" Theresa asked, interrupting Julie's reflection.

"What? I'm sorry. I didn't hear what you said."

"I asked if you disapproved of the way I let Mark weasel out of his chores."

"I'm not an expert on raising children, Theresa."

Theresa sighed and brushed a strand of dark hair out of her eyes. "Obviously I'm not, either."

Julie walked over and hugged her. "Maybe you love him too much. No matter how hard you try, you can't change facts. Mark's father walked out on both of you and that isn't your fault. Quit beating yourself up over something you couldn't control."

It was fairly late when she finally made it back home. Julie knew Kevin would be awake and was tempted to pick up the phone to check on his tooth. Her fingers were punching out his number when she forced herself to hang up. Although she was concerned about how Kevin was feeling and if the antibiotic was taking effect, she couldn't control what he did and didn't want to start trying. Kevin Royce was an adult; whether or not he paid attention to her warning and had his rotten tooth extracted was ultimately his decision.

SATURDAY WAS GLOOMY and overcast, but Julie and Theresa didn't let the weather dampen their mood. They were too busy even to notice how quickly time passed. In fact, when she'd finished helping Theresa, Julie had to rush home and get ready before Kevin picked her up.

"Simply mahh-velous!" Kevin exclaimed, circling her. "But do I really have to go to this party? I'd rather stand right here and stare at you for three or four hours."

"Are you always this bad?" Julie teased. It had been years since she had looked forward to a date with such enthusiasm, but one look at Kevin and the extra effort she had made in dressing seemed worthwhile.

He was commanding in his dark suit, starched white shirt and colorful silk tie. The very thought of him standing at attention, ramrod straight, attired in his dress uniform, gave her goose bumps. The years of military training added a touch of formality to his bearing even when he was relaxed, but she found his precise movements and confident manner reassuring.

Kevin Royce left no doubt in anyone's mind that he could handle himself and any situation that confronted him.

"Actually I can be very, very good." Kevin leaned over, careful not to muss her hair as he brushed his lips across her smooth, warm neck. "You smell delicious," he murmured and gently nibbled her skin.

"That's not fair," she murmured, sighed and ducked to escape.

Kevin watched her gather her purse and coat and admired the way her skirt molded her derriere, accenting her narrow hips and slender thighs. With the entire evening stretching interminably ahead of him, he knew he would be in serious trouble if he didn't control his rampant imagination. It wouldn't be an easy task, but she was worth every effort he could make to keep his hands to himself.

"I'm so glad you could come," Julie told Carlos when the three of them met in Theresa's driveway. "You'll like Theresa. But I want to warn you both she's not a shy, retiring wallflower."

Julie saw Carlos flash Kevin a doubtful look and chuckled. "Don't worry, Carlos," she went on. "That's not the same as saying that a blind date has a good personality. Theresa's beautiful."

Kevin nodded as if she had spoken to him and wrapped his arm around Julie's waist. "But not quite as beautiful as you."

Walking a few steps behind Carlos, Julie noticed Theresa peeking out of the window and could imagine what her friend was thinking. If Theresa were pressed to make a list of the physical characteristics she was looking for in a man, Carlos Romero would fulfill all the major requirements. He had thick black hair with just a touch of silver sprinkled through it and deep, dark brown eyes. Much shorter than Kevin, he was the perfect height for Theresa, and was as nattily dressed as if he just stepped out of a tailor's shop.

After Julie's introduction, Carlos said to Theresa, "Thank you for allowing me to help you celebrate your birthday."

"Too bad you're so annoyingly healthy," Theresa replied and winked at Julie. "Otherwise you'd have been in the doctor's office, and we wouldn't have had to wait six months to meet."

Julie could tell that Kevin was perilously close to laughing at Theresa's bold appraisal of his friend and steered him out of earshot. "I told you she would like him," she said as soon as they were on the other side of the room. "He's perfect for her."

"But will Carlos survive? I'm not sure he'll know what to do with a woman like Theresa."

"Oh, don't worry about that. Theresa's a very patient teacher."

Kevin couldn't control his laughter any longer. "Carlos doesn't stand a chance." He watched Theresa and Carlos talking and grinned to himself. Something was sparking between the two, and he wondered if an observer would have noticed the same electricity flashing between Julie and himself the first time they met.

After all the guests had arrived, Theresa concentrated anew on Carlos. "What do you think of our city now that you've been here a while?"

"It's a wonderful town, and the fact that Kevin's a homegrown boy eliminated most of the misery of starting a new business."

"Have you met my homegrown boy yet?" Theresa asked casually. Julie knew her friend had learned that many men were leery of dating a woman with a teen-age son.

"No, I haven't. How old is he?"

"Sixteen. I'll introduce you before he leaves for the dance."

Mark was talking to Julie. "May I interrupt?" Theresa inquired.

"Certainly," Julie replied, stepping back.

"Mark, I'd like you to meet Carlos Romero," Theresa said.

"Hi," Mark said vaguely.

Carlos extended his hand, but dropped it when Mark failed to respond. "I met a few kids at your school when I spoke to the seniors about a military career," Carlos said, probably trying to establish some common ground, Julie thought.

"That's nice," Mark said.

From the tone of his voice Julie was pretty sure that Mark considered anyone who chose to go into the military a social outcast.

She heard Carlos struggling to draw Mark into a conversation and was furious with the boy. "Mark," she said, gripping his arm in a viselike hold, "Mr. Romero owns a security business. He also raises and trains guard dogs. You know, the kind that are conditioned to attack when somebody offends the handler."

"Mom, where are the car keys? I need to leave or I'll be late for the dance."

"Mark," Theresa said and yanked him aside. "That was rude. I don't ask you to do much around here, but I expect you to be polite to my friends."

"All right. You made your point. Next time I see him, I'll take time for some male bonding, but not tonight. Now, where are the keys?"

"In my purse. And don't forget to fill the tank. You left it empty."

It was impossible to avoid overhearing what passed between Mark and Theresa, and Julie saw Carlos cringe. "He's a handful," she commented.

"Theresa shouldn't allow him to talk to her that way."

"He could use a reality check, all right," Julie replied.

"Like the firm hand of boot camp," Carlos said without any hesitation. "I trained dozens of spoiled young men, and nearly all of them matured into responsible, successful adults. Kevin was my star pupil."

"Kevin was spoiled?" Julie asked in mock horror. "I don't believe it."

"Nearly as obnoxious as Mark. Mark may have his mother's good looks, but he could definitely use some constructive criticism in the personality department," Carlos told her. "Is Theresa afraid of him because he's so much taller than she is?"

"Afraid? I doubt it," Julie said, grinning. "That lady may be little, but she's not frightened of anything."

"I'm sorry Mark was so rude," Theresa said, rejoining Carlos and Julie. "He has a one-track mind and it's fixed on that dance tonight."

Before either of them could comment, Kevin walked into the room. "The natives are growing restless, birthday girl. We all want to know what the surprise is."

"Then follow me." Theresa led the group into the living room and stepped onto a footstool. "May I have your attention, please? It's time to end the suspense and begin the scavenger hunt."

Theresa's plan was completely unexpected, and Julie glanced around at the startled faces. Although she had been on a scavenger hunt while she was at college, she suspected that some of the guests never had been challenged to scrounge for odd items.

"Carlos will give every couple a slip of paper with a list of articles," Theresa continued. "That completed list is what I want from each of you for my birthday. There are only two rules. You can't buy anything and you have exactly one hour to return. Oh, and as an incentive, the first couple back will receive these tickets to the theater."

"Good luck," Carlos said when he handed Julie her list.

She read the single line to Kevin. "Forty empty pop cans."

"You don't happen to be a good citizen and recycle aluminum, do you?" Kevin asked hopefully.

"I do," Julie said, "but I don't drink pop."

The couples around them shared their lists and Julie was amazed at Theresa's creativity. One request was for the front page from forty outdated newspapers, another was forty pencil stubs with worn-down erasers, and a third was forty different used books of matches.

"How long did it take her to think these up?" Kevin asked Julie in amazement.

"About forty years?"

Kevin booed at her joke and grabbed her arm. "I want to see that play, J.B."

While they waited for the cars parked behind them to clear the way, they plotted their strategy. "The best plan is to check the convenience store garbage cans," Kevin suggested. "We might get lucky and find one that hasn't had the empties picked up for recycling."

Julie glanced down at her expensive silk suit. "I, uh..."

He groped around behind his seat and pulled out a pair of clean coveralls. "Here, you can change on the way over."

She shook out the coveralls and ducked down in the back of the van. Julie felt like a juggler, trying to stay out of sight without wiping the floor with her hem or falling over when Kevin turned a corner. Finally she had the gargantuan cotton coveralls on and draped her suit from the passenger seat headrest.

Sitting down again, she held one foot in the air, pivoting her suede pump. "Quite a statement. Do you think they would label me as fashion forward or just a plain kook?"

"Definitely a kook with nice legs," Kevin said and grabbed her ankle.

"Thanks. I think."

She rolled up the sleeves until she had a thick wad of fabric around her wrists, then started on the legs.

"What if someone asks us why we're rummaging in the garbage?"

"Tell them the truth," Kevin said, and laughed at the look of misgiving on Julie's face.

They only found three empty cans at their first stop and two at the second, but by the third Julie's competitive spirit had emerged and she was tearing through the trash with a vengeance.

"Bonanza!" she cried to Kevin. "We're going to the theater and you're buying me lobster for dinner afterward."

They carried their booty back to the van and counted. "Thirty-eight," Kevin said in disgust. "Two lousy cans short, and we have to be back in ten minutes."

"I can't think of another convenience store between here and Theresa's."

"Wait a minute." He smacked his hand on the dashboard. "Theresa said we couldn't buy anything, but she didn't say a word about charging. When I was a kid my folks always had an account at the little store down the road from us. We pass right by Shorty's on our way back, and I think George still has an account there."

Freed from the necessity of pawing through garbage cans, Julie used their passage along the dark country road to get out of Kevin's coveralls, but was still zipping up her skirt when he shut off the engine.

"You're coming in with me. I want a witness that I didn't pay for these sodas. Our creativity will win first place."

"Isn't this cheating?"

"No, just bending the rules a bit."

Julie knew Theresa would laugh at their ingenuity. Straightening her blouse, she followed Kevin into the little country store. As she crossed the threshold, it was like stepping back fifty years in time. The floors were untreated wood, a dull patina of dirt and years of wear giving them a drab glow. Every available inch of floor and wall space was covered with an assortment of groceries, toys, magazines, books and imprinted sweatshirts.

"This is my kind of store," she said. "I'll bet some of this stuff has been sitting on the shelves since the sixties."

"1860 sounds about right," Kevin said softly. "No time for browsing, though."

He grabbed two cans of pop and plunked them down on the counter.

"Hi, Shorty. Remember me? Kevin Royce."

"Heard you were back. Good to see you, kid."

Kevin explained their unusual request and said, "Just put it on George's tab."

"Sorry, but I can't do that, Kevin."

"I'll come back in tomorrow and pay you. I'm sure George won't mind carrying me until then."

"No, he wouldn't. But I just can't add another dime to his bill. You know, Kevin, I always liked your folks. Mighty nice people and they paid up every month. Now George, he's not quite the same. It's been over four months since he's evened the score."

Stunned, Julie glanced at Kevin. His face was a mask, and she sympathized with his humiliation. "It's all right, Kevin. Let's just forget about it." She reached across and put her hand on his arm, but he didn't seem to notice.

"Are you saying George owes you money and won't pay?"

Kevin's tone was subdued, but Julie heard the tension in his words.

"How much is his bill, Shorty? I'll bring a check by tomorrow."

"Let's see," Shorty said and pulled out a ledger. "Four hundred fifty-three dollars. But you're not responsible for George's debts."

"See you tomorrow, Shorty," Kevin said and walked away, the pop cans forgotten.

"I was right about you all along, George Royce. You're a conniving swindler, using this city to line your pockets," Julie muttered as she followed Kevin.

CHAPTER SIX

THE DRIVE TO THERESA'S was silent and seemed interminable. Julie didn't know what to say and so elected to say nothing. They were the second couple to return, but the theater tickets had already been exchanged for a collection of forty used postcards. Julie congratulated the winners and turned to Kevin, ready to follow his lead.

"How are you and Theresa getting along? Did you manage to survive while I was gone?" Kevin asked Carlos.

"It's impossible to be bored when you're with her," Carlos said. "She showed me the patio she laid and asked my advice about the barbecue she wants to build. I've never known a woman who does her own remodeling."

Obviously Kevin was determined to pretend the incident at Shorty's had never occurred. Relieved, Julie pasted a smile upon her face. "Did she show you the pictures of what this house looked like when she bought it?" she inquired, turning to Carlos. "It was a disaster. The improvements she's made are incredible."

"With a little help from my friends," Theresa added, joining the conversation. "If you can't afford to hire professionals, you roll up your sleeves and get busy."

Carlos looked at Theresa with visible admiration and Julie could tell he wasn't intimidated, either by her friend's ambition or her unconventionality.

"If I put some more music on," Theresa suggested, "would you care to dance with me again, Mr. Romero?"

Julie sensed Kevin's mind wasn't on the party, but had to admit he was doing an admirable job of disguising it. Without asking, he tugged her onto the makeshift dance floor, too, and she easily followed his lead.

"Those two look happy," he said, nodding to Theresa and Carlos.

"I hope so," Julie said with a sigh. "Since Theresa's divorce, she's been too busy with her job and raising Mark to date very much. Behind that bravado, I know she's lonely."

Kevin pulled her nearer, absorbing her warmth and the comfort of her presence. He tried to relax, willing his tension to vanish, but couldn't forget the knot in his stomach. "How long has Theresa been single?"

"About ten years. Few men want to raise somebody else's child, and the occasional ones that came back more than once or twice were scared off by Mark's antagonism. He's not a bad kid, no drugs or alcohol or anything like that. He's just a handful, testing his mother's limits on a daily basis."

"If any man can handle Mark, it's Carlos."

"Sounds like he's exactly what both Mark and Theresa need," Julie commented.

"And what we need is a few moments of privacy. Any suggestions?" He couldn't go on pretending nothing was wrong. He had to talk to Julie.

"This way." Julie led Kevin upstairs to a spare bedroom and closed the door. She sat down on the daybed and waited for him to begin.

"I'm really sorry about ruining your evening." He sat down next to her and brushed her hair away from her face. "I don't know what else I can say."

"You didn't ruin anything, and there's no need for you to apologize. But I am concerned. Why should you pay George's bills? Shouldn't he be responsible for his own debts?" Julie could see Kevin bristle but continued. "Can you afford to subsidize George and his wife?"

"You don't have any brothers or sisters, do you?"

"No, but..."

"Then you can't understand. George is the only family I have. If he's in trouble, I have to help him. It's not a matter of choice. Besides, he would do the same thing for me if I needed his help."

"You're right, I don't really know what it's like to have a close relationship with a brother. But I can sympathize with what happened tonight. When I was twelve, my mother sent me to the butcher shop for a pound of hamburger and I was forced to come back empty-handed. No one had told me my father was on the verge of filing for bankruptcy and we had been living on credit for months."

She looked at Kevin, and when she saw the commiseration in his eyes, Julie resumed speaking. "My parents had sheltered me from the truth, thinking they were doing me a favor. Shortly after that, my father had his heart attack, and I've always wondered if the financial strain didn't contribute to his death."

"Then how can you say I shouldn't pay George's bills?"

"For one thing, as far as you know George is healthy and he's employed. He can pay his own bills. You have a new business, and I don't think it's wise to overextend yourself."

"You mean I should let Denise pay the debts with his death benefits. Is that what your mother did?"

Julie was dumbfounded by Kevin's response. "Since you feel privileged to be straightforward with me, I'll quit mincing my words. I don't like George. He abuses his authority and has a staff of goons posing as police officers covering his tracks."

"You had an unfortunate experience with Butler and you've labeled the entire police force crooked."

She could feel her cheeks flaming and an entire litany of insults swirling around in her head, but Julie clamped a lid on her rage. It would not accomplish a thing if she just responded with a nasty retort. Kevin could not be objective about his brother and she needed to get off the subject while she still could.

"I don't quite know what to say to you. It seems as though we can't spend the evening together without having a fight," she said. "This is not my idea of an enjoyable Saturday night, so I'm leaving. Should I call a taxi or will you drive me home?"

"Julie, I'm sorry," Kevin said, jumping to his feet to block the doorway. "Please don't go."

"Why not? So we can continue fighting? Do you know how many times we've apologized to each other? One or the other of us is always saying, 'I'm sorry.'"

"I'm not very good at expressing myself or show-ing other people I care. I suppose it's from years of disguising my real feelings. The military doesn't ex-actly encourage emotion."

Kevin was straining to be as honest and articulate as he could. If he continued to allow his concerns about George to intrude upon his relationship with Julie, he was going to lose her, and she had already become too important for him to allow that to happen.

Leaning against the door, Kevin struggled to find the right words. "Julie, I've dated a lot of nice women, but none of them compared to you. You know who you are and what you expect out of life and the people around you. I envy that, even if I don't al-ways agree with your opinions." Why did he have to sound so damn clinical?

"Every time I try to tell you what's in here," he said, thumping his palm to his heart, "it comes out sounding like a—a..."

Julie could tell how difficult it was for Kevin to ex-press his feelings. Kevin Royce was a man of action, not words, and she ached with the pain he was facing, a pain both physical and emotional. He had endured the agony of his tooth beyond the point any other person she had ever met would have been capable of. How much misery would he tolerate before he would acknowledge that his brother was not the perfect hu-man being he remembered, but a man corrupted by authority?

Did she herself have the strength to stand on the sidelines and watch Kevin suffer without interfering? Julie didn't think so. "We have a serious problem,

Kevin," she said. "The only way we can resolve it is to stop talking about George."

"How can you ask me never to mention my brother? I see him nearly every day," Kevin exclaimed, appalled by Julie's suggestion. "What if I promise not to get angry when you criticize George? He's not your favorite person. I can accept that."

She couldn't resist laughing at the image of herself berating George while Kevin stood meekly by. "Let's test your theory. Kevin, I find it inexcusable that George abuses his old friends."

"So do I if it's true." He crossed the room slowly and sat down next to Julie on the daybed. "Things sure do seem to be mixed up, don't they?"

"A little bit."

Even though Julie was clearly convinced that she had plenty of evidence of George's guilt, Kevin couldn't agree with her, even after tonight. He still believed George would never exploit his position as chief of police. He also realized he would hate himself if Julie walked out the door and out of his life.

"I had no right to make that nasty comment about your mother." Kevin hesitantly picked up Julie's hand and when she didn't dig her nails into his fingers, he brought her palm to his lips and kissed it. "The only way we can survive is for you—and me—to bend a little." He wrapped Julie's arm around his neck and buried his hands in the thick waves of her hair. "I've waited too long to find you. I won't allow anyone, not even my brother, to come between us, Julie." He touched her lips with his, then drew away, only to return immediately to taste her sweet mouth again.

She welcomed his kisses, mesmerized by the way he banished every misgiving the instant the silken tip of his tongue met hers. Kevin pressed one hand into her shoulder blades while his other tangled in her hair. He pulled her against the solid wall of his chest until Julie couldn't tell if what she felt was her own heartbeat or his.

"Nothing else matters but this," he said in a low voice and covered her mouth with his own.

It was insane and it was perfect. He gave up trying to reason away their differences and accepted the reality that he was falling in love with Julie Bennett. Lightly he kissed a path from the sculpted curve of her shoulder across to the hollow of her throat, hesitating when he felt her rapid pulse.

"You're feeling it, too," he said between more feathery kisses. "I know you are."

The extension phone on the end table reverberated in the near silence and, although Julie silently begged for someone else to answer it, she eased out of Kevin's arms and picked it up on the sixth ring. "Post residence."

"I need to talk to Mom."

"Hold on while I find her," she said.

She found Theresa downstairs, still dancing with Carlos. She hated to intrude, but Mark had sounded upset. "Your son is on the phone."

"What's wrong?" Theresa stopped moving, but didn't pull away from Carlos.

"I'm not sure."

Julie and Carlos were on Theresa's heels to the kitchen, where Kevin joined them.

"If he's in another jam, I'm selling him to the highest bidder," Theresa said, covering the phone's mouthpiece with her hand. "Anyone have an extra quarter they want to spend on an annoying sixteen-year-old?" She closed her eyes and put the receiver to her ear. "Mark, what's wrong?" While she listened to his answer, her toes were tapping in irritation, Julie observed. "It just quit in the middle of the road?"

Kevin flashed Julie a questioning look, but all she could do was shrug her shoulders.

"Did you get gas?" Theresa finally demanded. She was silent for a minute, then sighed deeply. "Hold on. I'll have to borrow a car." She covered the mouthpiece again and asked, "Anyone trust me with their car? Mark ran out of gas and I need to rescue him."

"I'll be glad to help," Carlos said. "But it might not be what you had planned."

"If you have a better idea, I'm open to suggestions. I don't know what to do with him anymore."

"Didn't I hear you warn him to fill the tank?"

"I certainly did, but he didn't want to spend his own money, and I forgot to give him my credit card." Theresa made no attempt to hide her anger.

"Where is he now?" Carlos asked quietly.

"He said he hiked about two miles to an all-night station."

"Mark needs to take responsibility for his own actions, Theresa," Carlos told her. "I spent nearly twenty years teaching young men like Mark how to take care of themselves. Give him your understanding and support, but make him accept responsibility for his own actions. Are there any girls waiting in the car with parents who might be worried?"

Theresa glanced at Julie and Kevin for guidance; Kevin said, "He's firm but he's fair, Theresa. I'd listen to him if it were my son."

"Mark," Theresa inquired, "did you take the girls home already?"

She waited for his answer, then handed the phone to Carlos. "He's all yours, Sergeant Romero. The girls are safely home, but he has a buddy waiting for him back at the car."

Julie was surprised that Theresa was allowing Carlos to intervene. She flashed a smile of encouragement to her friend.

"Mark, this is Carlos. Your mother has a house full of guests and can't leave. You'll have to buy yourself some gas and hike back to the car. Pour most of the gas into the tank, but save some, just in case you need to prime the carburetor. Do you know how to do that?"

Carlos looked at Theresa and saw her shake her head. "If it doesn't start, open up the hood, take out the air filter and pour a little gas down the opening, straight into the carburetor. Then the engine should turn over with no problem. See you when you get home." Before Mark could object, Carlos hung up.

"I'm not sure he even knows where the air filter is," Theresa said doubtfully. "I'd better go help him."

"No," Carlos told her. "His buddy is waiting for him, and between them they'll figure it out. Two sixteen-year-old boys can certainly manage to find the air filter."

"I suppose so," Theresa admitted. "But Mark has never tinkered with cars the way some boys do."

"I'm no mechanic," Julie said, "but even I could follow those directions. Have a little faith in him, Mom."

"We'll be right here if he has any more trouble. And I can guarantee he won't let the car run out of gas again for a long time." Carlos rubbed his hand up and down Theresa's back in a comforting motion. "Don't worry. He'll be fine."

The only people left at the party were Carlos, Julie and Kevin when Mark stormed into the living room. The men were putting the furniture back where it belonged and pulling down decorations, while Julie and Theresa loaded the dishwasher and cleared the table.

"Thanks for leaving me stranded in the middle of nowhere!" Julie heard Mark rant at Carlos before he'd even closed the front door.

"Hello, Mark. Glad to see you didn't have any problems."

"No thanks to you. Just because you're too stupid to do anything other than march up and down with a pack on your back doesn't mean I enjoy hiking for miles."

"You knew the car was almost out of gas and decided not to stop. It would have taken you five minutes to fill the tank and you would have saved yourself the effort." Carlos clearly had no difficulty in maintaining his composure.

When Theresa wanted to head for the living room, Julie stopped her. "Don't interfere," she whispered. "Carlos started this, let him finish it."

"And," Carlos continued, "if I'm stupid, why were you the one that ran out of gas?"

Kevin motioned to him, signalling that he thought the boy had been pushed far enough, but Carlos ignored him. "If your mother agrees, I'd like to spend a lot of time with her. That means you and I need to come to an understanding."

"Get off my case," Mark said and stomped indignantly out of the room.

Julie heard Mark's footsteps pounding down the steps to the basement and glanced at Theresa out of the corner of her eye. Although Theresa had claimed she wanted help with Mark, Carlos really had taken a firm hand with the boy and Julie was skeptical about how her friend would react.

"Bravo, Sergeant Romero," Theresa said to Carlos, rounding the corner. "It's time someone was on his case."

The events of the evening had left Kevin exhausted, and he whispered to Julie that it was time they got going. After a brief round of thanks, Kevin escorted Julie to the car. "What a night," he said, once they were on the road. "I'm going to see George tomorrow morning, but then I'd like to spend the day with you. Are you free?"

"For a picnic in the country with a man who has an international degree in kissing? I might be blackmailed into going."

The gulf between the two bucket seats made it impossible for Kevin to lean across and touch her cheek, rest his free hand on her shoulder or even talk softly. "Would you mind if we took your car? I don't want you so far away all day long."

"I'll even share the driving, so you can relax and enjoy the scenery."

"It's not the scenery I plan to enjoy," he said.

She waited for Kevin to come round the front of the van and open her door when they arrived at her duplex. In many ways he was a very traditional man, Julie thought. He treated women with respect and courtesy, always a gentleman, pulling out a chair and staying on the outside of the sidewalk. But he never hinted that he had any doubts about women being equal to men. Kevin was a refreshing and lovely blend of the best masculine traits.

He opened the door and Julie turned to him. Without a word, he wrapped his hands around her waist and practically lifted her off the seat, slowly letting her body glide down his until her toes barely touched the ground. She clasped her fingers behind his neck, stretching up to meet his lips and ending any hesitation he might have had about kissing her again.

"You have the most kissable lips, J.B.," he whispered, lightly brushing his mouth across hers. "I'm fighting one hell of a battle to let you go tonight." He deepened the kiss, encouraging her to match his need, his desire. Then, with a harsh, smothered moan of want, he pulled away.

Julie shivered when he released her and leaned against the side of the van. "I'd better go in."

"Are you sure?" Kevin cursed himself. Had he frightened her with his unexpected need to possess her, to tie them together so firmly that nothing could come between them?

"Kevin, I care enough about you to wait until what we share is something very special."

"What if I told you I care that much now?" Kevin asked, taking one finger and tracing the curve of her jaw. "I'm nearly forty-one years old, not a flighty teenager with overactive hormones."

"Kevin, I need more time. I can't rush into this without thinking of the consequences. We both live in a small town and we're committed to staying here, whether our relationship is successful or not. Who knows? Maybe you won't even like me after you get to know me better."

"I'm not looking for a pal," Kevin said, scooping her into his arms. "I've been searching for you for years. It's ironic that I've been around the world and found you right here in my hometown."

It would have been easy for Julie to yield to Kevin, to let him override her concerns, but she couldn't. Not yet. Kevin Royce was a dynamic, passionate man who would overwhelm both reason and logic, and Julie knew that once she had experienced the joy of loving him, her world would never again be complete without him.

"I'm not going to kiss you good-night because I won't be responsible for my actions," Kevin told her, taking her hand and leading her up the walk.

She smiled at the gruff way he spoke when he was trying to conceal his emotions. "A handshake will do quite nicely."

"Like hell it will," he said and lifted her onto the step above him, raising her to his eye level. "I lied."

She draped her arms across his shoulders, responding to the strength of the attraction between them. She felt her stomach clench when he touched her, her knees grew weak when she felt his breath brush across her cheek, then his mouth covered hers, urgently, possessively. How much longer would it be before she was imploring him to keep his promise and love her?

CHAPTER SEVEN

KEVIN LET THE VAN IDLE at the head of the long driveway while he studied his childhood home. Although the morning was clear, brazen sunlight illuminating each blade of grass in the overgrown pasture and every sagging fence post along the road, he felt as if he were looking at the world through a gray shroud of fog.

The Royce farm had never been a large, commercial endeavor, simply ten acres of well-groomed land in the country. Now it was a scraggly piece of property practically on the outskirts of town. Although he had dropped by a few times lately, it had always been at night when everything was hidden in darkness, and now he was shocked at the evidence of neglect.

The last time he had seen the house in broad daylight, Denise had just finished relandscaping the entire front yard. It had been awe inspiring, but that was over four years ago. Now weeds choked the flower beds, autumn leaves still littered the grass, the cold frames were empty, and an air of indifference clung to every new leaf and bud.

The house hadn't deteriorated as quickly as the grounds, but it was evident George wasn't putting much effort into maintenance. Christmas lights still outlined the front porch, and a broken window above the kitchen sink had a piece of weathered cardboard taped over the hole.

He shifted into gear and pulled around to the back of the house where he always parked. Before he could turn the engine off, Denise came bounding down the steps, dressed more for an evening on the town than a Sunday trip to church or even the supermarket. George had never wanted his wife to work, and Denise had always seemed content to stay home, so her elaborate appearance this early in the morning made no sense.

"George saw you pull up, Kevin. Coffee's hot. Bye," Denise said and jumped into her car, leaving Kevin staring through his rolled-down window as if he'd seen a phantom.

He had started to wonder if Denise had purposely been avoiding him. Lately she'd never been home when he dropped by. Now he knew he'd been correct. The woman who had married his brother nineteen years ago wasn't this gaunt creature; the Denise he knew was a bit plump and friendly, always happy to see him. Also, the Denise Royce he remembered didn't wear makeup thick enough and elaborate enough to raise the revenues of any cosmetics firm. And George's wife didn't own an expensive sports car like the one Kevin watched her drive away in. In spite of the fact that her husband couldn't afford even a plate of lasagna, Denise clearly wasn't lacking the finer things in life.

"What in the hell is going on around here?" Kevin muttered and raced up the back stairs two at a time. "George!"

"In here, Kev."

Kevin found his brother sitting at the kitchen table with a cup of coffee and the newspaper. George looked especially old this morning, almost fragile. "Was that Denise who just barreled out of here in a forty-thousand-dollar car?"

"Looks fantastic, doesn't she?" George said without lifting his eyes from the sports page.

"I thought she was perfect just the way she used to be," Kevin said. He couldn't keep his thoughts from racing. *If that's all that has changed, I would agree with you, big brother, but I'm disturbed. This place is starting to look as if a pair of bad renters live here. Old houses need constant attention, you know that.*

Kevin saw that his brother was blocking him out, hiding behind the newspaper. He poked it with his finger. "Want to save the sports page for later?"

"Sure. Something special on your mind?" George inquired calmly and poured himself another mugful of coffee. "Help yourself."

"Since I moved back to Tolt, I've had a few confusing experiences," Kevin resumed. "But nothing as astonishing as the sight of your wife. If I hadn't seen her step out the door, I don't know that I would have recognized her."

"Looks like a million dollars, doesn't she?"

There was a strained undercurrent to George's latest comment. Kevin sat down at the table with his brother. "Want to tell me what's going on?"

"Not particularly. What brings you out this way?"

"I was hungry and my refrigerator is empty. Thought I'd fix some breakfast and talk like we used to." Kevin realized there was no point strong-arming George, for he wouldn't say a thing if he decided to dig

his heels in the sod. But he knew George loved to re-
hash their childhood, talk with Kevin about the years
before their parents had been killed.

"Remember that time I picked all Mom's cucum-
bers and chopped them up on the sidewalk to make
pickles?" he asked, stirring the memories.

George grinned and tipped back his chair. "But she
wasn't nearly as mad that time as when you tried to fix
Dad's new lawn mower with a hammer. Good thing
she couldn't climb the tree after you, or you wouldn't
have lived to celebrate your sixth birthday."

"It sure got cold up there waiting for Dad to come
home. How was I supposed to know the difference
between a hammer and a screwdriver?" They both
started laughing and Kevin relaxed. "If I volunteer to
fix you my special Royce omelet, are you brave enough
to try it?" he inquired, getting up and poking his head
into the refrigerator.

"No sauerkraut this time," George said. "After
your German specialty it was six months before I
could face an egg."

"Always a critic," Kevin replied and started cracking eggs into a bowl.

He tried to pierce George's smoke screen throughout breakfast, but every time Kevin veered away from
the past and directed the conversation toward current
incidents, George pulled back. "I had dinner at Angelo's the other night and you almost bought the
meal," Kevin said, trying to keep any hint of accusation out of his words.

"How so?"

"A new waiter wanted to put my meal on your tab."
Kevin waited for George to turn red, get angry, or

stomp out of the room. The longer he stared at George, the louder the ticking of the clock sounded and the steadier George's gaze became. "Are you short of cash this month?" Kevin finally asked.

"A little. I made some investments on the stock market and they didn't pan out. Nothing to worry about. Angelo knows I'm good for it."

"Of course," Kevin said. He was pretty sure his brother was lying; the closest George ever came to investing was buying five dollars' worth of lottery tickets. George didn't know the difference between an IRA—an individual retirement account—and a CD—a certificate of deposit—a bull from a bear market. "But that doesn't explain why it's been nearly four months since you paid Shorty."

"I heard you were spending your free time with Julie Bennett, not driving around town doing a credit check on me."

"I'm not going to bother explaining how I know you owe Shorty four hundred fifty three dollars, but I promised him he'd have a check this morning. Which one of us is signing it?"

Seeing the stricken look on his brother's face, Kevin immediately wished he had kept his mouth shut. George wrapped his big hands around his cup and gripped it as if he were trying to crumble the ceramic to a pile of shards. But for all the apparent strength in his hands, his shoulders sagged. Kevin suddenly noticed how much more gray was streaking his brother's hair.

"Don't worry," Kevin said and thumped George on the shoulder. "You can pay me back when you get caught up on your bills."

"It might be a while."

"I know it's none of my business, but what's really wrong? Maybe I can help."

Pulling himself up straighter, George said, "I'll work it out. Don't worry. I've got a plan that will solve the problem."

"I hope so." Kevin glanced at his watch and began filling the sink with hot, soapy water. "I'll wash and you dry, then I have to leave. Can't be late."

"Julie?"

"Yes." Kevin waited for George to make a disparaging comment, but he didn't. The silence said more than any words.

When they were finished, George walked him to the door. "Next time I want cottage fries." He rumpled Kevin's hair the way he had done thirty years ago and Kevin cuffed his hand away. "I'm proud of you, kid."

"Enjoy your day off," Kevin told him and hurried to his van. He wanted to say he was proud of George, too, but couldn't. He wasn't sure he even knew who George was anymore. The man who had raised him had vanished; how long had he been missing? Kevin wondered.

Although it was nearly impossible, once Kevin left Shorty's he attempted to put his brother out of his mind and concentrate on the prospect of spending an uninterrupted, perfect spring day with a beautiful woman. Julie was ready to leave when he arrived at her door and he held his arms wide.

"Good morning, gorgeous," he said and folded her into his embrace. She was wearing fashionably faded, snug jeans and a loose sweater. The sweater concealed her enticing curves but Kevin didn't need to overtax his imagination to picture what was hiding beneath the soft pink folds. Julie was wearing flat shoes that made her seem even smaller in his arms. More than ever he wanted to defend her from any harm, to shield her from disappointment, but knew Julie wasn't a woman who needed his protection. She was competent, self assured.

"Don't I get a good morning kiss?" he said, smiling, finding her totally irresistible. It had only been hours since he had kissed her but seemed like weeks.

When she was young, Julie had worried that a relationship with any man would eventually become boring. She couldn't imagine how a woman could still find a thrill in kissing a man she had married years ago. But with Kevin she felt that the passion would never dim. Each time he touched her, each time he stroked her tongue with his, she was captured by a pleasure so fierce it was unbearable. Kevin was dangerous, and if she wanted to keep her sanity, she needed to douse the fire he'd lighted in her.

"Are we going to waste this lovely day?" she inquired, pulling free of his embrace.

"If this is wasting time, I'm game."

"Please, Kevin, it's time to leave."

"Why? Am I making you nervous, J.B.?"

"Yes."

"Good," he said and smiled his spectacular smile. "Then we're even."

He swooped up the picnic basket and thermos Julie had set by the door, snatched the keys out of her hand and began loading the car, leaving her standing.

"I already put a blanket and the cooler in the trunk," she finally said, chasing after him.

Her car was a small, unremarkable sedan, but she had been up early, washing and vacuuming it for today's outing. Theresa had given her plates of leftovers from the party, and they were carefully packed in the cooler along with anything else Julie had been able to scrounge from her cupboards. It was an eclectic assortment, but neither one of them would go hungry.

"Mind if I drive?" Kevin asked.

"No." Ordinarily, Julie didn't let anyone behind the wheel of her car, but Kevin drove with skilled assurance and a watchful eye, so she didn't hesitate. "Which way do you want to head?"

"Toward Bellingham," he suggested.

"Perfect. It should be a pretty drive. All those fields of tulips are breathtaking."

Kevin noticed Julie's camera sitting on the front seat between them and put it on the floor behind him. "That's better," he said and rested his hand on her leg. The need to have her close was beyond his control.

Julie sensed the change in Kevin's attitude. The first time they had met she had felt nothing from him except doubt and mistrust, then last night he had lowered his guard and let her glimpse his vulnerability. This, however, was something else again.

To still her apprehension, she tried to study the luxuriant green fields, the small farmhouses and the occasional herd of dairy cattle they passed. But nothing worked. Her stomach was twisted in a knot and her hands felt clammy. This man clearly didn't believe in half measures. His loyalty to George was conclusive proof of that.

As they headed out of Tolt, Julie pushed her misgivings aside. They followed the highway through the pastoral countryside, content to enjoy each other's presence.

Trying to piece together a pattern of his life, Julie asked questions about Kevin's years in the military. He didn't dramatize the horrors of his year in Vietnam and claimed he wasn't plagued by the nightmares many of his friends experienced.

"I was doing a job. There's no satisfaction in killing another human being, but there's honor in defending your country," he explained. "Vietnam's a beautiful country. Someday I'd like to go back."

"How did you have time to see anything other than the jungle?"

"I spent a few weeks recuperating in the hospital in Saigon and took advantage of day passes when I could wrangle one."

"You were hurt?"

"A piece of shrapnel caught me in the stomach. Just a scratch, really."

Julie had seen him without his shirt the night she had come to his apartment and hadn't noticed a scar. Without realizing it, she tried to envision where the scar was, and focused her eyes on the area below his belt.

"It's right here," he said, pointing to the right side of his abdomen. "Got an appendectomy out of the deal. Would you like me to pull over to the side of the road and show you my battle wound?" he teased. He picked up her hand, placing it over the spot he'd indicated. "Right here."

Julie could feel the hard muscles of his stomach clench at her touch and didn't immediately pull her hand away when he released it. "You're testing me. Trying to shock me."

"Wrong, lady," he said and quickly glanced at her. "I just want you to touch me and I don't care where."

The deep, husky pitch of his voice invited Julie to let her fingers stray, but she just slid them down to his upper thigh and let her hand rest.

"I was afraid of that," he whispered and covered her fingers with his. He squeezed her hand and guided it up and down his leg. "I can wait, but I need to know that it's not hopeless. Is it?"

"No."

"Before I drive off the road and get us both killed, maybe you should take a turn at the wheel. I'm too busy staring at you to pay attention to the traffic."

Kevin pulled onto the shoulder and started sliding across the front seat toward her. She knew he was going to lift her into his lap if she didn't escape, so she jumped out the passenger door, finding the tension between them unbearable. She leaned against the hood of the car, gulping at the rain-fresh breeze. When her heart had quit pounding and she trusted her voice again, she climbed behind the wheel.

"You must stop that," she said, facing him with a stern expression.

"Why?"

"Do you think that just because we're attracted to one another that it solves all our other differences?"

He wrapped his hands in her long, golden-brown hair and stared into her eyes. "We have no differences except the pleasantly obvious ones. If we were the only two people on the earth, we'd have no problems. But my brother does exist and neither one of us can forget him. What do I have to do to prove to you that he has nothing to do with us? When will you trust me?''

"I already trust you, Kevin. That's not it. It's just that all of a sudden you're pushing our relationship into high gear and I'm still coasting. Give me time to pick up speed, catch up with you.

"Or,'' she continued, brightening at the idea, "we could just leave our options open. Life shouldn't be rushed. It should be enjoyed.''

"I know,'' he said huskily and fingered her earring. "How well I know.''

Kevin did not attempt any further intimacies, and the remainder of the day was a delight. They explored the little towns along the way and stopped for lunch at Lake Whatcom. The sun was bright, the sky cloudless, but the breeze off the water cooled the air enough that they didn't linger at the picnic table.

Several small shops along the back roads intrigued Julie, and Kevin found he, too, enjoyed browsing through the cluttered amalgam of goods they found there. She had a fondness for art deco prints and found a particularly rare one hiding in an ugly frame beneath dirty glass.

"This would be perfect in my bedroom,'' she said, wiping the accumulated grease and dust off the glass. "What do you think?''

"I would look even better in your bedroom.'' Julie's eyes glittered at his words but Kevin jumped in ahead of her. "The opening was too good to resist. You can't blame me for trying.''

The highlight of the day came when Julie found a set of antique dental tools. They were just about to leave the store when she spied the tools in their leather case and bent down to study them.

"Kevin, quick. Look at this."

Kevin saw the instruments and shuddered. "You're not using them on me."

"They're for my collection. Eventually I want to make a display in the waiting room. Like a dentist's office looked around 1920."

"You mean a torture chamber?"

"Then people like you will be grateful for the advances we've made."

Kevin, warming to the idea in spite of himself, leaned closer. "If you put mannequins in the window dressed in costumes from that era, it would be interesting. It would set your clinic apart from every other sterile medical office."

Julie bounced on her heels in excitement. "Exactly. I already have the chair—it just needs to be recovered. I found an old drill that I've had restored to working order."

"If you put it in the front window and rearranged the waiting room, people passing by outside would spot the display and remember Dr. Julie Bennett the next time their teeth needed cleaning."

"Your opinion of my profession seems to be improving," she suggested, laughing. "Thanks for the vote of confidence."

"Oh, no," he said, raising his hands in defense. "I haven't changed my mind about all dentists, just you. The rest of your colleagues don't enjoy your privileged status."

It was nearly dark by the time they meandered back to Tolt. Kevin had one arm wrapped around Julie's shoulder, the other hand on the steering wheel. Julie was resting her head on his chest. They had been together all day, but he still wasn't ready to let her go. While he was unloading the trunk in front of her home, he scrambled for a way to delay his leaving.

"I only have an hour before I go to work. Think I could talk you into providing me with some caffeine?"

"Kevin, we should have come back a long time ago so you could take a nap. Why didn't you tell me you had to work?"

"Because I'd rather be with you than at home, sleeping my life away."

Julie smiled. "A cup of my famous cappuccino and you won't be able to blink until dawn."

Kevin walked around the living room and inspected Julie's home while she was in the kitchen. Up to now he had just had a glimpse of her duplex and was curious about the clues to her personality the room would yield. Clustered on one wall was a group of family photographs, and he smiled at the toothy grin of a happy little girl. In this picture she was about six, a pretty child, safely tucked in her father's arms. A small, mousy woman was clinging to them both. Julie resembled her father except for the large, unforgettable eyes she had clearly inherited from her mother. There were no photographs of Julie as a young woman, and Kevin remembered she had said her father had died when she was thirteen. The only other two were of her graduation from high school and college. In both of them she sat stiffly posed, clutching her diploma, and looking lonely. Had she really been that lonely?

"That's my family," she said, handing him a steaming cup of frothy coffee.

"Where does your mother live?"

"Florida. With her husband."

"Long ways from Tolt."

"About as far as you can get," Julie said. "My mother hasn't had much luck picking out husbands since Dad died. I hope my current stepfather treats her better than the last two did. He seems like a pretty good guy, so far."

Kevin didn't know quite what to say. Julie had clearly tried to defuse the bitterness she felt with a smile, but her confession deserved some comment. "Your mother looks like a nice lady."

"She is. Too nice for her own good. How do you like my secret brew?"

Kevin hadn't tasted the coffee and took a sip. Julie had closed the subject of her family as surely as if she had taken a key and locked up the trunk where she stored her memories. There was more to the Bennett family saga than she had revealed, but she was obviously not ready to share it yet.

"I didn't realize you were a gourmet," Kevin said, following her lead and smacking his lips. "It's delicious."

"I can't cook a whole lot but what I do, I do well. I can handle most anything you can fit in a wok. Years of living in a dorm, cooking with minimal kitchen space, taught me how to combine everything in one pot and still have an edible meal."

"Then we make an excellent team," Kevin said and held his mug aloft in a salute. "I produce the most delicious breakfasts this side of the Mississippi. I'm not bragging, but people line up outside my apartment on Sunday mornings, just waiting for leftovers. Disappointed the entire block when I wasn't home today."

Julie started laughing and had to set her cup down. "Humble, aren't you?"

"No, just honest. J.B.," he said and brought her hand to his lips, "today was perfect. I don't want to leave you."

"I wish you didn't have to go." The words just popped out, and she wasn't sorry.

"Would you consider spending the weekend with me, maybe in Victoria?"

"When?" She couldn't think of a more romantic city, close to home but a world apart. "Can you leave for an entire weekend?"

"Carlos and I already decided we need to hire more help. As soon as we can find the right people and train them, I'll have more free time."

"Do I have to give you an answer tonight?"

"As long as you say yes, you can take as long as you need."

She reached over and tucked back a strand of his dark hair that had fallen across his forehead.

"If I kiss you good-night, it just might take me another hour or two to get to work, and it doesn't set a good standard when the owner doesn't show," Kevin went on, rising from the couch. "Will you be up for a while?"

"Yes. Why?"

"I'll call. I like to talk to you when I know you're snuggled up in bed. It's the next-best thing to being there with you."

"You're incorrigible," she said, blushing at the thought.

"I know it, and you love every minute of it. Don't stay up past your bedtime, J.B."

Julie heard him close the door and kicked off her shoes to rest her feet on the cocktail table. It had been the most wonderful day. It all belonged in a storybook, and she wondered if she should pinch herself to make certain she wasn't dreaming.

The telephone rang and Julie raced to find it. She tracked the phone cord to her bedroom and smiled as she picked up the receiver. "You certainly don't waste any time, Mr. Royce."

"I'm getting a complex," Theresa replied. "Every time I talk to you, you're expecting me to be about a foot taller and a hundred pounds heavier. Where have you been all day? I've been calling you for hours."

"Why? Is something wrong?"

"If you call meeting the most tender, handsome man in Tolt something wrong, then I guess I've suffered a devastating catastrophe."

Julie chuckled at the girlish lilt in Theresa's voice. "That good, huh?"

"I haven't even started with good, my friend. That was just a brief description of his lesser qualities."

"What does Mark think of him?" Julie knew the key to any relationship Theresa had with a man was her son's response. If Mark didn't like the guy, it wouldn't take more than a week or two before Theresa was home alone again on Saturday night.

"Mark isn't speaking to me today," Theresa told her. "No matter what I do, he just pretends I'm not in the room."

"Did Carlos call you today?" Julie asked.

"Yes, he did. He told me to ignore Mark if he was going to act like I didn't exist. I'm trying."

Breathing a silent prayer of thanks to Carlos, Julie said, "I agree with him. Besides getting the cold shoulder, how was the second day of your new decade?"

"You're a perverse little snit, aren't you? Actually, I think I'm going to like this year. A lot. Where did you go with Kevin?"

It was late by the time Julie finished talking with Theresa. And the moment she set the phone down, it rang again.

"So, did you tell Theresa all about me?" Kevin asked.

"Pretty sure of yourself, aren't you?"

"Most of the time."

Julie heard another line ring, and Kevin put her on hold to answer the call. Seconds later he was back. "I have to go. Talk to you tomorrow. Dream of me, J.B."

CHAPTER EIGHT

WEARY, Kevin set the phone down and rocked back in his chair. He meticulously reviewed the facts one more time. Carlos had been on duty at Nickerson Electronics, supervising the guards and their dogs. He had noticed a light gleaming from under an office door. When he had stuck his head in to see who was working late, all he'd found had been a glowing computer terminal.

Carlos had very little knowledge of computers so the program was just a jumble of numbers and letters to him, but Kevin didn't recognize the sequence of symbols when Carlos rattled them off, either. It wasn't Nickerson's security system; Kevin had spent too many hours analyzing the files to not be able to identify them. Yet there didn't seem to be any logical explanation for any other program to be on screen. What was even more unnerving was that Carlos was positive the room had been dark and empty when he'd made his first rounds. The one crew working was the plant's third shift, and there was no one on duty with either the authorization or enough knowledge to access those files.

There was plainly more to the problem at Nickerson than just a malfunctioning security system. Computers only responded to their operator's instructions, and someone was tampering with Nickerson's. It was the only explanation for the dozens of random false alarms, and whoever was responsible was smart enough to leave no trail. Somehow, someway, an anonymous person, after dodging the guards and their dogs, had headed straight for that computer terminal.

Kevin didn't feel qualified to handle this job any longer. The only sensible plan was for Bud Nickerson to admit to the authorities that his company had a breach in its security and ask for help. It was late in the evening now, but Kevin didn't hesitate to call Bud. Accepting responsibility for a company that produced sensitive and potentially lethal products was the owner's duty, and Bud would have to take immediate action.

"It's Kevin Royce, Bud. Sorry to wake you, but this couldn't wait."

He told Bud the unsettling news and heard him reply, "I appreciate your conscientious attitude, but you're overreacting. Probably a secretary just forgot to turn off her machine. Happens all the time."

"This was Brent Olsen's machine." Kevin didn't think a programmer would be careless enough to leave his terminal on all weekend.

"Olsen? But he isn't even working right now. He's on vacation. Are you sure it's Olsen's office?"

"His name is on the door," Kevin said, exasperated. "This was one of your more complex systems. Doesn't that bother you?"

"Relax, Kevin," Bud told him. "Olsen's assistant was probably using that terminal to finish a new assignment. I asked him to modify our security program, make it close enough to our old one that it could be implemented without any drastic changes, but resistant to tampering. He's been working long hours and probably just forgot to log out. I'll call him.''

''You're the boss,'' Kevin responded. He didn't have to ask why Bud had never mentioned the change in programs. It was obvious. No one, not even Kevin and Carlos, was to have been informed that a new setup was running. So much for Bud's uncompromised trust. But he didn't blame the man. If his own company had been disrupted in this way, he would have been just as circumspect.

''Kevin,'' Bud resumed, ''this doesn't change your agenda. I want you back first thing tomorrow morning.''

Kevin reported to Bud's office thirty minutes before the office staff arrived and continued to do so for the rest of the week. There were no more disturbing, late-night telephone calls, no more false alarms, and no incidents with the guards and their canine colleagues. But as Kevin continued the search for what he was beginning to think might be a nonexistent program virus, he learned something disturbing.

The program that had been running on Brent Olsen's terminal hadn't been the security system, as Bud had assumed. It was a new one, similar to the Nickerson security program, but not identical to it. Kevin had worked with comparable defense programs when he was stationed in Washington, D.C., and recognized that this sophisticated series, when perfected, would be a much more powerful tool, outstripping every other computerized competitor currently in use.

By Friday he was exhausted from working all day at the plant and every night in the monitoring room. Although he'd spoken with Julie several times during the week, their schedules had never overlapped enough to allow them to spend even a few hours together.

"You decide when and where," Kevin told her when he called from his office on Friday afternoon to invite her to dinner.

"You know what I'd rather do than battle the Friday night crowd," she said. "Rent a couple of movies, make a big bowl of popcorn, and clog my arteries with melted butter." She could hear the fatigue in his voice and knew what he needed was a quiet evening. Besides, she didn't really want to share him with a roomful of other people. An evening alone with Kevin had been the prize dangling at the end of what had proved to be a long, tiring week.

"A woman after my own heart. You pick out the movies and I'll bring the Chinese food," he said. "I'll be there in an hour."

After selecting one action-adventure film and another more gentle drama, Julie let herself into her duplex long before Kevin was due, glad she had finally cleaned the place up this week. She doubted Kevin would appreciate how great a sacrifice that was. After maintaining pristine conditions at work, she was content to let things go a bit in her home.

She set the table, made certain everything was in perfect order, showered and leisurely changed into a pair of comfortable knit pants and matching lightweight sweater. Shedding her professional image, she brushed out her hair, completed her makeup and dabbed perfume at the base of her throat before the doorbell chimed.

Kevin's arms were loaded with two sacks filled with steaming cartons of Chinese food, but he nearly chucked them both aside to embrace her when she opened the door.

Over dinner Kevin shared what he could of his work, but was only able to confide a minimal amount, and Julie respected his need to keep the nature of his duties confidential. "Has Carlos mentioned Theresa?" she asked, switching to an open topic.

"Only about every other hour."

"Any comments about Mark?"

He shook his head. "Not really. Carlos doesn't offer me advice unless I ask for it, and I try to not poke around in his private life. We're together so much at work that both of us try to put as little strain on the partnership as possible."

"Wise of you," Julie said and began clearing the table. Kevin got up and helped her put the leftovers into the refrigerator.

A pleasant lethargy overcame her the moment Julie sat down on the couch. The sofa was old, but she had brightened it with chintz slipcovers. It was sturdy and comfortable, perfect for lounging and big enough for two people to relax.

Kevin kicked off his shoes as soon as the opening strains of the first movie's sound track could be heard, stretched his long legs in front of him and patted the couch with the palm of his hand. "Closer."

Julie scooted within arm's reach and settled back.

"Closer."

She inched a little nearer and he grabbed her around the waist, dragging her the rest of the way to his corner. "Perfect," he whispered and kissed her hair.

He settled back, one arm comfortably draped around her shoulders, and Julie relaxed, concentrating on the movie. Their conversation was limited to short comments about the plot until the final credits appeared on the screen.

Jumping up, Julie rewound the video and asked, "Want to see the other one?"

"Not really. I'd rather concentrate on you." Kevin didn't know if he could distract himself any longer, be content just to rub her arm, inhale the soft scent she wore and study her profile. He only had a vague idea what the movie had been about and had barely been able to make intelligent remarks about the plot. All he had really wanted to do was touch her skin, taste her lips and listen to her breathing quicken as he kissed her.

"Then I'll put some music on." Julie stalled for time, making an elaborate show of picking out a tape. All through the movie she had been waiting for him to lean over and kiss her and had been disappointed when he hadn't. But now that he had stated his intention she was nervous, unwilling to give in to her desire, yet unable to resist the temptation.

"Something wrong with your stereo?" Kevin asked and walked up behind her, wrapping his arms around her midriff.

"It's just hard to decide what type of music fits the mood." She heard the tremor in her voice and knew he wasn't fool enough to believe her.

"We won't do anything you don't want to." He swung her around and looked down into her worried eyes. "Don't you know that I would never hurt you?"

"This is all happening so fast. I'm not afraid of you. It's me. I can't accept just one night with a man and then walk away."

"You don't give me much credit," he said and tucked her hair behind her ears. "Do you really think that's all I'm looking for?"

"I don't know."

Kevin dropped his hands and released her. "Then maybe we'd better discuss this. I thought I'd made myself pretty clear."

"Now you're angry. I can hear it in your voice."

"I'm not angry, I'm tired. Tired of battling against something I can't change. My last name is Royce and that's the entire problem. If I was Kevin Jones, you wouldn't hesitate, but because George is my brother, I have to constantly prove myself to you."

"That's guilt talking. I haven't mentioned your brother." She crossed the room and pulled the curtain aside, peering out the sliding door. "We agreed that we wouldn't let George affect our relationship. I kept my end of the bargain, but you can't seem to keep yours."

"You're using George to keep me at a distance, Julie. Do you always turn your back on people? Can't you talk to me and look me in the eyes?"

Julie whipped about and faced him. "Kevin," she said, choosing her words with caution, "you're purposely picking a fight. This has nothing to do with either of us. What's really bothering you?"

She watched Kevin shed his mask of anger and saw the pain she knew was lurking beneath. He sat down on the edge of the sofa and stared at the carpet.

"I picked up some clothes from the cleaners a few weeks ago and they didn't want to accept my check. When I showed them that my bank card provided automatic overdraft protection, they grudgingly took it, but the clerk had to get approval from the owner first. When she stepped away from the desk, I picked up the piece of paper she had been looking at. It was a list of people who had written bad checks, and George's name was on it."

"You're not responsible for what George does."

"I'm not, huh? You say one thing, but—"

"I treat you like you need to prove yourself to me," she cut in, repeating his accusation.

Kevin looked at her expressionlessly. "The story gets better," he resumed. "The next time I went into that same cleaners, the surly clerk was all smiles and gracious hospitality. Seems George finally made good on his bad checks and overdue credit. How did he do that a week before payday?"

Julie sat down on the arm of the couch and drew her fingers through his springy, dark brown hair. "I understand why you might worry about George not paying his bills, but it seems a little odd that you're concerned when he does."

"He also paid me back the money I gave to Shorty. Where's all this extra cash coming from?"

"I doubt that you really want me to tell you what I think," she observed.

Kevin looked into her eyes and read the same conclusion he'd been trying not to draw. George had found a second source of income, and there was little chance it was on the police department's list of approved extracurricular activities. "That's what scares me so damn much."

"Besides," Julie resumed, "my hesitancy has nothing to do with your brother. I'm just a cautious person."

"Old skeletons? Older than mine?"

"Antiques." She slid off the armrest onto his lap and hooked her fingers around the back of his neck. "Some rainy day when I want to bore you, I'll tell you about it."

Whatever made Julie wary of accepting people into her life? It was plainly too deeply rooted for her to easily admit, and Kevin realized he couldn't overcome her fear by just pushing it aside. When she was ready, she would tell him. Until then, he would just have to prove she was safe with him.

"Now can I kiss you?" He slid one hand beneath her shoulders and cupped the back of her head with the other. Locking his fingers in her luxuriant curls, he kissed her languorously until she began to respond, gently darting his tongue between her parted lips.

Julie couldn't stand the temptation any longer and impatiently tugged his shirt out of his jeans. She wanted to feel his bare skin and sighed in pleasure as her hands skimmed his back, exhilarated by the heat of his flesh and the tight muscles that stirred at her touch.

She tipped her head back when he grazed his lips across her chin and felt once more the tingling ache in the pit of her stomach. Kevin's taut body was straining against her and she pulled him even closer.

"Soon," Kevin whispered in her ear, releasing her from his embrace.

"Did you hire anybody to help you this week?" she asked after her breathing returned to normal.

He smiled and circled his thumb on her knees. "One more for the monitoring room and we're all set. Carlos and I have been training the new guy, and I should be able to leave in two weeks."

"Two weeks?"

"Two weeks from now we'll be in Victoria. That's a promise." Kevin laughed and stood up, taking Julie in his arms as he rose and setting her upon her feet. "A lifetime, I know. For being so hesitant, you've sure become a greedy little thing. I like that."

Julie couldn't help but hear the wicked, husky note in Kevin's voice. Her ears burned and her toes tingled. "It's a date," she whispered, unable to say more.

After Kevin left, she laid her face against the cool metal of the front door and waited for her pounding heart to grow still and for her cheeks to cool. Julie rejoiced in the power Kevin had given her.

She awoke the next morning feeling more alive than she had in years. Sensing that if she stayed home, she would pounce on the phone every time it rang, hoping it would be Kevin calling, she decided to drop in on Theresa, who had an open-door policy toward family and friends. A van similar to Kevin's was parked in the driveway and when she walked by, she read the sign on its door. Her assumption that Carlos couldn't stay away was confirmed.

"Just in time to save me a phone call," Theresa said and flung the door wide open. "How about going dancing with us tonight?"

Carlos was sitting at the kitchen table, so Julie asked him, "Do you like salsa? A patient of mine was raving about a new club in Seattle that features a different Latin American band every week."

Carlos laughed and inquired, "What did you think? Romero's a Norwegian name?"

While they waited for Kevin to answer his pager and finalize their plans, Julie watched while Carlos and Theresa sketched out the barbecue Theresa wanted to build. Which type of brick to use seemed to be the most serious difference of opinion between them, but Carlos finally bowed to the home owner's wishes.

"You're paying for it, so have your way. I'm just cheap hired help," he said, and continued writing out the list of supplies they would need for the job.

"Good morning, Mark," Theresa said as her son entered the kitchen.

"Hi, Mark," Carlos said, lifting his head. "How's it going?"

Mark didn't acknowledge Carlos's greeting, but turned to his mother. "I have a track meet. Bye."

"What time will you be back?" Theresa asked.

"Late. I have a date tonight."

"Mark," Carlos said, grasping the boy's arm as he rushed by, "I asked you a question."

"I'm just wonderful, Mr. Romero. Thank you for asking. How are you?"

"Pretty good," Carlos replied casually. "Too bad you're not going to be home."

Julie was surprised that Carlos had ignored the sarcasm in Mark's voice. Mark's battle with his curiosity was so obvious that she had to choke back her laughter.

"Why?" Mark asked with difficulty, nearly strangling on the word.

"I thought we might talk to your mom about getting you a dog. She's not completely opposed to the idea, but she's concerned you won't take care of a pet and doesn't want the extra responsibility."

Theresa smiled at her son and added, "Carlos offered us one of his new puppies. You think about it."

Julie knew that Mark had been nagging Theresa for years to buy a dog and marveled at the sudden shift in her friend's attitude. Obviously, Carlos had managed to convince Theresa that it might be good for Mark to have a pet.

"Really?" Mark said, looking inquiringly at his mother.

"Maybe. A dog is a lot of work, and I don't have time to train a puppy. It would be up to you to take care of it."

"I will, I promise," Mark said. "Thanks, Mr. Romero."

"Wait a minute," Carlos said. "This is not a done deal. You have to prove to me that you'll give the puppy a good home. I'm picky about where my animals live."

The insistent blaring of a horn ended the conversation abruptly.

"That's my ride to the meet," Mark explained. "I have to go."

Julie understood what Carlos was hoping to achieve, but was worried the plan would backfire. "Mark makes a lot of promises," she said when the young man had disappeared. "Will he keep this one?"

"Not without signing a written contract," Carlos declared, facing Theresa squarely. "Right?"

"Oh, he'll keep his word. He's wanted a dog ever since he was a little boy and I've always said no. I just hated the thought of all the hair and muddy footprints."

Theresa's house was a visible testament to her sense of perfection, Julie reflected—everything was always clean and in its proper place.

"Kevin hasn't called back yet," Carlos observed. "Why don't you call him?" he suggested to Julie. "Try the office first."

She didn't have to twist Kevin's arm too hard to persuade him to come dancing. She assured him he'd blend right in with all the other people who didn't have the vaguest idea what they were doing on the dance floor, but were having a good time, anyway. Julie was smiling when she hung up the phone. And, realizing that three was a crowd from the way Carlos and Theresa had their heads jammed together over the list for the hardware store, she said goodbye and left the two of them alone.

ALTHOUGH SHE WAS anticipating an evening of dancing and lighthearted entertainment, things didn't work out that way. There was a message from Kevin on her answering machine when she got home late that afternoon, apologizing for ruining her evening. He explained that Maximum Security's only experienced employee had called in sick, leaving Kevin to cover the monitoring room.

So Julie headed for the local gym and a strenuous aqua aerobics class, followed by a circuit of the weight machines. Exhausted, she was happy to head home and snuggle in bed with a book by her favorite mystery author, the phone at her bedside.

While Julie tried not to keep staring at the phone and willing it to ring, Kevin scanned the computer screen. The most aggravating part of the job wasn't so much the boredom of night duty as the frustration of not being able to confide in Julie.

Most women he had known would have balked, fussing about having a date canceled at the last minute, but not Julie. Always supportive, never complaining, wasn't she even a little too happy with the distance his career put between them?

"How's my girl?" he wanted to know, smiling to himself the moment she answered the telephone on Sunday morning. They had talked until nearly midnight last night, but Kevin needed to hear her voice again.

"Sore, legs like noodles and arms like two pieces of lead. In other words, I had a great workout last night."

"Then you might want to book a hotel with a gym," he suggested.

"It's set? You can definitely get away?"

"June may not be the most reliable as far as the weather goes, but we're going. Would you mind making the plans? I don't think I could squeeze one more thing into my schedule."

"It sounds like fun to me," Julie said. She had not had the luxury of traveling any farther than the Oregon coast or eastern Washington except for one brief vacation when she was eight. The prospect of researching where they would stay and what restaurants were recommended by the guidebooks was exciting.

Refreshed and rested, Julie spent several hours at the library researching the city of Victoria, British Columbia, one of Washington's neighbors to the north. They had a choice of driving to the city of Vancouver and taking a Canadian ferry across the Strait of Georgia, booking space on one of the cruise ships that operated out of Seattle, or driving north to Anacortes and enjoying a leisurely trip through the San Juan Islands on a Washington State ferry. The scenic route through the islands easily won the contest.

The guidebooks were filled with information about the legion of hotels and restaurants in Victoria, and Julie had a difficult time deciding where to stay. After eliminating all the major hotel chains as too expensive and impersonal, she narrowed her search to two possibilities. Returning home, armed with phone numbers, she booked a room in a small, privately run inn close to the heart of the city.

The prospect of escaping with Kevin for an entire, uninterrupted weekend allowed her to face Monday morning with exceptional enthusiasm. She scanned her schedule when she sat down at her desk and was pleased to see the appointment book was filled for the whole week.

The name didn't stand out at first; her eyes were moving too fast to register any one individual, but something—a subconscious trip wire?—guided her back to Wednesday's schedule. Penciled in was the name Denise Royce. Julie had heard Kevin refer to Denise too many times to doubt that this was George's wife. How should she handle this new patient? she wondered.

Julie turned to Theresa for advice. "Just between you and me," she told her friend later that afternoon in the break room, "I have a potential problem with a new patient."

"Who?"

"Denise Royce."

"Sticky wicket, Dr. Bennett. Did she come to you on a referral?"

"Nope. What do I do?"

"You've left out some puzzle pieces, Doc. I don't see where there's a problem. Pretend you don't know she's married to a jerk, look in her mouth and send her one of your outrageous bills. Easy."

Julie fiddled with her hair, tucking some loose strands back into the braid. "There's likely to be a deductible on her dental insurance and..." She hesitated to tell even Theresa about George's financial difficulties, but knew she needed to talk to someone about her dilemma and didn't dare mention it to Kevin. "And I don't think she can afford to pay it."

Stupefied, Theresa looked at Julie in amazement before she started laughing. "Right! Have you met Mrs. Royce? There's no question about her not paying her bills. She's loaded."

"Wrong," Julie told her. "George owes everyone he knows money. Kevin paid his bill at Shorty's and two years' worth of back property taxes. That's just the two Kevin could afford to clear up. I know of three others, and I'm sure Kevin's kept quiet about more."

They discussed Julie's predicament, Kevin's naive involvement, George's squandering and Denise's apparent ignorance of the entire dreadful situation. But regardless of what her emotions were telling her, Julie couldn't ethically refuse to treat a person just because he or she might not be able to pay. It might not have been the soundest of business policies, but she had reconciled her conscience with her checkbook when she first opened her practice.

Without fanfare, Julie had worked on elderly men and women who couldn't have afforded proper dental care if she hadn't offered monthly payment plans. She had treated children, ignoring their parents' lack of finances, and had offered emergency care to residents of a local group home without charging extra for the late hours. She considered it her contribution to the community and didn't expect or want public recognition. But she did demand payment from employed adults who stepped into her office.

Every preconceived notion she'd had about George's wife withered and died the moment Denise Royce introduced herself at the beginning of the appointment on Wednesday. Denise was lovely, well-groomed and soft-spoken. Julie tried to picture Denise and George as husband and wife and shuddered at the thought.

"I believe you know my brother-in-law, Kevin," Denise said after Julie had completed the preliminary questions.

"Yes, I do." She wasn't about to admit they were more than casual acquaintances. She was positive that Kevin had not made George privy to his private life.

"What about my husband? Have you treated him?"

The way Denise asked, glancing up through her eyelashes as she spoke and nervously twisting the end of her belt, alerted Julie to the fact that Denise was well aware of George's feelings about her, but didn't necessarily share his opinion.

"No," Julie said, willing to play along for the moment, "I've never had the pleasure, but I've heard a great deal about Mr. Royce."

Denise did not reply, and Julie began her examination. Unless her patient was feigning ignorance, it seemed she was completely unaware of George's financial difficulties.

"When was the last time you visited a dentist?" Julie asked after Denise's teeth had been cleaned and she had reviewed the X-rays. Her teeth were in excellent shape. It looked as though Denise Royce's loyalty to the dental community at large made up for Kevin's betrayal.

"About two months ago."

Immediately suspicious of Denise's motives for being in her clinic, Julie said, "Then I don't understand why you're here. You take better care of your teeth than anyone I've seen in a long time."

"Didn't they tell you? There's nothing wrong. I just want you to put veneers on all of them. Don't you think I would look much better if you covered up the yellow tint and made my teeth sparkling white?"

Julie was tongue-tied. The more involved she became with the Royces, the more intimate her knowledge, the more ridiculous their lives appeared. Kevin needed to see an oral surgeon in the worst possible way and wouldn't go, no matter what Julie said, and Denise was requesting an expensive, unnecessary, purely cosmetic procedure.

"Are you aware of how expensive veneers would be?" Julie asked.

"That's not a problem. Would you like a deposit? I'll just write a check and you can apply it to the bill," Denise said and leaned over to pick up her purse.

Julie was staring at Denise Royce's check for three hundred dollars before she realized it. She watched Denise's trim figure retreat down the hall and wondered how she would ever explain this to Kevin.

KEVIN HAD ESCAPED for the evening and invited her to go for a long, energetic walk. Walking along hand in hand with her, he had explained that days of being trapped inside offices and windowless rooms had left him feeling like a mole.

Julie stopped and squatted to inspect a patch of pretty little flowers, grabbing at the chance to put her doubts about Denise and George aside. She gently ran her fingertip across the tiny petal and concentrated on the vivid pink, lacy blossoms, sensing that if she looked up at Kevin, said even one word, she would end up telling him everything. She also knew that he would accept the responsibility for paying Denise's bill.

"You're not fooling me," he said, bending down next to her. "I know exactly what you're thinking."

"If you're psychic, look into your crystal ball and tell me what the future holds." Mentally she crossed her fingers, hoping against hope that Kevin overestimated his powers of observation.

"I don't need any special gifts to understand what you're thinking, sense what you're feeling. If I look into your eyes and they're a warm, soft turquoise, I know you're happy. Icy cold like blue topaz means you're angry, and a gray tinge means you're frightened.''

Julie had no idea if Kevin's rainbow barometer had any validity, but felt as if she were teetering on the brink of an abyss, where one step forward would pitch her over the edge. Was she brave enough to take the plunge, or should she cling to the edge and wave him goodbye? Falling in love with any man was chancy, but Julie was positive that falling in love with Kevin Royce would be disastrous. Could she pull away, protect herself?

Julie straightened and tucked her hand around Kevin's narrow waist, hooking her thumb in his belt loop. She sighed softly. It was already too late.

CHAPTER NINE

"I THOUGHT we were only planning a three-day trip, not three weeks," Kevin said, glancing at the size of Julie's suitcases.

"If they're too heavy, I can help," she teased.

He scowled at her and snatched the bag. "Guess it doesn't·pay to be a smart mouth."

"Only if you consider this inadequate compensation." Julie strained to reach Kevin's lips and seized the moment to kiss him when his arms were burdened with luggage.

"Mind if we miss the boat?" he asked, nuzzling her neck.

She ducked away from his dangerous kisses and laughed, sprinting ahead of him down the steps. "I thought you were the king of punctuality."

"Only when it doesn't interfere with my life," Kevin said loudly, setting the bags down and locking the door behind him.

They raced north on the freeway unhampered by traffic, escaping early enough to miss the crush of rush-hour commuters. Only one car and a large truck were parked in front of them at the Anacortes ferry dock. Julie rolled down her window to inhale the tangy salt air, thanking the storm front that had blanketed the region with pelting rain yesterday for mov-

ing south. Rearranging her schedule to allow them to
escape on a Friday had been a Herculean accomplishment, and she would have been disappointed if the
weather hadn't proved as cooperative as her staff and
patients.

"Last time I was in Victoria, I was only eight years
old," she said as she stared across the water, searching for the lumbering boat. "We stayed at the Empress Hotel and my father treated us to high tea. It was
easy to pretend I was a princess because I felt like
one."

Kevin took his fingertip and skimmed it down Julie's nose. "I'll bet you looked like a princess."

"It was the last vacation I had with my parents.
First, Mom and Dad were too broke, then Dad died,
and from that point on, my mother was either just re-
covering from a divorce or too entranced with a new
husband to include me in her plans."

Julie seldom commented on her childhood, but
whenever she did, Kevin wanted to wrap her in his
arms and kiss away the painful memories. "Do you
visit your mother in Florida?"

"No. She's happy there, I'm happy here, and we do
better if we stay on opposite sides of the United States.
I love my mother, though," Julie rushed to explain.
"We call each other nearly every week."

"You deserve better," he said, wanting to throttle
Julie's mother for not loving and protecting her child.

"And George is first prize?" She wasn't sorry for
sniping at Kevin. What right did he have to criticize
her family when his own wasn't anything to brag
about?

Kevin sighed and stared out the window. George was an invisible specter, lurking in the wings of their relationship. Julie never missed an opportunity to remind him that she didn't like or respect his brother. The saddest fact was that his own opinion of George was deteriorating with astonishing alacrity. Reaching into his jacket pocket, he fingered the business card he had found on the office floor yesterday morning.

It must have fallen from George's wallet when he'd repaid Kevin for part of the back real estate taxes Kevin had taken care of. At the time, Kevin had been so startled by receiving the two hundred dollars that he hadn't noticed anything unusual. But later, the slick black business card with silver-embossed printing had caught his eye and Kevin had picked it up. It was from an international trading firm that had recently established offices close to Tolt in the nearby port of Everett. On the back a date and time were penciled in, and Kevin recognized his brother's handwriting. Kevin had felt a sudden chill. The time and date on the back of the card corresponded with the evening Carlos had discovered the defense program running on Brent Olsen's computer. Did that just amount to coincidence, or was George involved in the marketing of Nickerson Electronics's new program to a trading company that had found an eager buyer in the international arms market? Had George been involved in the break-in or was Kevin trying to jam the puzzle pieces together to support his own suspicions?

Glancing at Julie, Kevin stopped brooding and tried to smile. He'd been working too many hours and his judgment was warped. His brother wasn't any more capable of illegal activities than Carlos was apt to beat one of his dogs. A weekend away from Tolt with the most beautiful woman in the world would clear his mind so that he could discover a logical, sound answer to the entire episode.

"Here she comes," Kevin said, shaking off his melancholy as he spotted the ferry churning across the water.

Julie accepted Kevin's mild response as an unspoken apology and lightly rested her hand on his thigh. Silently she scolded herself for having fallen into the trap of allowing George to intrude on their time together and promised herself once more that it wouldn't happen again.

"What's the first time you can remember riding on a ferry?" she wanted to know, determined to create a holiday mood.

"Way back. My parents both worked hard, but they firmly believed in time off for good behavior. We took a lot of small family trips, and the islands were a favorite."

He grew silent as he negotiated her car along the narrow aisles of the ferry, nosing up to the front of the boat where a burly attendant was pointing to an empty spot.

"I don't know about you, but I'm ready to forget we live in Tolt, that either of us has a family," Julie said after he turned the ignition off. She coaxed him with a hopeful smile.

"Family? I have a family? What ever gave you such a bizarre idea, J.B.?"

"Never should believe gossip," she said and carefully opened her door. She wound her way past the other cars to meet Kevin at the base of the steep flight of stairs leading to the upper deck. The shrill blast of the boat's whistle sounded their departure and muffled their footsteps on the metal treads.

"Front or back?" Kevin inquired when they reached the landing. He took her hand and tucked it into the crook of his elbow.

"Never look back," she said and turned to the front of the boat.

Protected by a wall of glass was a flank of deck chairs, but Julie didn't want to hide inside. Instead, she urged him out onto the walkway suspended over the bow. The stiff wind tore at their clothing, thrashing her long hair about her face, and she captured it inside her coat.

"When I'm rich and famous," she said, raising her voice to be heard over the throbbing engines, "I'd love to have a place on the beach and watch wild winter storms from my cozy cabin. It would be a funky hideout of weathered shingles."

"Would it have a big fireplace?"

"Absolutely," she said, expanding her dream. "Do you think three bedrooms would be enough?"

They designed the cottage as they stood on the deck, nippy wind sneaking fingers of cold through their coats. After they had agreed on the floor plan, Julie reluctantly admitted she was turning into a chunk of ice.

"A cup of cocoa will fix you right up," Kevin said and they walked back inside the spacious, warm cabin.

Julie waited on the vinyl-covered bench and fished the ferry schedule out of her purse to study their route through the islands: Lopez, Shaw, Orcas, Friday Harbor and finally Sidney, British Columbia. The three-and-a-half-hour trip would take them through the Strait of Juan de Fuca, one of the most majestic regions in the Pacific Northwest. She closed her eyes to control the rattling of her teeth as a ripple of exhilaration collided with a shiver.

When Kevin returned, she cupped her hands around the plastic cup and prudently sipped the scalding-hot chocolate. It conquered her chill and she finally noticed that his hand was resting on her leg. His long, broad fingers weren't rough and scarred, but a stranger could tell he was accustomed to physical labor since his nails were clipped very short, his palms weren't soft and smooth, and there was an obvious strength to his grip. She lifted one of his fingers to inspect the ring he wore, not recognizing the dark stone, but familiar with the tiny gold crest, the Marine Corps insignia.

"What's this?" She tapped the stone and studied it closer. It was a deep green, nearly black with tiny flecks of red running through it.

"A bloodstone. It's the birthstone for March."

"I've never seen one before."

"My brother gave it to me for my twenty-first birthday." Kevin was almost afraid to admit it was a gift from George—even mentioning his brother's name might spark a rebellion. He hurried on. "Kind of scary to think you were still in grade school then."

Julie had given the ten-year age gap between them little thought and was surprised that Kevin would. "Does that bother you?"

"Do you mean that I'm a decade older than you are? Not a bit."

Twisting to face him, Julie saw that he was grinning and his eyes glinted with mischief. "Next I suppose you're going to give me that line about older men being like wine, improving with age."

"Not really. Marines are more like beef jerky. Tough to bite, impossible to chew, but satisfying once you acquire the taste."

"Carlos would box your ears if he heard you bragging like that."

"No, he wouldn't. It's his line."

They chatted about Carlos and Theresa. "He'll be good to her, but will she be able to accept Carlos's interference in Mark's life? Carlos won't sit back and watch Mark run roughshod over her. He'll walk out the door first," Kevin suggested.

"Carlos wouldn't be the only man Mark's successfully scared away," Julie commented.

"Mark doesn't intimidate Carlos. Have a little faith in the miracles a determined person can work," Kevin retorted, surprised.

"I guess I don't believe in miracles," she said and rested her head on his shoulder. "But I'm trying."

The unexpected shift in Julie's attitude revealed by the soft, melancholy admission was unnerving and Kevin held her even tighter. No one, absolutely no one, was going to come between them, he swore silently. They had both earned the right to be happy and were entitled to every moment of it.

They sat and stared out at the magnificent scenery, content just to be close, and the handful of other passengers never intruded upon their self-imposed isolation. When the sun chased the morning chill away, warming the sheltered observation area, Kevin retrieved a blanket from the trunk of the car. They staked out two lounge chairs in an empty corner and snuggled together in a private cocoon.

The sun beat down upon them, a blissful languor seeped into Kevin's tense muscles, and he felt the strain of the past weeks melt away. Sneaking his hand across the armrest dividing him from Julie, he twined his fingers through hers and tipped his head back to doze. He was hovering in that wonderful spot halfway between sleep and consciousness, his senses attuned only to his immediate surroundings.

Kevin barely moved his fingers over the tender skin of Julie's wrist, her pulse setting a steady cadence, and savored the texture of her flesh, soft and smooth like worn velvet. Outside he could hear water surging past the ferry and gulls screeching overhead, but nothing beyond their private oasis had any meaning for him.

Julie propped her book on her knees and thought about what Theresa had said to her last night.

"You're a ninny if you don't grab this chance and hold on to it."

About ready to phone Kevin and cancel the weekend, Julie had called Theresa first.

"I'm not ready for this," Julie had said. "I need more time. After all, I've only known him for little over a month."

"This has nothing to do with Kevin and we both know it. At least be honest with yourself."

"Okay, my wise friend, what pearls of insight are you selling?"

"First, good men like Kevin are scarce, and you don't ignore one who camps on your doorstep. Second, you're not your mother. I repeat, you are not your mother. You're independent and capable of taking care of yourself, but that doesn't mean you have to live in a convent your entire life to prove you can survive without a man. Caution is healthy, letting fear cripple you isn't."

Julie silently repeated Theresa's litany. "I'm not anything like my mother. I'm not anything like my mother," she said until she could feel herself begin to relax. It was only a first step, but when she looked at Kevin's tranquil face, she knew she was moving in the right direction.

By the time they arrived in Victoria after a twenty-mile drive from the ferry landing, Tolt was no more than a vague memory. The hotel Julie had booked was on Humboldt Street, just three blocks from the heart of the city, but a world apart. After the bellhop guided them to their room on the top floor, she knew she had made the right choice.

Silently she inspected the bedroom, its Edwardian antiques, down comforter, and the polished dark beams across the high ceilings. This was the most romantic setting she had ever seen. Battenberg lace was draped over the canopied bed and edged the curtains at the small-paned windows. A crystal vase was filled with a rainbow of fresh flowers and a tray of tiny sandwiches was covered by a silver dome, awaiting their arrival. Champagne was chilling in a fluted silver ice bucket flanked by two long-stemmed, platinum-rimmed glasses. Everything was perfect, just as she had ordered.

Kevin tipped the bellman and slid the dead bolt home. He leaned against the door and stared at Julie. "If this is a dream, don't wake me."

"Never?"

"Never," he whispered, crossing the room to take her hand in his and kiss the soft palm. He glanced up and saw that Julie's face had lost all expression; suddenly she looked like an expensive, molded figurine. Confronted by her own handiwork, an elaborately staged scene ready for lovemaking, she was terror-stricken.

"I hope this isn't your idea of lunch," he said, snatching the silver dome off the tray and wolfing down two of the delicate little sandwiches. Julie was clearly ready to jump onto the next boat back to Washington, and he needed to give her a chance to adjust to the idea—the fact—that they were sharing a hotel room, would be sleeping in the same bed. "I was thinking more along the lines of meat and potatoes. Let's find a restaurant."

He made a sweeping bow and saw a look of relief wash away the trepidation. He had to smother his laughter as she hurried past him.

"She's worth a little patience, Royce," he muttered quietly and dropped the hotel key into his pocket.

"Feel like walking?" Julie asked. "We could wander over to the Empress and branch out from there."

He didn't care where they went, as long as they ended up right back in their romantic room. The vision of Julie immersed in swirling bubbles in the bathtub after a long day of pounding the pavement was enough to make him agree to run round and round Victoria if that was what was necessary.

"You're in charge," he said and snatched her hand.

Their first stop was indeed the majestic, ivy-clad Empress Hotel. Overlooking the harbor, she was as grand as the British Empire had been in its prime. They admired the manicured, flower-festooned grounds.

"Your storybook castle," Kevin said, staring at Julie as she cupped a hand over her eyes and tipped back her head to look at the steeply pitched roof.

"Our room was right about there," she said, pointing to the opposite end of the huge building. "My father said this was the poor man's way of visiting England."

By four o'clock both of them had throbbing arches and pleasantly replete stomachs. They had eaten a hearty lunch then had browsed in the shops, looking at kilts and clan crests, Irish linen and Spode china, Indian art and miniature totem poles. Gifts had been purchased, and now they felt free to do precisely what they wished with the remainder of the afternoon.

"I thought I was finished with twenty-mile marches when I quit taking orders from Uncle Sam," Kevin said. "Mind if we ride back to the hotel?" He flagged a quaint horse-drawn carriage waiting at the corner.

"My blisters thank you," she said and gratefully climbed the steps to the small, black-leather-upholstered seat.

The nervous energy that had made her anxious to escape their room earlier in the day had dissipated. She wasn't a bit hesitant about returning. When she reentered the hotel room, she faced it with a measured calm, dropping her armload of packages onto the floor and gratefully kicking off her shoes. Kevin jerked his tie loose and unfastened his collar before he opened the champagne and filled two glasses.

"To us," he said. He held his glass in the air, waiting for Julie to pick hers up.

"To us," she echoed, clinking his glass with a smile.

She set her champagne down to prop the pillows against the cherry-wood headboard. "Make yourself comfortable. I have something I want to explain."

Kevin settled back close to her but not touching. "What's so serious, sweetheart?"

His use of the endearment gave her the courage to plunge in. "Do you remember how you thought I didn't trust you?"

"Vividly," he said softly.

"I promised myself I would never be dependent on a man. All the experts say we pattern our behavior after our parents, and I don't ever want to be like my mother."

"Wait a minute. I'm confused. I thought you liked your mother."

She hugged her arms around her knees and studied Kevin's angular face. Could he understand? Could anyone ever understand? She had spent years trying to unravel the maze of emotions and still wasn't sure she could put it into words, but knew she had to try. It was imperative for Kevin to understand who she really was and accept her need to maintain her own identity.

"I love and accept my mother for who and what she is, but that doesn't mean I want to repeat history," Julie said slowly, choosing each word carefully. "My mother can't survive without a man. The minute one walks out of her life, she's desperately searching for a replacement. She's so terrified of being alone that she marries any man who promises to take care of her."

"And a few times they've hurt her." He heard Julie sigh and knew he had understated reality. "All right, she's been stomped on."

"A mild version of the truth."

Kevin turned toward her. He wanted to see the color of those expressive blue eyes, monitor her emotions. "I'm not going to hurt you."

"No, you won't. You can't," she murmured.

"Because you won't allow it."

The pain on Kevin's face was obvious and she rushed to explain. "You're a part of my life because it's right for both of us, not because I need a man to support me, drive me to the grocery store, write out the checks. I won't ever give up my freedom, Kevin. I'll always work and have my own life."

"I should hope so," he said incredulously. "What ever gave you the idea I wanted it any other way?"

"You didn't. I just thought..."

"Then you do too much thinking, J.B." He took her hand and kissed each finger. "I like you just exactly the way you are. No changes necessary. If I want a clinging vine, I'll hire a gardener."

She inched down next to him and raked her fingers through his hair, all the way to the back of his neck. "I love the feel of these short little hairs. They're like bristles on a scrub brush."

"Thanks. Here I am, lying on a bed with a beautiful woman, and she tells me I remind her of a scrub brush. Your eloquence is making my head swell."

"I didn't mean..." she said and couldn't finish. His exaggeratedly wounded expression made her laugh, and the longer she stared at him, the more comic his puppy-dog eyes became. There were tears running down her face by the time she could speak again. The fact that they were tears of relief as much as laughter didn't diminish their effect. "I'm sorry. You really have nice hair."

He reached over to brush her tears away and slowly raised himself on one elbow. Dipping his head, he intended to claim her smiling lips in a deep kiss, but halted a whisper away. Her eyes glowed like twin opals, her lips were full, half-parted and her hair fanned across the white linen pillow sham. Every inch of her body was inviting him.

"I love you," he said.

She heard the force of his emotions in the deep, guttural way he spoke, as if the words were being torn from his throat. He wasn't making a lighthearted, flip comment, but was declaring a commitment to her, to them, to their future.

"I love you, too." How long had it been since she'd first realized she was in love with Kevin? She couldn't pinpoint the exact moment. But she knew her feelings had been bubbling for some time, despite the way she had clamped the lid on the caldron of her emotions, defying it to boil over. Her fingers traced the outline of Kevin's cheek, and she rejoiced at her marvelous fortune. Even in her most extravagant daydreams she'd never imagined finding such a magnificent, understanding man.

"I was beginning to get a little worried this was a lopsided love affair," he said and rested his chin on the crown of her head. Her hair was soft, smelling faintly of her perfume, and he buried his face in the burnished curls.

His powerful hands made circles on her back, and Julie could feel her residual tension floating away. "That feels good," she mumbled and snuggled closer. Her ear was on his chest and she could hear the steady pounding of his heart.

Hooking her leg across his, Julie reached up and began blindly fumbling with his tie. She had seen women who could unknot a man's tie like a pro, but didn't have the vaguest notion of how to begin. All the while she was tugging at the silky fabric, she could feel his hand making luxurious patterns on her light-weight cotton sweater.

The buttons on his shirt were easier to deal with, and she pulled them free, dancing her fingers down his chest until she reached his belt. A deep V of bare skin was exposed to her touch, and Julie rested her cheek on the sprinkle of dark brown curls. Her eyes were half-closed and the well-developed muscles of his chest rose like steep knolls from the flat surface of his stomach. She traced the curves with her fingertips and smiled when she felt his heartbeat accelerate.

"That's not fair," he complained lightly. "I always play by the rules."

With a quick kiss upon her delectable lips, Kevin eased Julie's leg aside and sat up. "My turn," he said and inched her sweater up her ribs until it was bunched at her neck. He tried to pull it over her head, but it caught on the tip of her nose; she stretched her hands behind her neck to undo a button.

With her elbows angled away from her body, her breasts were thrust forward, and he delighted in his first glimpse of rose-colored nipples peeking through sheer lace. She tossed the sweater aside and he gently flipped her hair back over her shoulders to allow him a full view of her luscious, beckoning breasts.

She expected him to make quick work of her bra, but he seemed to be fascinated with the pale pink lace bordering her skin. He fingered the trim until Julie thought she couldn't wait a second longer for him to take the clasp and remove the garment.

Kevin watched her nipples form hard little buttons of desire and resisted the urge to rip off the rest of her clothes. He had waited too long to find the right woman and was determined not to rush things now that they were finally together.

Straining toward him, Julie tickled the edge of his cheek with the tip of her tongue. His skin was coarse from the day's growth of beard and she outlined his jaw with tiny kisses. Her breasts brushed against the rougher texture of his chest, and she shivered in delight at the pressure of his muscles against her aching nipples.

Beyond control, Kevin jerked off his shirt and yanked loose the clasp on Julie's bra. He couldn't wait any longer to feel her smooth, soft skin molded against him. A streak of fire bolted through his body at the first contact. Knowing he could capture the prize that was waiting, eager for his hungry lips, but denying himself the pleasure, was exquisite torture. Finally he bent to kiss her, and when she matched his passion, he lost the battle for self-control. Cupping one breast in his hand, Kevin leaned forward to possess the other with his lips.

She responded to his sudden urgency as a river swells after torrential rains; her tentative explorations burst loose in a frenzy of wild, primitive longing beyond thought or reason. Julie was as frantic to feel Kevin's body merge with hers as he was to claim her.

The silence of the room was broken by his incoherent words of love. "I'm not sure what I ever did to deserve you," he muttered, squirming out of the rest of his clothes, "but I must have been a very, very good boy."

Leaning back, he watched Julie fling her skirt aside, following it rapidly with a sheer slip and panty hose. When she hesitated a moment, he reached over and slowly peeled the scrap of lace panties down her long, slender thighs. Kevin lowered her to the bed and angled himself above her, hovering inches away while his eyes feasted on her flawless body.

"All mine, lady love. You're all mine," he said, slowly parting her legs and wrapping her calves around his waist.

She clutched his shoulders, drawing him closer, closer, wanting to bridge every minute gap between them, and wriggled down a hairbreadth until she met his masculine desire. She began to rock her hips back and forth and Kevin firmly stoked her passion. "Now, Kevin. Love me," she breathed, her hands frantically guiding him deeper, deeper.

His brown eyes were wide open and he locked her in a gaze of satisfaction, owning his pride at their union. He was smiling, presenting her with the gift of his love, and she kneaded his tight buttocks with hungry fingers, encouraging him to increase his pace. She tried to keep her eyes open and memorize each expression that fluttered across his face, then lightning claimed her and she relinquished herself to its power.

Julie knew she was crying out his name and made no effort to stop.

"You're perfect, sweet thing," Kevin moaned as his own body arched and shuddered wildly. "Absolutely perfect," he said when he could finally speak again.

He sank to the bed next to her and she curved her body into his while he stroked the arch of her hip. "A penny for your thoughts," he whispered in her ear.

Julie recovered slowly. Now she knew that she had been wrong for all these years about eventually becoming bored with a man. She would never grow tired of Kevin, never be bored by his lovemaking and never forget their first, beautiful moment of complete surrender.

"Wiggle your finger if you're happy," he said. Her back was turned to him, so he couldn't see her expression.

"I may never move again," she said blissfully and closed her eyes.

"We have souvenirs to prove we did leave the hotel room at least once," he said.

She was returning to reality and managed to find the energy to run her finger up and down Kevin's forearm. "Would you be insulted if I took a little nap?"

"Only if you object to the way I plan to wake you up," Kevin said and cupped her breast in his hand, pulling her closer to the part of him that was signaling his renewed desire. "Just don't plan on sleeping too long." He thrust his hips forward and proved that any rest at all would be short-lived.

"You're bad," she said and giggled, then rolled over to face him.

"Is that a complaint?"

"Only if you rush," Julie said and began kissing her way down his chest.

By the time their hunger for one another was sated, the bedroom was camouflaged by shadows and a deep rumble from Kevin's stomach brought Julie up on her elbow to look at the clock. "Sounds like a complaint from the breadbasket." She patted his flat stomach and it echoed in hollow protest. Ducking away from his protective arm, she added, "I'm going to shower before dinner. I promise to save some hot water for you."

He lunged for her, but his effort was only half-hearted. The sight of her prancing nude across the floor was enough to make him collapse back onto the pillows to savor her long-legged, supple figure with his eyes. After a few days in Hong Kong he had grown immune to its raucous beauty; two weeks in Puerto Rico had inured him to tropical beaches; a month in the Netherlands had left him weary of canals, riotous flower gardens and windmills. But Julie Bennett of Tolt, Washington had captured his heart forever.

CHAPTER TEN

"IF AN AMERICAN DOCTOR wrote a prescription, would a Canadian pharmacy fill it?" Kevin asked, peering over the rim of his coffee cup at Julie.

It was a peculiar question and she hesitated before answering. "Well, I suppose if there were special circumstances a Canadian physician might cooperate."

"No, no. For instance, could you write a prescription and have it filled this morning?" Although he hated to admit he was suffering, Kevin didn't know if he could tolerate the gnawing pain of his tooth any longer. He'd spent the night pacing the hotel room with ice packed against his cheek while Julie slept, hoping that by morning the throbbing would ease or he could figure some way out of this dilemma without involving her.

The searing pain hadn't subsided, and the rain-streaked, gray morning matched his mood.

"No." Now she was positive she knew why Kevin was questioning international medicine and steeled herself to keep her resolution. "I'm sorry, Kevin. There's just no way I can get any antibiotics for you."

He stared out the restaurant window at the snow-tipped Olympic Mountains across the strait. They were having a late brunch in a white clapboard farmhouse before they drove to Swartz Bay for the ferry to

Tsawwassen on the mainland. Because they had slept late, they had missed today's only ferry sailing from Sidney back to Anacortes.

Kevin momentarily considered buying a pair of pliers so Julie could yank his tooth out right here and now, but realized he didn't deserve such a quick solution. She had warned him this might happen and it was entirely his own fault.

"When did it start hurting?" Julie asked, her tone sympathetic but firm.

"Saturday afternoon. And you don't have to tell me it's my own fault."

She calmly set her fork down and folded her napkin. "Let's go out to the car and I'll take a look at what's going on in there. Then we can hit a drugstore I noticed not too far back down the highway. We'll get what we can for the pain and start home. Ready?"

"You're supposed to tell me what a fool I am, bawl me out for ignoring my health, or at least be angry with me for ruining the day."

"And then I would write a prescription for more antibiotics, hover over you like a mother hen and make it all better. Right?"

He was holding hot coffee in his mouth, the heat temporarily masking the pain, and had to gulp before he could answer. "I promise I'll make an appointment first thing tomorrow morning."

"Wrong," she said and laid her hand over his. "Tomorrow morning you're having that tooth pulled. I care about you too much to allow you to stall any longer."

The whites of his eyes were bloodshot and his face was haggard with fatigue. If Julie hadn't known what was wrong, she would have suspected Kevin had been out drinking all Saturday night. Obviously he was miserable, but she wasn't surprised. Over and over again she had reminded him that eventually he would be forced to visit the oral surgeon and he had ignored her. Now there was no way to dodge reality.

"Let's go," he said gruffly and picked up the check.

With only sunlight filtered through a dense cloud bank to illuminate his mouth, Julie could see very little, but his jaw was starting to swell and she scolded herself for not spotting it earlier. *You're slipping, Dr. Bennett,* she thought.

"If that drugstore is open, we can get some Codeine Contin pills, stronger than anything available over the counter in the United States. It'll take the edge off," she said and tenderly cupped his flushed cheek in her hand.

They retraced their route, and Kevin waited in the car while Julie made a quick excursion into the pharmacy.

"These aren't going to do much good," he said, reading the label on the bottle that she handed him when she returned.

"They will. At least temporarily. And so will my grandmother's special remedy."

"Which is?"

"Tea bags. Once we get on the ferry, I'm going to buy a cup of tea and pack that tooth."

"Why don't you just hire a shaman and have him throw some magic powder on the fire?" Kevin inquired sarcastically.

"I know you're miserable, but don't use me as your whipping boy."

He clutched his forehead with one large hand and blindly reached out to her with the other. "I'm not angry with you. I'm disgusted with myself, but this is the worst it's ever been, Julie. I'm sorry, really sorry."

"So am I. And the sooner we get home, the sooner I can make arrangements with Dr. Hartmann. Ready?" He nodded his head in the middle of swallowing two capsules, not even bothering to open the can of soda she had brought him. She couldn't offer any physical consolation, her hands and eyes occupied with the busy Island Highway, but tried to sound compassionate. "Pain is a great motivator."

"If I said you were wrong, I'd be lying, but my timing sure stinks. Carlos is expecting me to work tomorrow night, and my client will be more than just a bit anxious when I'm not on the job bright and early Monday morning."

"You're taking tomorrow off, Kevin Royce. Doctor's orders."

"Yes, ma'am, Dr. Bennett, ma'am."

Kevin's lapse into Marine Corps formality sounded strange and Julie chuckled at his loud, gruff response. Ordinarily he spoke in a low-pitched, calm tone, and she had difficulty picturing him hollering at an entire platoon of men.

"Damn it, Julie," he mumbled, interrupting her reverie, "I wanted our last day together to be special."

"What do you mean by 'last day'?" A tendril of suspicion seized her. "Are you trying to tell me that I'm not going to see you again?"

"Of course that's not what I meant," Kevin said, stunned that she would even consider such a possibil-

ity. Did Julie think he told women he was in love with
them just to ease his conscience? "I was referring to
our trip, not our future. I love you, Julie."

"If that's the case, would you feel better if I pouted
for a while?" she said teasingly to cover her embar-
rassment. When would she be able to trust in Kevin's
affection? When would she quit waiting for him to
open the door and walk out? She hated her doubts,
but they continued to pop up the instant he mis-
phrased a comment.

"Pouting might help," he said lightly. "It also
might be a refreshing change for you to believe that it's
all going to be just fine. We'll be so happy that the rest
of it will be unimportant." When she didn't respond,
he asked quietly, "Can you believe that?"

"Part of me does."

"Only part?" he said, clenching his teeth to keep
from moving his mouth. Talking was becoming increasingly difficult. "Why not all?"

She concentrated on an unexpected curve, braking
to slow down. When she could refocus her attention,
she said, "Before we end up arguing, let's drop the
subject. Besides, my mother always told me it wasn't
polite to pick on invalids."

His nerves were stretched tighter than his brother's
budget seemed to be and Kevin jammed a tape into the
cassette deck to eliminate any further need to talk.
Hunching down on the seat, he leaned back against
the headrest and watched the wipers leap back and
forth across the windshield. Since they left the restaurant it had been drizzling, but a few miles back the sky
had turned leaden gray and the spring shower had
turned into a downpour. It looked more like an early

November evening than a Sunday afternoon in June and seemed appropriate for the way he was feeling.

Fatigue and medication made Kevin's eyelids droop, and Julie was grateful for the respite. He barely awoke when the car clattered onto the ferry, and before they were two minutes away from the dock his breathing was slow and even again. Quietly she slid out of the car and eased the door shut, leaving him alone while she stretched her legs topside and bought a cup of tea for when he woke.

On her return she rummaged in the trunk for the blanket and pulled her sweater out of the suitcase for Kevin to use as a makeshift pillow. His legs were angled across the front seat, his feet nearly resting on the gas pedal, his head propped against the passenger window. Realizing it was ridiculous for her to sit leaning against the door for the next hour and a half, she climbed into the back. Bending over the back of the seat, she stretched out Kevin's legs and covered him up.

Content to merely watch him sleep, see his eyelids flicker as he dreamed and monitor his breathing, Julie didn't consider leaving him alone. She was much happier here than she would have been surrounded by a crowd of noisy, uninteresting strangers.

"That's right," Kevin said softly and smiled. "That's my girl."

Julie jumped back, startled by the clarity of his speech. She stared at his eyelids and saw them flutter—Kevin was talking in his sleep. He didn't mumble incoherently like most people but spoke intelligibly.

"You have such pretty hair. Pretty, pretty hair."

She had to clap her hands over her mouth to keep from laughing at the saccharine tone of his voice as he droned on and on about pretty, pretty hair.

"Hush," Julie whispered and stroked his head. "Shh."

He was smiling in his sleep and she paused in her reading to study him. Sleep painted his face with a blush of innocence, and she could picture the little boy he had once been. He would have been the rascal who sat in the back row, always an elbow or a knee scraped, patches on his trousers from catching them on a nail or a tree branch, and smudges of dirt on his cheeks from diving for a ball during a baseball game. As a child he'd lived the life she had always dreamed of, and just being around him made Julie feel as if she hadn't missed quite so much, hadn't been nearly as lonely as memory sometimes suggested.

By the time the blast of the ferry's horn woke him, Julie had heard a detailed recap of their two nights together. She wondered whether the codeine was responsible, or if he was always this talkative when he slept. If so, it would be dangerous to trust Kevin with a secret.

"Nice nap?" Julie inquired and brushed her fingers through his tousled hair.

"I guess. I had a wild dream, but I can't remember what it was about. Yet it seemed so real."

"You can take one more of these," she said and handed him the bottle of painkillers, averting her eyes from his drowsy face and riveting her gaze on the horizon. She was afraid she was going to laugh and embarrass both of them with her confession. It was almost like being a Peeping Tom and getting caught.

"Already? Has it been four hours?"

"Only two and a half, but one more won't hurt. Unless you enjoy suffering."

"It's just that I hate this foggy feeling," he said and shook his head. The sudden movement made his jaw roar to life and Kevin mutely held out his hand.

With Kevin as navigator they made it through Vancouver's southern outskirts in near record time and drove to the border. The wait at customs was unusually short for a Sunday, and they were both relieved not to spend an hour or more in line.

"I'll call Dr. Hartmann's house and convince him you need to be seen tomorrow," Julie said when they were ten minutes from Tolt.

"As early as possible, please," he requested. "I left my van at the office so Carlos could use it if he needed. You can just drop me off there."

"You're going to work tonight?"

"I have to," Kevin told her. "If I'm going to be out of commission for a couple of days, there's no choice."

When Julie stopped in front of Maximum Security's office, Kevin tugged her across the car seat to his side. "We haven't discussed the future, what happens next," he said, toying with one of her gold hoop earrings.

"Can't we just take it step-by-step for a while? There doesn't always have to be a master plan."

"But I like to know where I'm going, what's around the next curve."

"And spoil all the surprises?" she asked. "I can't write out a set of orders and follow the time schedule. Isn't it better to just enjoy being together, relax and take time for what we have and wait to see where that leads us?''

"Is that a diplomatic way of telling me the subject's closed?" Kevin leaned over and captured her face between his palms. "You've put your old suit of armor back on."

"Just don't push quite so hard. This isn't a race, Kevin. It's our lives, our happiness, and I won't be rushed."

"But I need to make up for lost time. All my friends have solid jobs, houses, families."

"And mortgages, orthodontist bills, unsatisfying, dead-end jobs and would trade places with you in a second."

"Just let any of them try," he said and tightened his grip on her shoulders.

"I don't think this is the right time for us to be discussing the future. Codeine Contin makes people say funny things."

"Not a chance, lady," he said as clearly as his swollen jaw would allow.

Kevin emphasized his words by following the curve of her lips with his fingers, his touch feathery soft. He dipped his head lower and she shivered at the way his eyelashes brushed across her neck like the wings of a butterfly.

"You always smell so good," he muttered, nuzzling his way down her neck to the hollow of her throat. "How will I get into your apartment if I decide I need a nap later tonight?"

She smiled, straining toward him. "Wouldn't you rather forget about work completely?"

"A silly question. You're definitely more appealing than my desk, but . . ."

"Just so you don't forget me," Julie said with a sigh and softly whispered into his ear all the delightful things they could share during his nap. Her hands stroked his neck and back while her breathing caressed his skin.

"You'd make a saint forget his vows," he said fervently and tumbled out of the car.

She unrolled the window and called out, "I'll leave the porch light on."

The slight swagger of his narrow hips, the way his slacks accented his well-honed posterior was an inviting vision; Julie wondered what her patients would say if they were to see a photograph of Kevin's magnificent backside on her desk. Laughing at the thought, she started her car and drove home.

Otto Hartmann agreed to remove Kevin's tooth if Julie could bring him in very early and act as an assistant. The surgery would upset her schedule, but she knew it was the only way. If the procedure went like clockwork, she could have him settled in bed and get back to work without completely throwing her day out of kilter. Being gone on Friday had been bad enough; if she canceled tomorrow's appointments, people might start thinking she was unreliable.

ALTHOUGH he had every intention of staying for just a few hours, the moment Kevin walked back into the office his plans evaporated. He was back in a world that he controlled, back in a work mode and, after being at the mercy of a pain he couldn't dominate for the past twenty-four hours, it felt good to be in command again.

"Good, you got my message," Carlos said, looking relieved and bounding out of his chair to Kevin's side.

"Message? What message?"

"Didn't the hotel tell you I called this morning?"

"No," Kevin said and automatically started rubbing his jaw to block the ache.

Carlos exploded, offering a string of Latin expletives while he pawed through the files on his desk. "I called about eleven and asked you to head home immediately."

Ordinarily Carlos remained calm and outwardly serene even in the most tense situations, so Kevin knew that something must be seriously wrong. "We'd already checked out by then, so don't blame the front desk. What's happened?"

"Two of my dogs were poisoned."

"How in the hell did that happen? When?" Kevin knew how distraught Carlos became if someone even mistreated an animal and felt guilty that he had been absent when his friend needed him.

"Last night," Carlos said. "The vet figures it happened about midnight. They were on duty at Nickerson."

"Are they all right?"

"Yes, they'll both recover. Their handlers noticed they were behaving strangely in plenty of time for the vet to counteract the poison."

Kevin jumped to his feet, picked up a coffee mug and considered throwing it against the wall but stopped himself, carefully setting it down again.

"We're out of there. We're not equipped to handle this job."

"That was exactly my reaction, but Bud convinced me I was wrong."

"Then you're both fools. This is a job for the police, not a security company."

Pouring them each a cup of hot water, Carlos dunked tea bags into two clean mugs. "Here. This might help a little."

Kevin hadn't even realized he had been clutching his jaw the entire time he'd been talking to Carlos and stuffed his hand into his pocket. "It's coming out tomorrow."

"Good. What time?"

"I'm not sure yet. Julie's setting it up."

"Then we need to settle this tonight," Carlos said. "We can't call the police. What's happened to justify it? False alarms, a computer terminal accidentally left on and two sick dogs. That's not exactly high profile crime."

"But you know damn well there's more to it than that," Kevin retorted, gulping at the tea. He considered telling Carlos about the black business card he'd found after George's visit to the office; it was in his wallet, but he decided to say nothing for the moment.

"If we weren't doing a good job, would our elusive culprits be so desperate?" Carlos wanted to know. "Obviously our patrols are effective, if those guys have to try to poison my dogs to get rid of them. It's plain that the criminals managed to bypass the electronic system, but they can't get by us, and we're interfering with their plans. Now we just need to figure out who it is that's trying to break in and why."

"Or break out!" Kevin set his mug down with a heavy thud. "That's it! That's why I couldn't find anything wrong with the security program. Think about it, Carlos. Suppose no one was tripping it try-ing to get in. They were trying to find a way to skirt around it on their way out the door." It was the per-fect solution, and best of all, it cleared George of any involvement!

"Are you sure?"

"Positive. I'm a little slow, but I'm not a total dunce. We've been going at this from the wrong di-rection. If they were just petty thieves, they'd have moved on to another location."

With renewed enthusiasm, Kevin and Carlos spent the next several hours reanalyzing their security measures for Nickerson Electronics and devising a plan to maximize their advantage. There would be no set schedule of rounds; each night a new timetable would be implemented with every guard shifting lo-cations. By eliminating any preestablished routine they would increase their effectiveness.

"Enough," Carlos said eventually and yawned. "I'm an old man who needs some sleep."

"But this is just a beginning," Kevin objected. "Now we have to figure out who's trying to waltz out the door with a computer stuffed under his jacket."

JULIE HEARD the front door open and was immedi-ately wide-awake. "Kevin?" she called out. "Is that you?"

"I tried to be quiet," he said, making his way across the darkened bedroom.

"It's all right," she said and snuggled back under the covers.

She heard him undressing, then felt a breath of cool air stirring around her legs and the sagging of the mattress. Closing her eyes, she sighed contentedly as she caught the first whiff of Kevin's after-shave. It was a faint, slightly sweet aroma that made her think of a meadow on a lazy summer's afternoon.

"Finally," she mumbled and wrapped one leg over his, trapping them together.

He hated to pull up close to her and shock her sleep-warmed, bare skin with his cold body, but she erased his guilt when she wiggled her hips against his, molded her backside against his stomach without even a shudder, pulled his arm across her waist and waited for him to cup her breast.

Kevin had been expecting to lie awake the entire night, counting the slats in the window shades, but Julie's warmth, her silky skin, limber legs resting on his worked like a soothing balm, and he fell asleep to the light flutter of her breathing across his hand.

"THAT'S RIGHT. Just hold my hand," Julie said between gritted teeth. Kevin was squeezing her fingers so hard that she didn't know if she would be able to move them again, but fortunately he would be unconscious in just a few seconds. She watched his eyes close and pried his fingers apart.

"Here we go, big boy," she said and adjusted her mask.

Even though it was Kevin Dr. Hartmann was operating on, Julie had no difficulty in putting her personal feelings aside and concentrating on the procedure. There was virtually no danger and she enjoyed watching someone as skilled as Otto Hartmann at work. He was one of the best oral surgeons in the Pacific Northwest, and she was grateful Kevin was in such competent hands.

When they finished, she helped maneuver Kevin into the recovery area and sat with him while the anesthetic wore off.

Kevin was content to sleep on, but a voice wouldn't leave him alone. He tried to speak, to tell the voice to just go away, but couldn't.

"Wake up, Kevin. Time to open your eyes. It's all over."

The voice was Julie's; now she was wiping his forehead with a cool, damp cloth.

"Open your eyes, Kevin." Gently she rubbed his arm and smiled when he tentatively opened his eyes. "It's over. No more toothaches."

He sat up slowly, feeling muddled and disoriented. The nauseating taste of the gauze stuffed in his mouth was causing his stomach to rebel, and his arms felt as if he had been bench-pressing four hundred pounds.

"Here," she said and held out a spoon. "A few mouthfuls of chocolate shake should help the queasies."

The ice cream stemmed the nausea and Kevin didn't try to talk but tugged at Julie's hand.

She saw him point to his mouth and read the question in his eyes. "Everything's just fine. Your infected wisdom tooth is out, and in a few days you'll feel better than ever."

Profoundly relieved to have the worst behind him, he looked up at her and tried to transmit his feeling.

Julie accurately interpreted the message in Kevin's eyes. He was thanking her for helping him cross the barrier of his fear, and she knew it was no minor accomplishment. The discomfort had been nothing compared to his terror, and she respected his courage.

"When you're ready, try standing up slowly," she suggested. "We'll get you to the car and I'll drive you home."

Kevin lurched instantly to his feet. He didn't have any desire to linger in this place. By leaning on Julie and concentrating on slowly putting one foot down before he tried to pick up the other, he made it to the car.

After a slow climb up the stairs, Kevin stumbled over the threshold of his apartment. His mind was clearing, and he headed straight for the bedroom, yanked a pair of tattered sweats out of his drawer and, without a scrap of false modesty, pulled off his shirt and unzipped his jeans.

Julie followed him, assuming he was going to lie down. When he dropped his shirt onto the bed, she was once again captivated by his size and strength. Just seeing his bare chest froze her feet in place. She watched him try to kick his jeans aside, but they were stuck, and when he bent to untie his shoes, her warning came too late. He abruptly sank to the bed in a heap.

"I'm sorry, Kevin. I wasn't paying any attention and you forgot. Dr. Hartmann wasn't exaggerating when he said you needed to keep your head higher than your heart for the rest of the day."

"Like hell you weren't."

The gauze muffled his words, but Julie had no trouble interpreting. "Is ogling a sexy man forbidden?"

This time she couldn't understand what he said, but from the gleam in his anesthesia-dulled eyes, his meaning was clear.

"There'll be no activity of any sort today," she said with mock sternness. "I'm going to make a bed for you on the couch and I want you to stay there."

He looked so helpless with his little chipmunk cheeks and sad eyes that she hated having to go back to work when he needed her. Julie loved being an integral part of his life. Kevin, loving and generous man that he was, was filling a spot in her heart that she hadn't even known was vacant until now.

After she had him settled on the sofa, she filled a glass with cold apple juice and set it on the table next to him. "Drink as many liquids as you can, but don't sip too hard on the straw," she instructed him.

She was kneeling next to him and Kevin reached out to her. His broad hands spanned her back, pulling her close.

"Oh, no, you don't. You're a sick man."

He shook his head slowly back and forth and his eyes twinkled.

"In case your stomach starts acting up, I'm leaving this coffee can right here," Julie told him.

Sneaking one hand underneath the hem of her skirt, he skimmed his fingers up her stockinged thigh until he came to the flare of her hip.

"Kevin," Julie scolded, trying not to laugh as she batted at his hand, "behave yourself. Anesthesia is supposed to make people sleepy, not frisky."

He slowly withdrew his hand, inch by inch, but made certain Julie could tell he was doing so under protest.

"I hate to leave you," she said as she handed him the remote control for the television set, "but I have to go to work. I'll call you when you need to take your next pills."

He nodded his head and smiled as best he could.

As soon as she could escape the clinic, she headed straight back to Kevin's. He was wide-awake when she arrived.

"Not too bad," he said slowly and carefully, pointing to his face.

She sat down next to him and tested his forehead for any sign of fever. He was cool, his eyes were bright, and the ice packs he'd been using were keeping the swelling to a minimum.

Kevin clicked off the television. "Boring."

"Would you like me to read to you?" She had tucked a light mystery novel into her purse to read on their trip, but had never finished the first chapter.

He scanned the back cover and nodded, a faint smile on his lips and an even brighter one in his eyes. "Mom used to read to me. Hardy Boys."

Julie was learning what special people Kevin's parents had been. Everything about his childhood seemed to have been perfect; he'd had a horse, dogs, cats and chickens, streams to explore, loving parents and an older brother he worshiped. No wonder he defended George. His brother was the last remnant of the security and happiness he had known as a child.

Opening the book, Julie began reading aloud and Kevin settled back, a feeling of peace and contentment washing away the dregs of pain. They were in the middle of the second chapter when Carlos and Theresa stopped by.

"Well, well," Carlos said, gripping Kevin's hand in a brief display of affection, "he really did it."

Theresa set a tray filled with cups of custard on the coffee table. "Dinner is served," she said. "And you don't have to worry about calories or cholesterol." Patting her slightly rounded hips, she turned to Julie. "Would you check to see if I need any teeth pulled? Sounds like a good excuse to go off my diet."

Carlos wrapped an arm around Theresa's waist and squeezed her affectionately. "You need to diet like Kevin needs to grow some more."

"Isn't he adorable?" Theresa said and quickly kissed Carlos's cheek.

Some men would have been flustered by Theresa's enthusiastic affection and praise, Julie thought, but she didn't see Carlos twitch a muscle even to let her friend go. She had never seen Theresa look so happy. The worry lines around her eyes were fading, and the tension that usually clung to her the way a piece of old gum stuck to a shoe was missing, replaced by a happy energy and an added bounce in Theresa's step.

"Remember what we were discussing last night?" Carlos asked Kevin.

Kevin nodded.

"I have some information for you. Our friend doesn't want you to rush back in until you feel better, but he thought you might want to do a little reading."

Julie saw Kevin knit his eyebrows in a frown and wondered what job was so sensitive that the men were obligated to talk in vague generalities.

"Good idea," Kevin commented.

"The reading material's locked in the van. I'll be right back."

Before Carlos had the door completely open, George filled it.

"Hey, kid, why didn't you let me know you were sick?" he inquired.

Kevin's eyes darted to Julie; he saw immediately the loathing she was trying to subdue. Having Julie and George in the same room was as lethal a recipe as putting two fighting cocks into the same ring. The only question was, which of them would launch the attack?

"Unexpected," Kevin muttered, trying to speak clearly. "Have a seat."

Julie saw George's eyes scan the room, passing across her without a flicker of recognition. "Good evening, Mr. Royce," she said distinctly.

"Excuse me," Carlos said, stepping into the breach. "George Royce, I'd like to introduce Dr. Julie Bennett and Theresa Post."

"Theresa knows Mr. Royce quite well, Carlos, and I'm sure Mr. Royce remembers me. Our encounter was unforgettable," Julie said pointedly, refusing to let Carlos smooth things over. She waited for George to respond, but he continued to ignore her.

Kevin caught George's attention and shot up an eyebrow, warning him to tread carefully.

"Here," George said and handed Kevin a brown paper bag. "Thought it might help the pain."

Pulling a bottle of scotch out of the sack, Kevin beamed. "Just what the doctor ordered."

"Not this doctor," Julie said and held out her hand, wondering what kind of an idiot George was.

"Or this nurse," Theresa added. "Alcohol and pain medication can be lethal, Kevin."

He relinquished the bottle and shrugged. "Thanks, anyway."

"Nothing wrong with the healthy people in the room taking a little taste. Just to make sure it's not spoiled," Carlos added and forced a laugh.

Theresa and George laughed, too; Kevin tried to smile and chuckle, but Julie just moved her lips upward, the pretense of amusement never reaching her eyes.

"Excuse me," Julie said, feeling as if she would explode if she stayed in the room another moment. George was still refusing to even look her way. "I haven't been home to change or check my messages. I'll be back in a little while." She grabbed her purse and practically ran from the room.

"Dr. Bennett always seems to be in a hurry, doesn't she? Drives fast and talks fast. Wonder how many citations she's earned?" George inquired.

"Everyone has heard the story, Chief," Carlos said and frowned. "There's no point in repeating it."

"Just professional curiosity. And, speaking of curiosity, how's it going over at Nickerson? Figure out who was trying to break in?"

"Can it," Kevin said and glowered at George.

"Chief," Carlos said, intervening, "Kevin and I don't discuss business outside the office."

"I'm sure you can trust Theresa," George responded. "She doesn't care what goes on over there."

"Theresa, it's not just you," Carlos explained. "Kevin and I have a business based on trust and we don't betray our clients. Ever."

"I understand," she said. "I know a lot of secrets. Working in a doctor's office demands discretion."

"See," George said with a laugh. "All of the people left in this room can be trusted."

Kevin forgot about the pain in his mouth and jumped angrily to his feet. He grabbed George's arm, pulling him towards the door. "Isn't Denise expecting you home for supper?"

"Okay, okay, I can take a hint, Kev. Want me gone before the little lady gets back. Call me when you're bored with her, and I'll introduce you to some of Denise's friends."

He could feel his hands clenching into fists; if any other man but George had made that comment, Kevin would have flattened his face. "You need an attitude adjustment. We'll talk later in the week."

After George had left, Kevin felt obligated to excuse his brother. "Little personality conflict. I guess George needs a few lessons in tact."

"Before you give anybody lessons, you'd better sit down, Kevin," Theresa said, taking his arm. "You're white as a ghost."

His mouth was aching again, and he picked up the pad on which Julie had written down what time he could take his next pill. It was over an hour away. He pressed the ice pack to his face, steeling himself to wait.

"Files," he muttered. He knew he'd done too much talking and tried not to move his mouth any more than necessary.

"You two discuss business while I putter in the kitchen," Theresa said, politely excusing herself.

By the time Julie had calmed down enough to be certain she wouldn't throttle George or snap at Kevin for having been unfortunate enough to have such a lout for a brother, she had changed her clothes, packed an overnight bag and watered her plants. Kevin wasn't responsible for George's behavior, any more than she was accountable for her mother's. The day her mother had moved to Florida had been a blessing, and Julie wondered if she could arrange to have George transferred to Miami.

Returning to Kevin's apartment, she found Carlos and Kevin hunched over a stack of manila folders and heard Theresa singing in the kitchen.

"Don't stop," she said and leaned forward to give Kevin a quick kiss. "I'd better check on the scrubbing wonder in there before she starts stripping the wax off your no-shine linoleum."

"I see your blood pressure's back down," Theresa said when she saw Julie.

"Temporarily. But I'd rather hear about how things are going with you and Carlos."

Theresa didn't stop wiping down the stove as she spoke. "Better than I ever dreamed possible. I was willing to settle for someone who would help me with the bills, keep the car in running order and tolerate Mark. Then I met Carlos."

"That's wonderful, Theresa." Julie jumped up and sat on the edge of the counter. "I need some advice," she said suddenly.

"If it's about men, don't look at me. I couldn't deal with my husband and I haven't had too much luck with my son. Before Carlos moved to town, I was seriously considering selling Mark to the highest bidder, taking my two-dollar profit and running away to join the circus."

"What do you think we'd get for one nearsighted, balding, stupid cop?" Julie asked.

"We don't have enough money to pay them to take George."

"How much am I worth?" Kevin wanted to know, glowering from the doorway.

CHAPTER ELEVEN

"I CAN'T ANSWER THAT," Theresa said with an impish gleam in her eye. "You're priceless."

Theresa was visibly trying to defuse Kevin's anger, but Julie doubted she would succeed. "Sorry about the crack," she said to him after Theresa scurried from the kitchen. "It was just a joke."

She expected Kevin to lecture her on George's innumerable sterling qualities but all he did was refill his juice glass, take a sip and shuffle back to the couch. Not wanting to involve Theresa and Carlos any further, she allowed him to shelve the discussion, knowing there would be numerous other opportunities to argue about George.

"Mark is so excited about bringing his dog home," Theresa told her after they were all seated in the living room. "He goes over to Carlos's house after school every day to work with his puppy."

"Good for him," Julie responded.

"That's what he said?" Carlos asked.

"Mark told me that he rides his bike straight to your house from school."

"He does. Sometimes." Carlos looked Theresa straight in the eye and added, "Other days he never shows."

"You're still giving him the dog, aren't you?" Theresa's voice rose in alarm.

"Maybe. The condition was that Mark prove he's mature enough to care for a pet, and I haven't seen that degree of responsibility. But it's a few more weeks before the pups will be ready to be weaned. He has some time left."

Julie saw Theresa flush; her friend's back stiffened.

"You can't make a promise and then go back on your word." Now her friend was indignant.

"I never made a promise. I was honest with him from the beginning," Carlos pointed out. "Animals aren't toys that can be put away in the closet when Mark gets bored. If he's tired after this short a time, what's going to happen in the next ten years?"

"I'll have a talk with him," Theresa said.

"Why don't we discuss this later? Besides," Carlos went on, "it's time for us to leave. I want Kevin to rest so he'll haul himself back to the office as soon as possible."

Kevin settled for waving goodbye to Carlos and Theresa without speaking. The pain in his mouth had roared to life again, and he didn't want to jiggle the ice packs. Tomorrow he would slog his way back into the mainstream regardless of how he felt, but tonight he was more than content to hold down the couch.

From the minuscule balcony, Julie watched Carlos and Theresa walk to the car. She thought about their relationship. Carlos was calm, even-tempered and gentle, the opposite of the feisty Theresa. They seemed well suited. Theresa had been waiting for a man like Carlos, and her wish had been granted. Julie, on the other hand, hadn't been searching for a man like Kevin to complicate her life, a fantasy and a nightmare all in one.

She sighed and leaned forward to prop her elbows on the railing. It was too late to walk out of Kevin's life now. She was in love with him. But how in heaven's name was their love ever going to survive?

"Come here, J.B.," Kevin called, beckoning her inside.

"I'll be right there. I was just searching for the evening star."

Julie shuddered briefly; how often Kevin tapped into her innermost feelings! The more time she spent with him, the more she was coming to depend on his hidden strengths, the way he had of sensing when she needed him the most, anticipating her moods and saying just the right thing to banish a moment of despondency. It was almost as if there was an invisible link between them, a thought she found a little unnerving.

Recalling the childhood chant her mother had taught her, Julie murmured, "Starlight, star bright..."

Before she could finish, the telephone rang and she rushed indoors to answer it.

"It's Carlos. He says he wouldn't bother you if it wasn't an emergency." She handed the phone to Kevin.

He listened silently for a few minutes, then said, "I'll be right there."

"You're in no condition to go anywhere," Julie intervened, grabbing his arm.

"I need a favor. Will you drive me over to Nickerson Electronics without any questions? I'd go alone, but I feel a little too woozy from that last pill to take any chances." He was fighting to speak as normally as possible, to seem as capable as he could with his mouth stuffed full of gauze and his brain dulled by medication.

"Can't Carlos handle the problem?"

"No."

She searched Kevin's glassy eyes. Though she knew he should be resting, she saw he was going to leave, with or without her help. "All right. If you promise to call me the minute Carlos delivers you back home."

He reached over and grazed her cheek with his fingertips. "What did I ever do to deserve you?"

"Followed doctor's orders," she said and smiled at his feeble, crooked grin.

Kevin changed his clothes and thought about what Carlos had told him. On the way to Theresa's, the man on duty at Maximum Security had contacted Carlos on his car phone after Bud had called, looking for Kevin. Somehow the security system at Nickerson Electronics had been reactivated without Bud's authorization, and every siren in the entire complex was wailing.

"Ready?" Kevin asked, still tucking his shirt into his jeans when he rejoined her.

Julie left him outside the main gate of the Nickerson plant after assuring him she wouldn't mention to anyone the hubbub going on inside the fences. Horns were blaring from each building, brilliant lights illuminated the plant, and Carlos was waiting for him with a phalanx of guards, each struggling to control a barking dog. Two police cruisers blocked the entrance to the compound, and George Royce was propped against one of them, talking into a hand-held radio.

Julie turned her car and sat idling at the corner, wondering what to do with the rest of the evening. She had been looking forward to coddling Kevin, not to sitting alone in the silence of her duplex. Since Theresa had been with Carlos when the original call had come through, squashing their plans for the remainder of the evening, too, her friend must also be sitting at home alone. Julie made a right-hand turn and aimed her car toward her friend's house.

Julie heard shouting the moment she opened her car door. Although she couldn't distinguish the exact words, she recognized Mark and Theresa's voices and rushed up the front steps.

Without knocking she let herself in, tracing the angry sounds to the kitchen. "Hey, you two," she said, announcing her presence, "the entire block can hear you. It might be a good idea to tone it down before your neighbors call the police."

"Julie," Theresa exclaimed, "thank goodness! Maybe he'll listen to you."

"What do you do, Mom? Call all your friends and discuss what a rotten kid you have? Do you keep a diary of everything I do and then pass it around at work?" Mark yelled.

"Mark Allen Post," Julie said firmly, "I won't tolerate that kind of screaming when I'm in the room. Lower your voice, and then we can discuss your problem like rational adults."

"Shut up, Julie!" Mark hollered even louder. "This is none of your business!"

"Wrong," Julie whispered and snatched him by the front of his shirt, obliging him to face her. "You just made it mine. Sit down."

She glowered at him in her most menacing manner, defying Mark to disobey. The moment he threw himself into a chair, Theresa sat down, as well, and put her head upon the kitchen table, hiding her face in her crossed arms.

"Thank you," Julie said. "Now, what's going on?"

"That stupid creep Carlos said I could have one of his dogs and he's welshing on the deal."

Theresa lifted her head. "That's not what I said," she maintained. "Carlos told me that you haven't been going over every day after school like you said you would. You're the one who's not keeping the bargain. If it wasn't for Carlos, I wouldn't even have been considering letting you have a dog."

"The only days I missed were when I had track meets," Mark said sulkily.

"You had a meet every afternoon last week?" Theresa challenged him.

Mark swung his foot back and forth, first thumping the leg of the table, then tapping the rung of the chair. His arms were folded across his chest and he was staring at the floor, lips tightly clamped.

"Well, did you?" Julie demanded.

Thump, thump, thump.

"Mark, answer me."

Thump, thump, thump.

"Go to your room," Theresa told her son.

"Thank you, Mommie dearest," he sneered, got up and sauntered away.

Julie waited until she was certain Mark couldn't overhear what she was about to say. "Are you all right?"

"I should have let Carlos handle this. All I wanted to do was warn Mark that he might lose his chance for a puppy if he didn't follow the rules. I never threatened him that Carlos wasn't going to give him the dog."

"Does Mark ever accept responsibility for his actions?" Julie inquired. "Did he mow the lawn before your party?"

"No. But . . ."

Julie held up a hand. "Hey, I'm no expert. It's just that I'm a step away from this craziness and can see a few little problems that maybe you're too close to notice. Carlos is trying to force Mark to accept the consequences of the choices he makes. If Mark falls on his nose and is disappointed, it might be high time."

"I know you're right, but it's so hard to have him learn everything the hard way," Theresa said.

Julie saw tears in Theresa's eyes and handed her a tissue. "You can't protect him from every bump and bruise. Let Mark make his own decisions and accept the consequences. He'll learn. Besides, Carlos likes Mark and knows what a great kid is lurking underneath that lump of sixteen-year-old rebellion."

Loud music blasted from Mark's bedroom and Theresa jumped out of her chair. Julie grabbed her before she made it across the room.

"He's just doing that to annoy you. Come on, let's go for a walk and forget about teenagers," she proposed. "I want to hear all the details about how it's going with the other man in your life."

As they strolled down the quiet street, Theresa grinned tremulously and inquired, "Do you remember your first kiss?"

"My first kiss or my first good kiss?"

"Why, Dr. Bennett, I do believe Kevin has uncorked the wild woman hiding beneath that white lab coat."

"Why, Ms. Post, I do believe you might be right."

"What I like most about Carlos," Theresa went on more seriously, "is that he doesn't ask me to be someone I'm not. I don't have to apologize for having a teenage son, I don't have to make excuses for being divorced, and I don't have to pretend I like watching sports programs on television."

"Impressive credentials," Julie commented. "Sounds close to perfection."

"He is."

By the time Julie and Theresa returned from their walk, it was nearly ten o'clock. Julie was pleasantly exhausted.

Her key was still wedged in the lock of her door when the phone began ringing. She navigated her way through the darkness to take the call before the answering machine did.

"Hi, J.B.," Kevin's deep voice greeted her.

"Hi, yourself. How are you? It sounds like you're trying to talk without moving your mouth."

"I'm fine. Sore, but I've known worse."

"Are you home?" she asked.

"Not yet. Just wanted to touch base with you and tell you not to worry. I'll call you in the morning. Sweet dreams."

Before she could scold him or even respond, Kevin hung up. She stared at the receiver. Would anything short of a full body cast slow that man down?

The next day was a blur of activity, affording Julie precious few moments to indulge in worrying about Kevin. Her backlogged schedule finally caught up with her, and she didn't even have time to take a break. She gulped down a tuna sandwich at her desk between patients, rather than leave the office for lunch.

Kevin called and left a message with her receptionist. He had worked all night and was home just long enough to grab a few hours sleep before heading back to work. Julie crumpled up the pink slip and chucked it into the trash, irritated that he was reestablishing his old patterns; it was abundantly clear that everything else came before his health.

Tuesday evening, after her last patient had skipped out of the examining room to proudly tell his mother he had no cavities, Julie called Kevin's office.

"Maximum Security Systems." It was Carlos.

"Hi, Carlos, it's Julie. Is Kevin around?"

"No, but he left a message for you. He wants to know if you can have one of the superdeluxe shakes you guaranteed would keep him from starving ready at nine o'clock. And Julie, make it a double. That man gets real testy when he's hungry."

Julie laughed. "A double chocolate malt special will improve his sense of humor."

"Wear your armor just in case."

She chatted briefly with Carlos, then looked at the clock and realized she had plenty of time to finish sorting through her accumulation of mail before she left the office. The quiet times at the clinic never

bothered her; in fact, she treasured the moments when
the phone lines weren't blinking, her hygienist wasn't
waving another chart at her for evaluation, and her
patients weren't blanching and clenching their fists at
the sound of the drill. It was soothing to be at the office when no one was there.

Her desk was soon clear of clutter, and she still had
an hour before Kevin would arrive. Rather than rush-
ing home, she altered her traditional route and followed the twisted maze of residential side streets back
to her duplex.

As she paused at a four-way stop sign, she studied
a plain little bungalow that the owners had charm-
ingly personalized. She wondered what Kevin would
think of the tiny house. A picture of him mowing the
grass while she set out violet hyacinths and bright yellow daffodils in the planter boxes prompted a wistful
sigh, and she found herself smiling.

"Julie Bennett," she said aloud, giving herself a
slap, "quit acting like a moonstruck teenager. You're
years away from such a domestic little scene. In fact,
you might be an entire lifetime away from it."

Jamming the gas pedal down to put as much distance as possible between herself and the bungalow,
she accelerated faster than she intended, and her car
squealed through the intersection. She glanced nervously into her rearview mirror, just in case George or
one of his cohorts was trailing her. She sighed with
relief when no flashing blue lights signaled her to pull
over and by the time Kevin rapped on her front door,
had regained her composure.

"What's for dinner?" he asked, sniffing the air ex-
pectantly.

"Instant Breakfast à la mode."

"What? No steak? No corn on the cob?"

She raised her hand and barely tapped his bruised cheek, watching him flinch in anticipation of the pain. "If I cook it, you'll have to eat it."

"Every little boy's dream. Ice cream for dinner," Kevin said and smacked his lips as he accepted the dish from her.

"Have you had any real problems?"

"Enough to last a lifetime. But nothing I can discuss."

"I meant with your mouth."

"Oh, this? Heck, no. Other than not being able to eat much, it hasn't bothered me a bit. Don't know why I didn't get those pesky devils yanked years ago."

Julie almost choked. After all the wheedling, begging and threatening she'd done, trying to persuade Kevin to see Dr. Hartmann, she couldn't believe what she was hearing.

"Kevin Royce!"

"So you were right. I'm throwing up my hands in defeat. Would you like me to print a public retraction of all the nasty things I said?"

"That would be very nice."

"Too bad," Kevin said and grinned as best he could. "You'll have to settle for one very private apology."

He drained the glass and casually put it down on the counter before he pulled Julie close to him. It had only been two days since they'd left Victoria, but it seemed like two weeks, and he was ready to kidnap her for another weekend of exhilarating solitude. He buried his face in her hair and molded her body to his, absorbing the feel of her firm breasts pressed against him, the silky texture of her hair, and the fresh scent that reminded him of the lilac bushes his mother had planted underneath his bedroom window when he was very young.

"You're exactly what the doctor ordered," Kevin said, squeezing her even tighter.

Ten minutes ago Julie had vowed to keep Kevin at a healthy distance, but the moment he touched her, her resolve was forgotten. All she cared about now was satisfying her need to be closer, hug longer, and love more.

"I missed you," she whispered, nuzzling the rough surface of his sweater.

Kevin drew her into the living room and eased her onto the sofa, pulling her shoes from her feet as soon as she was leaning back against the cushions.

"The mouth is out of commission, but the rest of me still functions," he said.

He took her foot and began kneading the sensitive arch with the knuckles of his clenched fist. Julie had never had her feet massaged before. She had never imagined how sensual an experience it could be. Kevin moved from one foot to another until she was nearly purring with satisfaction. Then his fingers strayed up her legs to her tired calf muscles. His hands slipped back and forth across her hose. She held her breath, silently begging him to glide higher each time his fingers wandered up her thigh.

"Panty hose must have been invented by an anxious father, trying to protect his daughter's virtue," Kevin muttered when he reached up to try and slip them off.

Julie laughed and quickly squirmed out of the offending garment. "Better?"

"Much."

"Are you always so attentive to hardworking ladies?" she asked, watching his fingers skim around her thighs in ever widening circles.

"Actually I'm quite particular. She needs to have long, auburn hair, big, beautiful blue eyes and legs that can melt chrome off a bumper."

She chuckled at his compliment. "You're crazy."

"About you."

Sitting up, Julie brushed a stray lock of his thick dark hair off his forehead and kissed the tip of his nose.

"You really should be resting. I'm not going to be held responsible for abusing a patient," she said. "Lie down."

"If I do, I'll fall asleep."

"And what's wrong with that?"

"I have other, more pressing matters to attend to," Kevin said and flattened his body against hers, shoulder to shoulder, chest to chest. "Dr. Hartmann told me that moderate physical activity was acceptable as soon as I was ready," he murmured as he unbuttoned her blouse. "And I'm definitely ready."

Kevin cupped the ripe fullness of Julie's breasts in his hands, delighting in the way her nipples hardened into diamondlike jewels when he touched them. His mouth was too sore to kiss her breasts, and he had to content himself with rubbing one of the rosy-tipped crests against his cheek. Julie arched her back, clearly inviting him to continue.

His demand finally outstripped his control and Kevin peeled off his jeans, starting what proved to be a fast-growing pile of discarded clothing. Julie's skirt and filmy half slip were the last to join the heap. Glorying in her beauty, he lay down again and claimed her love.

"Not too bad for a sick man," she commented softly as she cuddled in his arms a little later.

He reached back and pulled the afghan over them, unwilling to move even as far as Julie's bed. "Just for that, I'll have to prove to you that sick men try harder than healthy ones."

CHAPTER TWELVE

KEVIN OPENED HIS EYES with a start, trapped halfway between sleep and consciousness, confused by the unfamiliar surroundings. Sitting up, he blinked several times before it registered. This was Julie's place, and he had spent the night on her couch. The last thing he remembered was Julie getting up to pour him a glass of juice.

He wrapped the blanket around his waist and wandered into her bedroom, expecting to find her curled beneath the comforter. The bed was empty and neatly made. Puzzled, he checked the kitchen and found a note telling him that she had early appointments. Glancing at the clock on the stove, Kevin slammed into action. It was nearly nine-thirty and Carlos was waiting for him at the office.

"Sleeping Beauty arises," Carlos said when Kevin finally appeared.

"Sorry. I overslept."

"No problem. Julie called and told me you might be late. I postponed your meeting with Bud."

"Fantastic," Kevin said, but felt far from overjoyed. "We need to talk before I see Bud. I think I finally realized what's wrong at Nickerson. While I was shaving, the truth broke through this thick skull."

Carlos never lounged back in his chair like Kevin, who usually propped his feet on the desk or an open file drawer, so Kevin wasn't surprised when his partner sat down, took out a pad of paper and pen and wrote the date in one corner before he nodded in readiness.

"First, we all thought there was something wrong with the security system, yet I couldn't find a glitch or virus. When that theory didn't wash, we assumed that some unknown perpetrator was trying to break into Nickerson and redoubled our efforts. Right?"

"That's right," Carlos confirmed.

"Then we twisted that around one hundred eighty degrees and theorized that someone with access to the security system was trying to get out, bypassing the traditional checkpoints without being detected. But we still didn't know who it was."

Kevin's adrenalin was surging by now, and he had to physically restrain himself from jumping up and pacing the room. "At first I assumed they were after the machines. But we were missing the obvious. Hell, Bud can afford to lose a few computers without closing his doors. But I've got a strong hunch it's not the computers. They're after the new software. After reading those files the other night, I know that program would give them the capability to develop and manufacture armaments. Seems like a fellow might be able to retire quite comfortably after he peddled those goods on the international market." He stopped and waited for Carlos's reaction.

"Sweet saints preserve us!" his colleague said, dropping his pen. "You're serious!"

"I'm not positive, but it would explain why that security system was reactivated. An employee at Nickerson with the knowledge and opportunity reactivates the computer and during the chaos makes a copy of the disk. He also might have computer parts tucked under his coat or in his lunch box. It wouldn't take long to waltz out the gate with enough components to construct a unit, and we know they need a particular type of computer to run that program. Detroit has lost entire automobiles off the assembly line that way."

"Who?"

"That's what frightens me the most. There's one person objecting to calling the authorities. Just one man who doesn't seem to want to cooperate in a logical manner."

Carlos's shoulders sagged as he took in what Kevin was saying. "Bud's sabotaging his own firm?"

Kevin didn't want to think about it. All he wanted to do was turn his back on the whole mess. But he couldn't walk away. His conscience wouldn't allow it. "That fiasco Monday night was not a freak accident. The timing was too damn convenient. I was out of commission, you had the night off. Very few people had that information. That's a fact. Another fact is that it wasn't a bored teenager playing with daddy's computer who accidentally tapped into Nickerson's system."

"Didn't you devise a code to prevent any unauthorized people from tampering with your work?"

"Sure did. But what good does that do, if the person you're trying to keep out has the codes? From the very first day I argued with Bud about contacting the authorities and he refused. The blind faith he's shown in me is stupid," Kevin said.

"I can see why it looks bad, Kevin, but there isn't any proof that Bud's involved."

It was impossible for Kevin to sit still any longer. He jumped to his feet and nervously began pacing back and forth. "Exactly. What do I do? Ruin a man's reputation and his business on a hunch? What if he's not guilty? What do I say? Gee whiz, Bud, I'm sorry we put you into bankruptcy by falsely accusing you of computer espionage."

"I really don't think it's Bud," Carlos said again, getting up and uncharacteristically pacing alongside Kevin. "He's got too much to lose."

"I hope you're right, but what if you're not?"

Two hours later, Bud Nickerson was roaring loudly enough at both Kevin and Carlos to shake the windows of the entire plant. "Go ahead and dig as deep as your slimy little minds can go. You won't find a shred of evidence to support this insanity."

"We had to get it out into the open, Bud," Kevin insisted. "If you were in my position, what would you think?"

"Gentlemen," Bud said, lowering his voice to a dangerous-sounding growl, "I might come to the same conclusion, but I'd wait until I had proof to support my theory before I said anything."

"We looked at the facts," Carlos told him. "What are we supposed to think when you refuse to let the police help you?"

"I assume you're prepared to accept a reality check yourselves," Bud said, standing up and towering over the two, who had remained seated while he exploded.

"Absolutely," Kevin agreed and met Bud's intent stare.

"I won't call in the police because I don't trust them. They're slow responding to my calls and they're inexperienced. Even if the evidence was sitting under their noses, they wouldn't recognize it. Besides, Tolt's distinguished chief of police doesn't exactly inspire confidence. George owes money to everybody and his uncle. Does that clarify my position?"

"Partially," Kevin said, feeling Carlos's eyes trained on him. "If you don't trust my brother, why do you have such faith in me?"

"I checked you out before I ever talked to you. You're nothing at all like your brother."

Kevin chose to ignore the backhanded compliment. "I never tied your hesitancy to George's financial difficulties." He faced Bud squarely but continued. "Do you still want me working on this job?"

"Of course," Bud said emphatically. "You're the one who's acting spooked. I will give you your due, though. Not too many men would have had the nerve to accuse me of being a thief. You and Carlos make a good team, but I'd leave the public relations work to Carlos."

Kevin's reservations about Bud disappeared, but he still believed someone was after the program, not the hardware. "Do you agree with me that it's possible one of your employees is trying to steal the new programs?"

"I doubt it. The few people who have enough information about it are completely trustworthy. Besides, we haven't been working on it for a couple of

weeks, and the only copies are locked in my safe,"
Bud told him.

"I'm not convinced," Kevin said.

"And I am," Bud replied, sitting down again.
"Your theory is too farfetched, Kevin. This is just a
disgruntled employee or computer hack playing with
us. It's annoying but not serious."

Kevin knew Carlos didn't consider his dogs being
poisoned a prank, and neither did he. Bud's casual
attitude was strange.

"You seem to be very relaxed about all this, Bud,"
Kevin observed. "Why? You have a great deal to
lose."

"I already considered the possibility that someone
might be trying to steal the new weapons program. I
talked to Brent Olsen, the man who developed it, and
he assured me there is no way anyone could possibly
steal that information. He bugged the program so
thoroughly that they'd have to have the series of codes
to even open it up."

"Could I talk to him myself?" Kevin inquired.

"Not for another six days or so. He's on vacation.
After the long hours he put in, I gave him two weeks
off to float around on his boat in the middle of Puget
Sound. He just checks in from a marina every few
days."

"If I don't charge you for my time, would you let
me search the personnel files, looking for a string of
debts, outlandish spending or other suspicious signs?"
Kevin requested. Bud agreed, albeit reluctantly.

Carlos and Kevin nearly filled the van with personnel files, then drove back to Maximum Security. Alone

in their shared office, they started hammering out a feasible schedule for the next week.

"We can split the night shift at Nickerson," Kevin suggested. "Our crew here is capable of managing this operation without us. That installer you hired is good, he can tend to this week's calendar without my help if we juggle a few appointments."

"I never thought I'd say this, but we've got more work than we can handle," Carlos said. "There's a developer in Issaquah who called for a bid on thirty-five houses."

Kevin tried to smile, but the swelling on the right side of his face was still bad enough to prevent it. "Every dream's coming true and you're complaining?"

"We've hired four new employees in the past two weeks. The expansion's a little fast."

"But we're good," Kevin said, beaming. "The chance we took investing in all that advertising is paying off. A healthy bank account doesn't make me nervous."

"Profit is generated by volume," Carlos agreed.

"I'm going to get started on those files while you check on your mutts," Kevin said, picking up the first manila folder from the gargantuan mound.

"There's one other item we need to discuss," Carlos said, taking the folder from him and setting it down again. "You haven't said a word about George."

"What's the point?"

"The point is that we've staked our professional integrity on our claim that we can be impartial enough to protect our clients."

"That's right. Whoever is responsible for trying to break in or out of Nickerson Electronics will be caught."

"That's going to be hard, Kevin. While you're busy finding the culprit, you just might point the finger at George's negligence. That would cost him his job."

Kevin leaned over and stared hard at Carlos, somehow summoning enough self-control to keep his temper. "George is a good cop. He's having a rough time right now, but it's nothing that can't be fixed. I can handle it."

JULIE BENT OVER THE SINK in the exam room, scrubbing her hands longer than usual in a bid to marshal her thoughts. Denise Royce was waiting in the chair for Julie to begin the expensive procedure of applying veneers to all her teeth. The only reason Denise had slipped in so soon, before Julie could question Kevin about George's ability to pay the bill, was because Denise had asked to be put on the list of fillers for last-minute cancellations and had responded to the receptionist's call this morning. Well, she thought, at least Denise's deposit check hadn't bounced.

"Well, Mrs. Royce," Julie said, snapping on the bright overhead light and tipping back the chair, "I was sure surprised to see you on today's schedule."

"You have such a nice staff," Denise said and smiled. "I told them I wanted these ugly, stained teeth covered up just as soon as I could, and your receptionist promised she'd call."

"She does a good job," Julie said, forcing herself to disguise her annoyance. "I'll have to remember to thank her. Mrs. Royce, do you realize dental insurance won't cover this procedure, since it's for cosmetic purposes?''

"That's no problem. My husband will pay you.''

Just like he paid Angelo and Shorty, Julie thought. "As long as there's no confusion that you'll be responsible for paying the bill.''

"Don't worry, Dr. Bennett. The chief of police can't afford to damage his reputation by ignoring his obligations.''

Julie winced at Denise's naiveté. Ignorance of their husbands' financial affairs had been common among women years ago, but she couldn't imagine a contemporary woman being as oblivious to her husband's debts as Denise clearly was about George's. George was duping his wife as successfully as he was hoodwinking Angelo and a dozen other merchants in Tolt. And what irritated Julie the most was that she was being drawn in, as well. If she had any courage at all, she would refuse to treat Denise Royce.

"First we need to take a full set of impressions, Mrs. Royce,'' Julie said, approaching Denise with the mold.

The appointment was brief, just the beginning of the lengthy and costly process of creating a flawless smile for George's wife. After Denise had left, Julie made a brief stop at the receptionist's desk with some specific instructions.

"Regardless of what Mrs. Royce says, the first available slot you have is three weeks away,'' she told the young woman.

"But Dr. Bennett, I thought you always wanted to get our patients in as soon as possible and keep the calendar full.''

"Stall this time. There's a good reason.''

Julie hurried to her next patient, but all afternoon she vacillated, unable to decide how to deal with Denise. Dropping her professional dilemma into Kevin's lap wasn't exactly fair, but George was his brother, and maybe Kevin could intervene, sparing all of them a potentially ugly confrontation.

She would broach the subject tonight after putting Kevin in a mellow mood with his first solid meal since Sunday. She had talked with him briefly this morning, and he had hinted how good it would be to eat some real food, especially now that Dr. Hartmann had expressed his approval.

"It still can't be anything too spicy or tough to chew," she had warned. "Tell me your heart's desire in the bland, mushy category."

"How about good, old-fashioned tuna and noodles with tiny peas in it, the way Beaver Cleaver's mom used to make?"

"Are you serious?" Julie said, laughing.

"Just make sure you fix a double quantity. Theresa always teases me about looking like Paul Bunyan, and I have an appetite to match my nickname."

How easy it was to please Kevin, she thought later that evening while she assembled the casserole. He was the most considerate, undemanding man. All he asked for was her love—a love to match his own. Starting, she acknowledged that her own feelings for Kevin were threatening to overwhelm her. Kevin was becoming precisely what she vowed no man would ever be to her—indispensable.

She'd been catering to him for weeks. And now she'd been about to place the responsibility for her business decisions on his shoulders. In fact, she was about to cast herself in her mother's starring role as the queen of dependency! The realization was terrifying.

"Well, Julie Bennett," she said as she set the table, "you caught yourself just in time."

By the time supper was ready she had made her decision. She couldn't ignore or deny her love for Kevin, but she could certainly place it in its proper perspective. She wouldn't mention Denise's appointments; that would be abdicating responsibility for her own life. If she couldn't solve this problem herself, she had no right to be in business.

"Ambrosia," Kevin said, breezing into the apartment and heading straight for the oven, cracking it open to sniff.

"Everything's ready. Have a seat."

"Not before I sample the appetizer."

He pulled her into his arms and slid his hands possessively down her back and over her hips.

"You'd better eat before it gets cold," Julie said, drawing away.

"Did you have a bad day?"

"No. Why?"

Kevin waited for her to quit bustling back and forth from the kitchen to the dining room. "Hey, it's me," he said, reaching across the small table and tipping her chin up. "Remember? Kevin? Tell me what's wrong."

"I'm just fine," Julie said, keeping her eyes trained on the table.

"What is it?"

"I really can't discuss it. Besides, you wouldn't want to know."

"Try me," he said.

"Do you think your job is the only one that requires a degree of discretion?"

He began filling his plate while he considered her question. "Not the only one, but I don't understand what's so private about filling people's teeth."

Julie couldn't stop herself. "I see. I'm supposed to spill my guts about every little thing that goes on in my life, yet you hide behind client confidentiality. 'Don't ask any questions, Julie. I have to work tonight but, I can't say why, so please don't ask.' Great degree of equality we have going."

"Whoa, whoa," Kevin said, holding up his hands. "Is that what this is all about? The long hours?"

"No, not at all. It's about my right to privacy. You didn't respect me enough to accept that I couldn't talk about what was bothering me. How would you like me to hound you with questions? And I don't like being mauled the minute you walk in the door."

His fork halfway to his mouth, Kevin's hand froze in front of him. "Are you going to hang me for giving my lady a squeeze?"

"Without asking? Maybe." Julie glared at him. She wanted to fight with Kevin, wanted to make him angry and send him racing out the front door. She wanted her life back, just the way it used to be.

"Let me make certain I'm understanding you correctly. You want me to ask your permission every time I touch you?"

Although she was busy shredding her napkin in her lap, Julie kept her expression calm and steady. "Isn't that the polite thing to do?"

"That's the stupid thing to do."

"Fine, I'm stupid now, too."

There was no way he was going to survive this insane argument; he didn't even know what they were quarreling about. Kevin slowly put his fork down, placed his napkin on the table and stood. "I'm leaving. You aren't making any sense at all, and I refuse to fight with you over nothing. I can't read your mind, Julie. If you decide you want to talk, I'll be at Nickerson's."

He leaned forward and wrote a phone number on the back of a business card. When she wouldn't reach up to accept it from him, he left it lying on the table.

Julie wondered why she felt so miserable when she was doing the right thing, reestablishing her identity as a single, successful woman who didn't need a man. Kevin was a wonderful person, and she didn't want to alienate him completely, but he was getting too close. She was beginning to depend on him to solve her problems, help run her life.

She was confused by her desperate need, both to break free from Kevin and break out of the oppressive loneliness of her surroundings. Before, evenings of solitude had always been enjoyable. Invariably there'd been something to keep her busy. But not any longer. She was almost beginning to hate the cozy home she had worked so hard to create.

"Thank you, Mr. Royce," she said aloud, jumping to her feet. "This is all your fault."

She banged around the kitchen, jamming plates into the dishwasher and food into the fridge before she began cleaning the apartment with a vengeance normally seen only at boxing rings or professional football games. When there was nothing left to scrub, dust or vacuum, she turned her attention to her car. The long weekend had left it in a somewhat grimy condition, so Julie grabbed a handful of quarters before she made her way to the all-night car wash.

Her reliable sedan was soon sparkling clean, but she still felt as if she had enough energy to scrub the hundreds of aisles in Seattle's Kingdome. Finally returning home after stopping at an ice-cream parlor and making herself bilious by eating a giant hot-fudge sundae with a double scoop of nuts, Julie faced the truth. Her life was never going to be the same. She couldn't rewrite history and she couldn't pretend she didn't need Kevin Royce. All she could do was salvage what she had left of her independence and make certain he didn't erode it any further. And that was going to be about as easy as making George pay for Denise's dental work.

She dialed the number on the card Kevin had left and nervously waited for him to answer.

"Yes?"

"Kevin? It's me. Are you still speaking to me after the way I behaved tonight? I'm really sorry I acted like such a shrew. I don't know what it was."

The line went dead and she stared at the receiver in shock. He had hung up on her! While she redialed the number, her foot was tapping a rapid, nervous beat on the floor.

"Yes," a deep masculine voice answered abruptly.

Julie realized with relief it wasn't Kevin who had hung up on her the first time, but this man. "May I speak with Kevin Royce, please?"

A click followed by a dial tone was her answer.

Little though she knew about Kevin's work at Nickerson Electronics, she realized the man's behavior was peculiar. Kevin's investigation wasn't open to public scrutiny, but it wasn't any secret that he was spending nearly every spare moment there. Her fingers itched to dial the number again, yet she hesitated. The inner alarms that she had learned to trust were all signaling a warning.

She decided to call Carlos and tell him what had happened.

"Carlos, this is Julie," she said after he answered on the seventh ring. "I'm sorry to bother you, but something unusual happened when I called Kevin at Nickerson Electronics."

Quickly she explained about the strange man who had hung up on her twice. "Which number did Kevin give you?" Carlos asked urgently.

Julie repeated the phone number, reading it straight from the card. "Did he make a mistake?"

"No," Carlos said softly.

She heard the tension in his voice, and the tiny hairs at the back of her neck rose.

"Julie, I want you to try that number one more time. If you reach Kevin, tell him exactly what you just told me. If the other man answers, I want you to listen to his voice, listen carefully and try to get him to say something more. Then call me right back."

"Bye," she said, punched the Disconnect button and dialed again.

"Hello?"

She gasped with relief at the familiar sound of Kevin's voice. "Kevin! Where were you?"

"I stepped down the hall to get a cup of coffee. Why?"

Julie told him what had happened.

"Could you describe the man's voice?" Kevin asked. "Was there anything distinctive about it?"

"It was soft and very deep, but I only heard him say two words."

"Thanks, J.B.," Kevin said. "If you hadn't called, I might never have known. Listen, you decide what you'd like to do Saturday morning, anything your heart desires, and I'll pick you up about nine."

"But you don't even know why I called."

"Yes, I do, and it's all right. We'll talk about it Saturday. I'm sorry, but I've got to call Carlos before he ruptures his spleen. Sweet dreams, love."

Kevin shook his head at the strange workings of fate. If Julie hadn't been in a snit this evening, if they hadn't fought, he would never have left her the number of the direct line into the computer room at Nickerson Electronics—and the unknown intruder would not have been discovered.

"Carlos," Kevin said a moment later, "meet me outside the gate in thirty minutes. Julie's call struck pay dirt."

CHAPTER THIRTEEN

KEVIN PROVED HIS THEORY while he waited for Carlos. Someone had definitely monkeyed with the computer while he had been out of the room, and it took less than ten minutes to discover exactly which file was so engrossing to the stranger with the soft, deep voice. The computer automatically recorded the last use down to the precise date, hour and minute. Kevin scanned the directory until he found the security system file. Sure enough it had been the last entry. The intruder had been activating the old security system again. The fellow was getting sloppy, and that could only mean one thing. He was running out of time.

Kevin called Bud to fill him in on the latest developments.

"Thank Julie for me," Bud told him.

"I will. Not only did she prevent another fiasco, but tonight's discovery eliminated at least half of your employees as suspects," Kevin replied.

Bud arrived at Nickerson half an hour later. "I've got every area supervisor double-checking their rosters," he said.

"That leaves the cleaning staff and myself. Carlos and I are going to personally check off the people walking out the gates tonight. The person that doesn't match up with the list is nailed."

The rain was drizzling down the collar of Kevin's lightweight jacket as he stood at the gate and studied the smudged piece of paper. Every single name had been checked off; the head count had been exact. Each person had been accounted for, and not one of them had access to the code needed to enter the computer system.

"I should have known it was too easy," Kevin said when he met Bud again. "If the guy is smart enough to have made it this far, he's good. I just thought that we finally had lady luck on our side."

"Any ideas of what to do next?" Bud asked.

"Yes," Kevin said and sighed resignedly. He explained that earlier in the day he'd spoken to a man he had worked with in the Marine Corps. His former colleague had armed him with a means of programming his own virus to prevent any further tinkering. Kevin would completely erase the old files and confiscate every copy of the program—at least, every copy they could find. "Now it's up to you, Carlos. We'll have a guard on the door to the computer room at night, and I'll check the system every evening. Our fellow will be forced to pass by one of our guys with the goods in his possession. There won't be any ruckus to distract attention, and he's bound to slip. Eventually."

But would his preventive measures be enough? Kevin wondered privately. The computer could be used to develop sophisticated military weaponry like cruise missiles, radar tracking systems and submarines. Illegal bidding for the technology Nickerson Electronics produced must be high, and greed prompted men to take foolish risks.

That was one question Kevin had been trying to avoid. Was his brother George desperate enough to have become involved? The thought made Kevin physically ill, yet he couldn't ignore the signals any longer. On the pretext of verifying a client's credibility, he had run a financial check on George. The extent of his debts was staggering. "Damn it, George. Why?" Kevin demanded as he firmly closed the metal door of the computer room. "What's wrong?" But the antiseptic, climate-controlled computer room was about as talkative as his brother.

Kevin beat Carlos to the office in the morning to tackle the hunt through the files of everyone who had been working last night at Nickerson. It was a bit like looking for agates on the beach. All the rocks looked the same until you scrubbed away the surface layers of sand and salt from each one and held it up to the light for closer inspection. Hidden among all the ordinary stones was the prize, the one Kevin was determined to nab.

It was five o'clock when Kevin closed the last manila file folder. He was exasperated. The entire day had been wasted in poring over every scrap of paper in the file. Each one of Bud's employees seemed to be worthy of a humanitarian award. Bud treated his people well, demanding top quality, and apparently received what he paid for—first-class service from solid citizens who were loyal to their company.

Whether Bud liked it or not, Kevin was through. He had tried his best, had used every legal means available to a private citizen to flush the guy out, and his hands were still empty.

He punched the intercom to the monitoring room and inquired, "Carlos, do you have time to walk with me?" Since their office was small, they had virtually no privacy to discuss business matters and had resorted to going for walks to escape being overheard.

"Give me five minutes, Kevin," he answered.

The day was cloudy, and a light mist watered the emerald-green grass, the brilliant ruby azaleas and the fluffy, pink cherry trees. Maximum Security was situated on the edge of one of Tolt's older residential districts, and Kevin and Carlos were soon striding down a block of stately homes.

"So what's up?" Carlos wanted to know.

"Nothing. Absolutely, positively, nothing—and I'm finished."

"It's your call. If Bud doesn't like it, let him fire us."

"He needs to call the U.S. Commerce Department."

"Why?"

"If the goods are going out of the country, it's their bailiwick," Kevin replied.

"You're not nearly as dumb as you look," Carlos said and laughed.

"Waall, thanks a lot, mister," Kevin drawled in his best John Wayne impression.

"Haven't heard one of those out of you in quite a while. Your stitches must not be bothering you."

Kevin stopped walking and frantically looked at his watch. "I forgot. I'm supposed to get my stitches out today. Call Bud, have him meet us somewhere away from Nickerson. Make it for tonight. I'll call you later for the time and place."

He sprinted back to his van and barely made it to Dr. Hartmann's office before closing time. The visit only took a few minutes. He called Carlos before he left the parking lot.

"Go home," Carlos said. "Bud wouldn't wait for the verdict and I relayed your message. He said he'd make the call first thing Monday morning."

"Just like that?"

"Yeah. Apparently he already spoke with his attorney about his liability and doesn't want to court danger any longer."

"Hallelujah!" Kevin exclaimed, smiling.

He drove straight to Julie's, hoping to surprise her. But she wasn't home. Even though he knew she didn't work late on Friday nights, he backtracked to the clinic and followed the curving road to the lower lot.

Sure enough, parked in a far corner was her nondescript beige sedan. He used his mobile phone and dialed her office number.

The incessant ringing invaded her thoughts. Julie tried to ignore the irritation but couldn't. Whoever it was, and she was confident it was a wrong number, had more patience than she did.

"Hello?" she said, making the word clipped and unfriendly.

"Aren't you having a good time tonight? Did somebody replace me as the world's worst patient?"

"Kevin? I thought you were working late."

"A slight change in plans. How about meeting me in the parking lot in thirty seconds?"

Julie pulled the curtains aside and saw headlights blink at her. "Best invitation I've had all week."

He was waiting for her just outside the doorway and gathered her into his embrace before she had dropped the clinic keys into her purse. His worried frown had been replaced by an impudent grin, she noted, and his eyes weren't shuttered with concern, but sparkling with laughter and promise.

"Come here, stranger," he said and tucked his arms around her waist.

His leather jacket was soft against her cheek, the scent of his cologne reminded her of a thicket of evergreens washed clean by a summer storm, and the reassuring comfort of his muscle-corded arms banished her exhaustion. "What are we going to do with this unexpected bonanza?" she inquired. "It's a sin to waste a Friday night."

"I'm going to eat the biggest steak I can buy."

"That's right," Julie said, laughing. "Your stitches came out this afternoon."

"And I want real food that has to be chewed."

They decided on a steak house that featured a large salad bar, drove separately to Julie's duplex and, after leaving his van there, followed the main highway to the edge of town. The restaurant was crowded, so they decided to wait in the dimly lit bar until a table was free. Soft music and the chatter of Friday-night revelers lent a partylike atmosphere to the lounge. Julie made her way through the densely packed tables to a small booth against the far wall.

It looked as if half the town was celebrating the end of the work week. Kevin scanned the crowd for any familiar faces. The only person he recognized was Butler, the police officer who had been the cause of the feud between George and Julie. He was sitting at the bar. Fortunately Julie's back was turned to him, but Butler's booming laugh echoed above the commotion. Julie, however, didn't seem to recognize it, and Kevin thanked fate for small favors. His good fortune continued when Butler got up and ambled out of the lounge.

Once they were seated in the restaurant, where they could talk normally, Kevin explained his unexpected freedom. "It's back to normal hours," he said, holding up his glass of beer in a toast.

"You mean only sixty hours a week?" She raised her eyebrows doubtfully.

"Look who's talking! A bit like the pot calling the kettle black. I closed up shop before you did tonight. And who snuck out of bed early the other morning?"

Julie didn't want to admit that she'd worked long hours this past week by choice, not by necessity, and shrugged her shoulders in a gesture of defeat. "Let's not talk about our jobs."

"I think we'd better. You seemed to have quite a definite opinion the last time we were together."

"I was wrong and I apologize. End of discussion."

Pushing her wouldn't accomplish a thing, Kevin realized, temporarily accepting her abrupt dismissal. What had triggered her sudden misgivings? he wondered. This was more than George, more than working long hours himself and not being able to talk about the details of his day. But it would have to wait until she was ready.

"Did you hear the latest in the Romero-Post saga?" Kevin asked, taking a new tack.

"Do I want to hear this?"

"Probably not, but you may as well be prepared. Mark was caught letting the air out of his teachers' tires."

This time Julie didn't find anything funny in Mark's antics. "When?"

"After school today. The principal called Theresa and she called Carlos. Seems like the young Mr. Post will be busy scraping old linoleum off Carlos's basement floor for the next few weekends to pay for having the flats fixed. And starting Wednesday afternoon, he's going to be bagging beans and rice at the food bank."

"I pity the other volunteers," Julie commented. "Mark isn't the most cooperative young man when he doesn't want to do something."

"I doubt it. Seems the food bank is his track coach's pet project, and the two of them will be working together."

Julie grinned at the thought of Mark being coerced into contributing his time. "He'd do anything to keep from getting kicked off the team."

"The theory is that he's going to be so busy, he won't have time to get into trouble."

"I'm reserving judgment. I've a feeling Mark is still two leaps ahead of every adult he knows."

"You certainly seem to know a lot about mischievous teenagers," he said.

"I've had a bit of experience with jealousy. The first time my mother was engaged after my dad died, I did everything possible to scare the guy away. Too bad it didn't work."

"You're still angry with your mother, aren't you?"

"Not anymore."

The answer to the riddle of Julie's hesitancy, the emotional distance she tried to keep between them, had a lot to do with her mother, Kevin realized. He searched Julie's solemn, wistful face for a clue. She'd experienced a tremendous upheaval during a critical stage in her life; scars were undoubtedly there, hiding beneath the veneer of rationality. He admired all she had accomplished and wanted to be at her side when it dawned on her that there was one last hurdle to clear before she was truly free of the past.

But pounding her with an emotional sledgehammer wouldn't accomplish his goal, so Kevin lightened the mood by recounting a few of his own escapades as a senior at Tolt High School. "Mark has no imagination," he commented. "Putting seven ducks in the principal's swimming pool was inspired. Do you realize how big a mess ducks make when they're excited?"

"Kevin Royce!" Julie tried not to laugh. "You didn't!"

"I most certainly did."

The remainder of their meal was punctuated with laughter. By the time they left the restaurant, Julie could feel every pair of eyes in the room tracking them out the door.

"I think we both disgraced ourselves," she said when they were alone in the car. "Everybody was staring at us."

"They were jealous."

"Probably." She outlined Kevin's square jaw with one finger; how alive, how carefree he made her feel! "Do you know what I'd like to do?"

"No, but I can always hope," he said.

"Pack a suitcase, put gas in the car and just start driving. I wouldn't decide where I was going until I saw a road that looked interesting and then I'd follow it. I'd drive until I found a cabin by a river or a cottage just off the main drag, a place where the bedspreads don't match the curtains and you can put a quarter in a machine to make the bed vibrate for ten minutes."

"Running away sounds good to me, too."

"Are you patronizing me?" Julie asked, surprising him.

"If George was your brother, wouldn't you want to skip town?"

It was the first time he'd ever joked about George, and the wisecrack made her smile. "We could always send him to visit my mother in Florida."

"But he couldn't afford the bus fare." Kevin started to laugh even though it really wasn't funny.

Julie was wise enough not to join in; the pain behind his humor was too evident. "Let's go home," she proposed, putting the key into the ignition.

The moment Kevin clicked the dead bolt on Julie's front door into place, she took him by the hand and led him down the hallway.

"It's been a long day," she said. "Doesn't a nice, hot shower sound refreshing?"

Without a word, Kevin fumbled for the light switch. She stopped him and he waited in silence while she struck a match and lighted a large candle sitting on the counter next to the bathtub. The room seemed to dance with the flickering light and he watched as she slowly, teasingly pulled her sweater over her head, stretching her arms and arching her back. She dropped the sweater and unzipped her skirt, peeling off her slip and hose in one smooth motion.

He reached out and followed the curve of her waist with his palms, drawing her panties down as his hands moved from the enticing fullness of her hips to the tight muscles of her thighs. She stepped out of the garment as Kevin kissed the hollow of her throat where he could feel her pulse beating, then nibbled his way to one lace-covered nipple.

"My turn," she whispered. She ducked out of his grasp, swiftly tugged off his lightweight sweater and slowly undid the buttons on his shirt. When his chest was bare, Kevin pulled her against him and cupped her buttocks with hungry fingers, nearly lifting her off her feet. He seized her mouth in a demanding kiss as his hands rocked her body back and forth in an erotic rhythm.

"Game's over, princess," he said and set her back on her feet to hurriedly finish undressing.

His impatience—and the evidence of his desire— were obvious. Julie turned on the taps and waited just seconds for the pounding water to warm. They stepped into the tub hand in hand and he closed the glass door, enshrouding them in a fantasy world of billowing clouds.

She faced the torrent, letting the water pound her body while Kevin languorously explored her back and shoulders with soapy fingers. He massaged and stroked her neck, rubbed and caressed her buttocks and thighs before his hands stole around her waist to skim her breasts and stomach. Her knees felt as if they were about to collapse, and she turned to face him, wrapping her arms around his neck.

"I love you," he said softly.

Hands racing he soaped his own body as thoroughly as he had hers. Only when he needed to rinse the suds away did she reluctantly loosen her hold, but only for a heartbeat. He turned and lay down, drawing her onto him, until her legs straddled his hips.

Julie felt herself ready to welcome him and her head reeled. She was being catapulted to that fringe of consciousness where no other thought intruded. Here nothing else mattered—nothing but her need, her desire, for Kevin.

"Now, baby," he moaned, his fingers gripping her hips. "Now."

She tipped her head back to glory in the moment. She couldn't hear his breathing and could barely see him through the blanket of steam. All she could do was feel the strength, the need, the energy of this man.

"I love you, Kevin Royce," she whispered. "I—" A dazzling light flared before her eyes.

"Wow!" he exclaimed a moment later as he traced a line from where their bodies met to the tip of her chin. "Was that my reward for working hard all week?"

Julie collapsed on top of him, quivering. "That was a Friday night special."

"A hell of a lot better than the meat loaf my mother used to feed me on Fridays," he said. He brushed her long, wet hair out of his face. "The water's growing cool. Do you think it's about time to get out?"

"If I can stand."

Kevin slid her off his chest and scooped her into his arms. He had never felt this content. She turned her head, nestling it against his chest. On the way by she snuffed out the candle, then grabbed an armful of towels, draping one around him.

"Why are you so quiet?" Julie asked, digging in the drawer of her nightstand for a hairbrush.

"I was just thinking of how lucky I am that I never had the nerve to visit a dentist. Otherwise we might never have met, and that would have been the greatest loss of my life."

Her arm, poised above her head, froze in midair and she found her eyes suddenly full of tears.

"You make me feel anything is possible," she whispered. "Even forever."

Gently taking the brush from her hand, Kevin sat up and began lightly drawing the bristles through her tangled curls. "That's because forever is more than possible. It's a promise."

CHAPTER FOURTEEN

PRODDED AWAKE by a tantalizing aroma, Julie slowly relinquished her cozy world of dreams.

"Good morning," Kevin said the instant she opened her sleep-clouded eyes. He was sitting on the edge of the bed, holding a cup of fresh coffee close to her nose.

"Hi," she mumbled, combing the hair away from her face with her fingers. "Mine?"

He smiled and handed her the milk-laced brew. "I'll be back in a few minutes, after you've had time to join the living."

She watched him walk away and raised her mug in a salute. Kevin's buttocks were embellished by a pair of faded, snug jeans, but he was bare from the waist up, and the display was quite striking. A tiny hole with a hint of flesh winked at her just below where his wallet rode. Kevin was obviously wearing nothing underneath the denim. By the time he was out the bedroom door, Julie's eyes were completely clear.

Last night had been incredible, the most wonderful experience of her life. Last night Kevin had promised "forever." Dare she believe him? Wouldn't it undermine her hard-won independence?

She glanced at her chest of drawers; her mother's photograph smiled back at her. It was a lovely picture, but Julie was bitterly aware of the price her mother had paid.

"The weatherman says we're going to have showers with some minor clearing in the late afternoon. What does that do to your plans?" Kevin inquired, returning. He was carrying a plate of toasted English muffins, and sat down on the bed to share breakfast.

Dismissing all thoughts of her mother, she said, "In Washington, if we wait for it to quit raining, we'll spend the rest of our lives staring out the window. I'd rather be out there, getting wet."

"Spoken like a true, web-footed native," he said with a grin.

"I've heard the Swap Meet in Everett advertised on the radio all week."

"A bargain hunter's bonanza," Kevin said in his best W. C. Fields voice. "People travel from far and wide to partake of its splendors."

"For seventy-five cents we can spend all afternoon poking through other people's junk. That's how I furnished this apartment."

Kevin stopped licking the butter off his fingers and stared at her in disbelief.

"Stick with me, big boy, and you'll go places," Julie said in a lousy imitation of Mae West.

His eyes glittered dangerously, and she started to laugh. Slowly Kevin took the coffee cup from her hand and set it on the floor with the rest of the dishes. Crawling across the bed, he stalked her the way a wild animal stalks its next meal.

"If we want to get a good parking space, we should be leaving soon," she said, giggling as she ducked under the covers. "Really, Kevin, we need to leave."

"I don't like parking close, anyway. Do you?"

The sound of jeans being unzipped brought her eyes peeping out from under the edge of the sheet. "Walking is one of the best forms of exercise."

"But not the best," he growled making Julie squeal as he joined her under the blankets.

HOURS LATER, Kevin's feet ached from wandering the warren of aisles. All he wanted to do was escape the hordes of people. Slamming the trunk of Julie's car on her collection of treasures, he turned to her, still shaking his head in amazement at the eclectic assortment of goods they had seen. There had been fresh vegetables, bedding plants and broken appliances, antique furniture and gaudy costume jewelry, vintage clothing and used books. Everything imaginable had been for sale.

"I can understand your fascination with antique dental tools and equipment," he said, "but keys? What's so engrossing about old keys?"

"When I get enough, I'm going to paint them all a dull black and make a display. Who else do you know with a collection of antique keys?"

"Absolutely no one."

Julie's enthusiasm for collecting was becoming contagious, Kevin realized, but he didn't intend to admit his growing interest. When he was very young, he had spent every dime of his paltry allowance on bubble gum so that he could trade the baseball cards. The last time he had seen the old shoe box he'd filled with them he had been in high school and cleaning out the attic. Were they still there? Or had Denise tossed them away years ago?

As they were driving home, he asked, "What do you collect besides dental equipment and keys?"

"Not much. Leather-bound books and things for home."

"What kind of things for home?"

"That's the mystery of it," she said. "I never know what I'm going to find."

"If I ever turned you loose in my folks' attic, I wouldn't see you for weeks. My mother saved everything."

Julie doubted she'd ever set foot inside that house, let alone prowl through the attic. No matter how close she and Kevin were, her relationship with George would never thaw to that point. It was hopeless. The best she could hope for was a stalemate, and even that seemed unlikely.

"The house is half mine," he said, as if interpreting her silence.

His defensive tone didn't surprise her. She decided the best thing to do was to change the subject.

"Look at the hot air balloon," she said, pointing to a brightly colored blob in the sky.

"Don't." Kevin grabbed her hand, kissing the palm. "We aren't going to argue about George. I just don't want to go through the rest of my life never feeling comfortable mentioning his name."

"I don't expect you to."

"How do you cope with your own family situation? You act like your mother doesn't exist. Doesn't it ever drive you crazy? Aren't you lonely on holidays?"

"Of course. I'd love to have a big family with brothers and sisters. But I don't. My mother did the very best she could, and I let it go at that."

"Want to give me a few lessons?" he suggested, squeezing her fingers.

"No. You need to come to terms with George on your own. What's right for me might not be the best thing for you."

She put her arm around him and leaned her head against his shoulder. For all the potential happiness she could see with Kevin, there was too much room for heartache.

They didn't speak again until they were back at her place. Kevin handed Julie the keys to her car. "Carlos gets the rest of the weekend off and I'm in charge. I'm going to miss you."

"I'll miss you, too," she said, stretching up to kiss his lips. "But maybe it's a good idea for us to spend a little more time apart."

"I don't like the sound of this."

Julie dragged her hand through her hair and tried to find the right words to explain her feelings. "This is a dead end, and we're both about to run into the brick wall."

"Damn it, Julie," he said and gripped her elbows, forcing her to look at him. "I won't let go just because you're not buddy-buddy with my brother. That's absurd."

"It's more complicated than that."

"Then explain it to me."

"I can't. I don't know that I can even explain it to myself."

He slammed the car door hard enough to alert the entire neighborhood. Julie shuddered. Kevin Royce wasn't a man who would accept defeat without a fight.

"You are not walking out of my life. Whatever's wrong can be handled. I'll fix it," he declared.

"This isn't your problem. It's mine."

Kevin snatched the keys away from her and ran up the walk to her front door. He unlocked the door and waited in the entry for Julie to catch up with him.

"You're doing it again. What's your obscene preoccupation with creating a fight when nothing is wrong? We get along better than any other couple I've ever known," he said vehemently, "and I'm not leaving until you tell me what in the hell's going on!"

Taking a deep breath, she struggled to put her feelings into words. "I can't deny that we seem to be quite well suited for each other."

"What's this? A bit of professional detachment? Do me a favor. Be honest."

"I am being honest. It's not going to work, and I want you to back off before it gets out of control."

Kevin whirled on her and captured her mouth in a sudden display of anger. One hand kneaded her buttocks with insistent fingers, while the other scanned the flesh beneath the back of her blouse. "I've been out of control since the first time I saw you," he said fiercely, "and so have you. If you deny it, you're lying. So quit analyzing and tell me what you're feeling!" he demanded.

"Right now?"

"Yes, right now."

"I, uh, I mean, it's h..." she stammered.

"I love you, Julie Bennett. I love your hair, your eyes, your skin. I love your stubborn streak, your passion for your work and your lust for me. I love the way you whisper my name when we're making love and the look of total pleasure I see on your face when I kiss you. Now, if all that isn't real, then I had a lobotomy somewhere along the line."

"Someday, just to indulge me, would you let me win an argument?" she inquired, admitting defeat.

"Maybe," he said and kissed her again. "Promise me I'll see you Monday night."

"I promise."

Kevin looked at the clock on the wall and groaned. "I'm late, and Carlos is going to be jumping from one foot to the other. He has plans with Theresa and can't leave until I take over."

"You can blame me for being late," she said and smiled.

"I'll call you tomorrow. And don't think so much, J.B. Trust your hormones. They don't lie."

Julie started to laugh and he kissed her once more on each cheek.

"That's better," he said, running his fingers through her hair.

Puttering around the empty apartment after Kevin had left, Julie wondered what she was going to do to fill the rest of the weekend. How had she managed to stay busy and content before Kevin came into her life? He'd only been gone for a few minutes, and already she was at odds with herself. For the first time in her life Julie understood how her mother must have felt.

"Get busy," she told herself, and put some lively music on the stereo to banish the silence.

Julie started to strip the sheets off her bed but stopped when she picked up a pillow and smelled Kevin's cologne lingering on the fabric. Hugging the pillow tightly, she curled up on the bed and closed her eyes until pounding on her door brought her to her feet and down the hall.

"I knew you were home," Theresa said. "I saw the lights and could hear the music."

"Are you okay? I thought you were going out with Carlos tonight."

Theresa's lips quivered and she tried to smile, but Julie could tell something was seriously wrong. She had never seen Theresa cry.

"I brought this. Want some?" Theresa held out a bottle of champagne, waving it back and forth. "It's a leftover from my birthday."

"Only if you quit shaking it up. Sit down in the living room and I'll pour each of us a glass."

After she managed to wiggle the cork out of the bottle, Julie filled two glasses. She found Theresa curled up at one end of the couch.

"To men," Theresa said, raising her glass. "To all the men I'll never understand."

"Want to talk about it?"

"Carlos and I had a fight."

"About Mark again?"

"Why do you automatically assume it was about Mark?"

Julie saw the anger in Theresa's eyes and retreated. "Just guessing."

"Well, you're right. It was about Mark. My little cherub borrowed Carlos's van without asking."

"Did he get into a wreck?"

"No, the van was parked in the mall parking lot when we found it. Not a scratch on it."

"That's a lucky break for Mark."

"That's what I tried to tell Carlos. Since no damage had been done, it wasn't really all that awful. But he wouldn't listen to me. He jumped in his truck and just left."

Julie jerked the empty glass out of Theresa's hand and stomped into the kitchen. While she filled the teakettle, she counted backward from one hundred to get control of her temper.

"What are you doing?" Theresa called out.

"Making tea. No more alcohol for you. Your brain's fuzzy enough as it is."

Julie returned to the living room, determined to be honest with her friend. Tiptoeing around Theresa's feelings had proved to be detrimental, both to Mark and his mother, and Julie was tired of biting her tongue.

"Theresa, I love you like a sister and I hope you can accept the truth. You're turning your son into the biggest self-centered monster it has ever been my displeasure to know. You haven't listened to a word the counselor or principal at school have been saying, and you won't allow Carlos to discipline him. What he did tonight was steal a car. That's grand theft auto. If Carlos wanted to go by the book, Mark would be cooling his heels in juvenile hall right now."

"Thank you, Dr. Bennett. I wasn't aware of that."

Theresa's sarcasm was uncharacteristic, but Julie chose to ignore it. "Is Mark the golden child?" she continued. "Is he above the laws that all the rest of us must obey? When are you ever going to draw the line?"

"Good night, Julie. It's been swell," Theresa said. She slammed the door on her way out.

Julie had never had a serious disagreement with Theresa before, but she didn't regret her comments. For over a year she had been listening to the same routine, and had never challenged Theresa, always putting their friendship above her own opinion. It was high time for somebody to point out that Theresa was doing her son more harm than good by allowing his behavior to go unpunished.

"Why me?" Julie asked herself. She walked over to the dining-room window to peer up at the sky. She was disappointed when she didn't find a full moon; her mother had always claimed the full moon brought out the beast in even the nicest people.

Grabbing the detective novel she'd started reading to Kevin, Julie poured herself another glass of champagne and crawled into bed to forget her personal problems in a fictional city being stalked by a murderer. Her tactic worked, until the next morning, when she found herself perched by the phone, waiting for it to ring. By noon she hadn't heard a word from Theresa or Kevin and decided staying home any longer was ridiculous.

Exercise was the best tonic for tension. She headed to the health club for a session with weights and as many laps in the pool as she could manage, losing herself in the repetitive rhythm.

A message from Kevin was on her answering machine when she dragged herself back home, but she didn't hear a word from Theresa. By Monday morn-

ing, Julie was ready to apologize, even though she
didn't believe she had been unfair. But Theresa called
in sick. Quite certain Theresa wasn't ill, she knew her
friend was going through a difficult time and respected her need for privacy.

"I sure hope you're not in the mood to go anywhere," Kevin said when he spoke with Julie late that
afternoon. "I've had it. The only person I want to see
tonight is you."

"Sounds perfect," she said. "Shrimp curry sound
good?" Anticipating a busy week with little time to
shop, Julie had tackled her least-loved household
chore Sunday afternoon and stocked her refrigerator
and freezer.

"I'll be late," Kevin told her. "I'm just heading into
a meeting and I'm not sure how long it'll last. If you
get hungry, eat without me and I'll nuke mine in the
microwave later."

Ending the conversation with Julie, Kevin watched
the federal agent shake hands with Carlos and Bud
Nickerson. He was both pleased and alarmed at the
rapid response Bud's phone call to the Commerce
Department had received.

"Mr. Royce, I think we're ready," Frank Edwards
said, sitting down at Carlos's kitchen table.

Edwards had asked to meet in a private place, away
from Nickerson Electronics, and Carlos had offered
his house. Situated on the outskirts of town, there was
little chance of unexpected intrusions.

Kevin made his statement to Edwards as briefly as
he could. Bud and Carlos added their observations.
Then the lengthy period of answering Edwards's
questions began. Kevin peered at the husky man's

ruddy face and tried to guess what was going on behind the federal agent's pale gray eyes, but Edwards never gave a hint. He was aloof, efficient and unreadable. There wasn't a glimmer of amusement or annoyance throughout the entire interrogation.

"That's all for tonight, gentlemen," Edwards said, standing up and snapping his briefcase shut. He handed Bud the list of documents he wanted and left quickly.

"A real personality boy, isn't he?" Bud said, jamming the list into his pocket. "What do you think he's going to do?"

"Catch the bad guys," Kevin replied. He tried to sound relaxed and glanced at Carlos and Bud to see if they believed him. Neither of them responded. "Cheer up. It's my family name that's at the top of the list."

"Kevin, I had to explain why we didn't call the local police. I thought you'd understand," Bud said. "Don't forget that you were the one who insisted on calling these guys."

"So why am I the only one smiling?"

"You're a better actor," Carlos said dryly, emptying the ashtray Frank Edwards had filled.

"Wrong," Kevin retorted. "I just have more faith that the obvious answer isn't the only one. Good night."

He left before he said something he might regret later; Carlos's and Bud's assumption that George was negligent or even more involved was upsetting. For the last seven years of his military career he'd been in a position where he couldn't share information about his job with anyone. But during that time, Kevin had always been able to walk out the door and leave the problems behind. Not any longer. Now he lugged them around like a pack filled with enough gear for a five-day bivouac.

Julie's mood was almost as glum as his, and as a result the atmosphere during their dinner was strained and tense, the silence filled with unspoken comments. Finally Kevin couldn't stand it any longer.

"Want to talk about it?" he asked.

"Not really."

"It might help."

She looked at Kevin and wanted to hide from the world in his arms. This temptation to run to him was exactly what scared her the most.

"It involves Theresa, and the two of us need to work it out," she explained.

"She spent the day with Carlos. They patched up their differences."

"That's wonderful."

"Then why don't you sound elated?" Kevin asked.

"Losing a friend isn't a good reason to party. I accused her of not listening to what people were saying about Mark, ignoring the warnings."

He reached across the table, taking her hand and guiding her to the huge rocking chair. He sat down and pulled her onto his lap. "Don't worry. Theresa will be back. She's got a blind spot, but she's not petty or vindictive."

"I hope so."

Kevin smiled and closed his eyes, resting his head against the back of the chair. "When this is all over, I'd like to take a week and escape to somewhere very private. Do you ever go on vacation?"

"The office will be shut down the last two weeks of July."

"Do we have to wait that long?" Almost two months seemed like an interminable delay. But unless Frank Edwards was exceedingly lucky, it would be much longer before Kevin could realistically leave town.

Julie snuggled her head into his shoulder, absorbing the warmth of his body, willing herself to let go, relax. If she could, maybe Kevin would release the tension she could feel knotting every muscle in his body. Whatever his dilemma was, she suspected that George was involved. Would she ever hear the true story?

They comforted each other without saying a word. Finally Kevin could feel the lump in his throat dissolve and the tight band around his head grow looser. "You're the best tranquilizer I've ever had," he murmured and sighed. He brushed the hair away from her neck, kissing the bare skin exposed to his lips.

Julie dropped her head to one side, electric excitement chasing the lethargy from her body. Kevin had admitted being addicted to her. What would he say if he knew how she missed his kisses when she didn't see him for a day, how she longed to feel his lips on her breasts?

"You're a wicked lady," he said between kisses. "No one tastes as sweet as you do."

Everything was perfect when they were alone. She forgot about the world beyond the sheltering walls of her home. George and Denise Royce didn't exist. Her fear of surrendering control of her life faded. All that mattered was Kevin. She clutched him tightly around the neck when he stood up to carry her to bed.

Comfortable though he was in Julie's bed, tired as he was, Kevin couldn't fall asleep. He listened to her even breathing and slowly pulled his arm free of her head, until he could roll to the side of the bed. Her apartment seemed more like home than his, he realized as he stretched out on the sofa, intending to watch a late movie. He clicked through the channels and found nothing of any interest. Annoyed, he shut the television off.

Dishes and food still covered the table, and he hoisted himself off the couch to clean up the clutter. Carefully, moving slowly to minimize the noise, he scrubbed dirty pans, loaded the dishwasher and wiped the counters and stove.

The clock on the microwave warned him that if he didn't get to sleep soon, tomorrow would be a long day. But Kevin couldn't turn off his imagination. Every time he closed his eyes he pictured Frank Edwards snapping handcuffs on George. Kevin had felt like a traitor, sitting back and listening to Bud Nickerson detail the seemingly endless reasons he had for not wanting to involve the local police department.

The shock of hearing the accusations voiced to an authority with the power to indict George had tested every ounce of Kevin's self-control. Rationally he knew that if he were in Bud's place, he would feel the same way. But that didn't make the knowledge any easier to swallow.

"What's wrong?" Julie inquired softly.

She had heard water running in the kitchen and assumed Kevin was getting a drink, but when she'd outstretched her hand, the sheets were cold. He had obviously been awake for some time.

"I'd better leave," he said. "It's silly for both of us to be up. You'll pull the wrong tooth tomorrow on some poor slob and it'll be my fault."

"Thanks for the vote of confidence. I hope your customers have more faith in your skills than you do in mine."

Kevin knew she was referring to more than his teasing comment. Julie loved him and wanted to ease his pain, the same way he tried to comfort her after a bad day. But it was impossible. It was unethical to breach Nickerson Electronics' security, and he didn't want to give her any more ammunition for her feud with George.

"This has nothing to do with you," he said.

"That's the first time you've ever lied to me, Kevin."

"Now we're even."

She tightened the belt on her robe and faced him. "And what's that supposed to mean?"

"Your little performance the other night when you told me we weren't right for each other. Did you really think I'd believe that?"

"Is that what's bothering you? My fear of making a commitment to you?"

"Finally, the truth. I don't recall asking you to make any promises. I love you, and I assume you're telling me the truth when you say you love me."

"Isn't that a commitment? I was raised to believe that loving a person carried certain responsibilities. Like honesty and fidelity."

He leaned against the counter and wiggled his finger at Julie. "Over here. I want to be able to see your eyes when you answer this next question."

Suddenly Julie wished she'd never dragged herself out of bed. There was no avoiding him, and she turned to meet his penetrating stare. "You misunderstood what I was trying to say."

"I don't think so. You think I'll eventually leave you."

"Pretty logical assumption. Under the circumstances."

Kevin knew that their entire future hinged on the next few minutes. He was scratching the surface, but buried underneath Julie's defenses was something she had kept so well hidden that she herself had trouble recognizing it.

"Not really. I don't have time for casual affairs. I love you and want to spend the rest of my life with you."

"Right," Julie said and laughed bitterly. "The sacred wedding vows."

"No, the sacred fact that I love you."

Kevin's eyes were piercing her, boring through the layers of protection she had built up. "For how long? A year? Two?"

"Maybe. Or thirty. Love doesn't come with any guarantees. Are you so afraid of being hurt that you won't allow yourself to take a chance?"

"That's right." Saying it at last was a relief. Julie closed her eyes, gulped and grew calm.

"Why? What did I do to you?"

"You expect me to accept certain facts without question. Your work and your brother. And I do. Now you have to grant me the same privilege. This has nothing to do with you."

"Like hell it doesn't!" Kevin was tired of being reasonable and understanding. "This has everything to do with me. You don't trust me, do you? You've never trusted me since you found out my last name was Royce."

His pain erased her hesitancy and Julie opened her arms wide. "Let's go back to bed. I want you to listen to what I have to say without interrupting me or asking any questions, and you might as well be comfortable, because it's going to be a long story."

After they were comfortably snuggling together, Julie told him the story behind each of her mother's marriages. She vented her frustration over the way men had manipulated and used her mother and the way Joan had expected her daughter to accept it. Joan walked a certain way for men, she wore her hair a special way for men, dressed in pink to please them— or maybe it was blue or black. Every action, every move was calculated to keep a man happy. Constantly careening from one man to the next, she had had no time to develop her own goals, had had no extra energy to devote to establishing a career for herself. The woman who had been Joan Bennett simply reflected the man she loved, and when he disappeared, there was nothing left of her.

Kevin listened in astonishment. "Your second stepfather gambled your entire college fund away?" It was hard to believe, and he had to bite back his anger.

"That's what he said. After the money was gone, so was he."

"I guess a few setbacks might make a girl skittish."

His understatement was so absurd, and his lack of cloying sympathy so refreshing, that Julie started to laugh. When she could speak again, she said, "Just a little." She wiped the tears from her eyes. Tears of happiness? Or tears of relief that her story had finally been told?

CHAPTER FIFTEEN

"I DON'T SEE IT ANYWHERE," Kevin called to Denise.

He'd been thinking about his baseball cards since Saturday and had decided that searching for them would provide a logical excuse for spending enough time alone with Denise to casually question her about George's debts. But he had wasted an hour and accomplished neither goal. Denise didn't say a word about their financial difficulties, and Kevin couldn't find his collection.

"They're here somewhere, Kev. Along with fifty years' worth of other junk." She brushed the dirt from her hands onto the back of his shirt and headed for the stairs. "But you'll never find them without sorting through everything."

"You didn't throw them out, did you?" he suggested. "Just tell me, so I can quit searching."

"No, I didn't throw them out. Honest. Come on, I'm thirsty. Want some iced tea to wash the dust out of your throat?"

Kevin followed her down the steep, narrow stairs to the second floor and stopped on the landing when he saw water stains on the ceiling. "When did the roof start leaking?"

"Oh, I don't know. Last winter some time. Want a sandwich?"

"I'd rather have a few straight answers."

"What did you say?"

"I asked you when you planned on fixing the leak."

"My, oh, my," Denise said, her tone softly intimidating, "Kevin gets angry when he can't find his baseball cards, doesn't he?"

"Knock it off, Denise. You sound like you're talking to a four-year-old. I asked a simple question and I'd appreciate a simple answer." He stared at Denise, waiting for her reaction. Had he overstepped the boundaries of their relationship?

"Really? And precisely what's troubling you?"

"Start with the sports car you drive. How much did that cost?"

He watched her pour her glass of iced tea down the sink and pick up her purse. Her expression never changed.

"I really don't think that's any of your business, Kevin. I'm sure you wouldn't want me to be late for my appointment with Dr. Bennett."

"You're seeing Julie Bennett? What for?"

Denise's face brightened and she set her keys down on the counter. "I hated my ugly yellow camel's teeth, and she's going to make them look like a model's."

After he listened to Denise describe the procedure, he said, "I'm surprised your insurance covers that."

"Oh, it doesn't. It's going to be expensive, but a beautiful smile is worth it."

Anger flooded him. "Then how will you pay for it?"

"George'll figure it out. He always does."

"Just like he paid the property taxes and your bill at Shorty's? What about Angelo? Does he pay for dinner there?"

"I guess so."

As if he'd been listening to the conversation with a remote-control device and knew when to intervene, George pulled into the driveway in his police cruiser and stomped up the back stairs. "You should have told me you were coming by, Kevin."

"I didn't think I needed an invitation."

George appeared to ignore the remark and said to Denise, "You going somewhere?"

She walked over and kissed her husband on the cheek. "Did you forget today was my visit with Dr. Bennett?"

"Sure did," George said and smiled at his wife.

After Denise left, Kevin concentrated his anger on the person he saw as the appropriate victim. "You knew about it and you didn't stop her?"

"Seeing a dentist isn't against the law."

"I'm surprised you let your wife set foot in Julie's office. Or is it easier on your conscience to cheat someone you don't like?"

"Get out, Kevin. You don't have the slightest idea what you're talking about."

George held the door open, but Kevin didn't budge.

"Then explain it to me. Tell me why you owe everybody in this town money, George. Justify using your friends. What's wrong, Chief Royce? Do you have a guilty conscience about cheating on Denise? Do you buy her presents to keep her happy while you visit another woman?"

The two brothers glowered at each other until George snarled like an angry animal and curled his knuckles into a fist.

"Before you take a shot at me, consider the consequences," Kevin said, grabbing his brother's fist in midair. "Remember those papers we signed when I turned eighteen? You agreed to put two hundred fifty dollars a month into my savings account until there was forty thousand dollars there. Can I go to the bank and withdraw that money?"

The lawyer who had been the executor of the Royce estate had devised the scheme to reimburse Kevin for his half of the house without imposing a hardship on George. In all the years, Kevin had never once asked for an accounting or even doubted that his brother had made the payments. Until he had returned to Tolt, he had been certain every dollar would be waiting for him.

"You don't understand." George sighed raggedly. "Those investments..."

"Don't," Kevin said and shook George's hand off his arm. The long weeks of ignoring his brother's double-dealing were finished. "I don't care what you do with your life, but leave Julie alone. She's already suffered enough because of you. She came to you for help, but not only did you turn your back on her, you spread vicious lies that could have ruined her career. What happened to your integrity and dignity, George?"

"So I made a mistake. No harm done."

Kevin took his finger and jabbed the police badge pinned to his brother's uniform. "Just make damn sure none of your men makes another mistake. If I

ever hear of anyone harassing her again, he'll be a so-
prano when I'm finished with him.''

Without waiting for George to respond, Kevin
stormed out of the house and broke every speed limit
between the farm and his office. He was itching for
one of Tolt's finest to pull him over, but they were,
predictably, as inefficient as ever. Kevin screeched into
the parking lot without as much as a raised eyebrow
from anybody he passed.

''Where's Carlos?'' he demanded, brusquely,
thumbing through the stack of messages their new
secretary handed him.

''He's out of the office, Mr. Royce. Mr. Edwards
phoned, and Mr. Romero said to tell you to meet them
at the regular place.''

Kevin didn't want to frighten the woman into quit-
ting and tried to wipe the glower off his face. ''You're
doing a good job,'' he said. ''It's nice to have a reliable person keeping us organized.'' He knew he hadn't
succeeded in calming her when she ducked her head
and began typing the minute he finished speaking.
Carlos would have his hide if he scared her away.
Kevin tried again. ''Ignore me, please. It's been a bad
day.''

''They left nearly half an hour ago, Mr. Royce.''

''One of us will call in for messages,'' he said and
jogged back to his van. Carlos lived fifteen minutes
from Maximum Security, which Kevin considered a
long commute by Tolt's standards. He used the time
to call Julie's office.

''Is Dr. Bennett with a patient?'' he asked Julie's
new receptionist.

''She sure is.''

The receptionist's casual inefficiency was particularly annoying today, and the urge to vent his frustration nearly overpowered him, but he resisted it. "Just tell her Kevin Royce called." He was too late. Denise was already in the chair, and Julie had joined the list of people who subsidized George's life-style. Why had she accepted Denise as a patient? It didn't make sense. Julie knew she didn't have a prayer of getting paid.

Frank Edwards's unmarked, government-issue car was parked nose up to the back bumper of Bud's Mercedes-Benz, and Kevin joined the lineup. He sprinted across the wet grass and around to the back of the building.

All three men had their heads bent over typewritten sheets of paper. They looked up the moment he entered the room.

"Fill me in on what I missed," Kevin said, grabbing the closest empty chair.

"Why don't we just move on? I'll brief Kevin later," Carlos suggested.

Kevin saw a look of relief light Bud's eyes when the federal agent nodded. Whatever it was they had been discussing, they didn't want to include him. Although it irked him, he wasn't about to make embarrassing demands; once they were alone, Carlos would come clean.

Frank Edwards advised Bud that his phones, both at work and at his residence, would be monitored. A background check of all employees was already in progress, the security staff was being bolstered with some new personnel, federally trained, and the Tolt police department would be carefully scrutinized.

Kevin could find no fault with any of these moves, but he wondered how many others Edwards wasn't revealing. He wasn't naive enough to think the Commerce Department would take a small outfit like Maximum Security into its confidence.

"You've still got friends in The Aerie," Edwards told Kevin after the meeting was over.

From the comment Kevin understood that Edwards had talked to more than just casual acquaintances. Only people with unrestricted security clearance would know the nickname of the fluorescent-white maze of rooms hidden in the basement of the government building where Kevin had worked. Whoever had christened it "The Aerie" had been forgotten years ago, but the amusing name lived on.

"I was there for three years. It's a good group."

"So I've heard," Edwards said. "They'd welcome you back."

"Enough," Kevin said abruptly.

"Goodbye, Royce. Later, Romero," Edwards said. He followed Bud Nickerson out the door.

"What exactly did I miss?" Kevin asked Carlos as soon as the other two men were gone.

"If our friends from out of town are right, the name Royce isn't going to be very popular around here when the truth is revealed. George is going to have a lot of questions to answer for his department's procedures."

Kevin shrugged and opened the refrigerator, searching for a soda. "Does that surprise you?"

"For a man who nearly rearranged my face at the hint George was careless, you seem to be rather indifferent."

"Things change. Did you know that Denise is having an extensive dental procedure done, and Julie's her dentist of choice?"

"Well, I'll be—" Carlos whistled. "So George finally changed his mind about her."

Kevin set down the frosty can and glared at his friend. "It's a cosmetic procedure. A very expensive cosmetic procedure."

"And George's insurance won't cover it, right?"

"Isn't that generous of him to spread his debt around? He made sure Julie is doing the work, because he doesn't care about cheating her. Just like Shorty and Angelo aren't any more important than roof moss to him."

"If you don't mind, I'm going to stay out of this one. Last time I made a comment about George, you exploded, and my advice about Mark nearly caused a permanent breakup with Theresa. My average is down this week. Besides, it's time to start mixing dinner for the gang." Carlos motioned for Kevin to follow him. "We can talk while I measure."

Kevin had never known another dog breeder and wasn't sure exactly what was established procedure, but he couldn't imagine anyone being more fastidious than Carlos about what his animals ate, the vitamins they received and the size of their portions. Feeding his dogs was much more complicated than just throwing dry food into a bowl and refilling their water buckets.

"How's Mark doing?" Kevin asked, hoisting himself onto the bale of hay Carlos had piled in one corner of the shed.

"He'll be all right. But it's as much Theresa's problem as it is Mark's."

"Can she see that now?"

"She's starting to," Carlos said, lining up the clean bowls. "It takes time to break old patterns. I quit smoking twelve years ago and I still reach for a cigarette when I'm nervous. I can't expect her to end sixteen years' worth of overprotecting her son, just because I snap my fingers and tell her it's wrong."

"You really think Mark will come around?"

"You did."

Kevin saw the corners of Carlos's mouth twitching from the suppression of a smile and picked up the gauntlet. "I was never that bad. I was indulged a bit maybe, but not spoiled."

"Do you remember the time . . . ?"

Their reminiscences about incidents when Kevin was in boot camp had them both boisterously laughing in minutes. Kevin realized Carlos had orchestrated the banter to relieve tension and silently thanked his friend.

"I think I'd better warn Mark what a vengeful person you can be," Kevin said. "He doesn't know there isn't a chance this side of Saturn that he can win."

"I think he realizes that," Carlos said, balancing four dog dishes on his arms like a waitress in a busy diner. "Grab a few."

As Kevin helped Carlos feed the dogs, the grumbling of his own stomach reminded him he hadn't eaten since morning. After settling their plans for the next two days of the work week, Kevin followed his homing instinct to Julie's.

"You smell better than supper," he said. She was standing at the sink; he came up behind her, pivoting her to face him.

"That's quite a compliment from the king of the clean plate club."

He nibbled her earlobe, well aware of what her response would be.

"Dinner's ready," she said, trying to keep back a wistful sigh. At that moment, all she hungered for was Kevin.

"Too bad," he said, kissing her neck one more time. "I'm still enjoying the appetizer."

They dawdled through the meal, content to chat about inconsequential things. Kevin wished he could just blurt out that he knew about Denise, tell Julie about his disillusionment with George and their confrontation, but knew that unless she elected to confide in him, Julie's business was just that—her business. And besides, his feelings toward his brother were too raw to share.

The sparkle was missing from Kevin's eyes. Julie smiled at him, thinking he looked like an eight-year-old whose puppy was lost. The list of people who had the power to hurt Kevin was short: Carlos Romero, George Royce and Julie Bennett. Two names could be scratched off that list immediately.

"Want to tell me about it?" she asked softly. "I'm a good listener."

"Not yet," he said.

"My receptionist told me you called just after Denise came in. Does that have anything to do with what's bothering you?" It was the first time she had ever mentioned that his sister-in-law was a patient, but she didn't want to hide the fact from him any longer.

He refilled their coffee mugs and held out his hand, inviting her to leave the table. "Denise told me about it this morning. How are you going to handle this when George doesn't pay the bill? We both know he can't afford it,'' he said, glad to finally have the subject out in the open.

''The same way I would any other patient. I'll wait a few months, then turn him over to a collection agency. When tax time rolls around I'll write him off as a bad debt.'' She couldn't believe how detached she sounded.

''I'm sorry you were dragged into this mess, Julie. Just take comfort in the fact that George's career as a tax credit is coming to an end,'' Kevin told her.

Seeing that his cryptic comment puzzled her, he added, ''Don't frown,'' and rubbed her forehead with the tip of one finger. ''When I can, I'll explain. I know I shouldn't have said anything, teasing you with a hint when that's all I'm free to say. But trust me. It's almost over.''

Julie smiled at him, apparently swallowing the questions she was dying to ask.

''Let's go somewhere. Anywhere,'' Kevin suggested, jumping up.

They prowled up and down the night-hushed streets in Julie's car, talking about everyone and everything but George. Julie related the episode of Denise's first appointment, including her anger with George. She had expected to feel freed of her pent-up rage when she finally had the chance to speak her piece about Kevin's brother, but didn't. Kevin's grim silence robbed the moment of any satisfaction.

''I promise that you'll be paid,'' he said. ''Everyone will be paid.''

"I'm not talking about money. That's not the point at all. I just want to see an end to George's shenanigans. It's a crime the way he uses people in this town."

She saw Kevin wince and realized what she had said. "There's an investigation going on, isn't there?"

He had followed a two-lane country road to a café miles from Tolt. "This place has the best pie," Kevin said as he parked the car. "If the owners haven't changed, they make a wonderful lemon meringue on Wednesdays."

Kevin was obviously avoiding her question. Accepting this, Julie looked around. She couldn't recall ever passing this little café.

"Where are we?" she asked.

"About thirty miles from Tolt. My father used to stop here every time he went fishing."

Julie opened her door and jumped out of the van. "Do you think they have coconut cream?"

Hand in hand they entered the restaurant. Kevin led them to the last burgundy vinyl booth. "I don't like to sit in the middle. I feel like I'm entertainment for the other people in the room," he said. "And now I can kiss you whenever I please."

The only way he could put George out of his mind was to concentrate on Julie. Briefly he tasted her half-parted lips, but any further exploration was for the moment interrupted by the waitress.

"Do you know what I'm going to do once we get home?" he said after their order had been taken.

"Help me do the dishes we left on the table."

"Nope. That'll come later."

She batted her eyelids, feigning ignorance. "It's too late for anything more strenuous."

"You won't need to go jogging tomorrow morning. I'll see that you get enough exercise. Consider me your personal trainer."

Julie smiled at his impish grin. "What if I say I'm too tired for a workout?"

"I don't think that'll be a problem."

Kevin leaned over, putting his lips against her ear and confided precisely what he was going to do. His enthusiasm for life had clearly returned. Julie wrapped her arms around his shoulders.

"Is that a promise?" she inquired, smiling.

"A money-back guarantee, lady."

They shared their pie, feeding each other bites and laughing at just about everything. Julie was just about to prod Kevin out of the booth when she heard a masculine voice from the booth behind them. She couldn't see who it was, but the soft, deep tone sent shivers up her spine. Stiffening involuntarily, she struggled to place the voice. It tickled the edges of her memory, teasing her with a vague familiarity. She held a finger to her lips, asking Kevin to remain silent.

The man was neither patient nor friend, but she had memorized the sound of his voice for a good reason. Grabbing a napkin and rummaging in her purse for a pen, Julie waited for him to speak again and confirm her hunch. Quickly she scribbled a message to Kevin.

"He's the one. That's the man who answered the phone at Nickerson."

There was no way they could leave without being seen so Kevin wrote back, "We'll stay until they leave. Don't say a word. We don't want to let him know we're here."

Kevin fought to control the urge to peek over the divider. Then a second man spoke, and he wasn't surprised or even disappointed when he recognized Butler's voice.

Julie recognized it, too; she searched Kevin's face for confirmation and he mouthed the name.

"It shouldn't take much to get old Georgie boy to change the duty roster," Butler went on. "He's been cooperating with me so far."

Kevin glanced at Julie and saw her strain to catch every word.

"I can only make the delivery to our friends if you get the goods out on time," the other man warned. "I'll reimburse Royce for any inconvenience."

Julie could almost feel Kevin cringe and gripped his hand. Why did they have to be here tonight? Of all the other places they could have stopped at, Kevin had to pick this one.

Butler spoke again. "Here's Royce. Let me do the talking. He'll come cheap."

"Our friends want another ten workstations, so don't be stingy. There's enough money to keep him happy."

Everything Kevin had been dreading was coming true. Anger gripped him in its clutch. His illusions about George were dead. He had no doubt that his brother would accept the money.

Julie didn't dare look at Kevin. She knew she couldn't without crying, so she stared straight ahead. Not only was George Royce cheating people he knew and had sworn to protect, he was betraying everything Kevin had spent twenty years of his life defending.

"You're doing great," Kevin told her in another note.

She picked up the pen again and scribbled a question. "Did you know George was involved?"

Kevin shrugged and took her hand.

The grip of his fingers grew excruciating as footsteps approached, but Julie didn't squirm. She was concentrating on controlling her breathing, mastering the rage that threatened to overwhelm her.

"Evening." It was George.

Julie could hear him slide across the booth and clamped her eyes shut.

"Glad you could make it," Butler said. "We need to talk about changing the duty roster Friday night, so I can work at Nickerson."

"Getting a little picky about your second job, aren't you?" George asked. "Or is this more than just moonlighting?"

"That's right, and I'd be very grateful if you'd let me have this night off," Butler replied. "If you have a deposit slip, I can show your bank account that I'm ten thousand dollars grateful."

Kevin's blood was pounding in his ears; his brother was selling himself for ten thousand dollars tonight? How much had been at stake on previous occasions?

"Friday night the alarms are going to be singing at the main gate. You take your time getting there, and if you happen to notice anything at the side entrance on Grant Avenue, you'll just ignore it. Be real convincing and there'll be another ten coming your way," Butler went on.

"Without me you're dead," George said firmly "Make that twenty and you've got yourself a deal."

"Forget it," Butler retorted.

"You'll be busy at the station for at least ten minutes," the third man suggested. "That'll be worth something, too."

"We speak the same language," George observed. "I'll be ordering a new bank statement. Make sure I'm happy."

Butler and his associate waited nearly five minutes after George left, discussing the details of how they would get the computer terminals out the side gate.

Kevin listened, itching to jump over the divider and bash their heads together. He had been right all along. They had stolen the defense program and needed the specialized computers; without them the software was useless.

"Royce is asking for too much," Butler said.

"Drop it. If you'd been smart enough to figure out how to plug my terminal into the modem, we would have been finished by now. I'm the one taking all the risks. Bud thinks I'm bobbing around on my boat."

Well, well, Kevin thought, *the man Julie recognized has to be Brent Olsen, Bud's top programmer.*

"You have the program and two computers. Isn't that enough?" Butler demanded.

"Our friends want ten more terminals. Then this is all history. We can both go back to our regular routines and sympathize over the disastrous tragedy at Nickerson Electronics."

"I want it all out of the country before the day shift comes on," Butler insisted. "Can you arrange it?"

"As long as you don't make any more stupid mistakes."

''Me? You were supposed to get that program weeks
ago.''

''Listen, we both want to go on living in this town.
If you stay calm, your piddly little salary from the
police force will have a tidy supplement. I'll be waiting outside the gates. All you have to do is get the cartons that far, which shouldn't be too difficult. Kevin
Royce and those damn dogs are off the job, and Bud
will be busy with the Department of Commerce guy.
I've eliminated all the variables.''

Are you sure? Kevin silently inquired.

CHAPTER SIXTEEN

THE RESTAURANT was nearly empty; the booth behind them had been vacant for what seemed like hours. Still, Kevin and Julie waited. He couldn't take the risk of being spotted and ruin the perfect opportunity to catch the thieves before any real harm was done.

"Just a few more minutes," he said. "Then, while you're paying the bill, I'll call Carlos."

"Why Carlos? Why not the authorities?" Julie asked.

"Carlos will contact the federal agent who's in charge of this case and arrange a meeting for tonight. Okay?"

Julie was speechless. Even as she walked to the cash register and paid the waitress, she still couldn't manage to push a word past her paralyzed throat. Kevin was sealing his brother's fate; she would never have thought it possible. She waited just inside the door for him to finish with Carlos.

"Ready?" He wrapped his arm protectively around her shoulders and hustled her across the dark parking lot. When they were locked in the car he said, "Carlos is at Theresa's, and I don't have time to take you home. Do you mind waiting there?"

"Of course not," she said. She didn't know what else to say and settled for silence, unsure about how

Theresa would react. They hadn't talked since the blowup over Mark, and the strain between them was still unresolved. But Kevin's problems overshadowed hers.

Julie's doubts disappeared the instant she walked in the back door of Theresa's house.

"Gin rummy or canasta?" Her old friend was sitting at the kitchen table shuffling cards, a pot of tea steeping next to her.

"You always win, but I'm a sucker for a good game of cribbage," Julie told her.

"You don't stand a chance," Theresa said with a wink.

"Enjoy yourselves, ladies." Carlos stood and kissed Theresa. "We'll be back before you can miss us."

"Impossible." Theresa waved him on his way.

Kevin planted a quick kiss upon Julie's forehead and followed Carlos out the door without saying anything.

Mark appeared. "Mom, I'm going to be in the living room doing my homework. Hi, Julie. Bye, Julie." He executed a clowning bow, and the two women smiled briefly, but their laughter died when Mark came over and kissed his mother on the cheek. "Sorry tonight was spoiled, Mom."

"Was that Mark?" Julie inquired when they were alone.

"That was my son. I don't think you've ever met him before."

"Pretty dramatic shift."

Theresa poured tea into her cup and stirred it with her spoon, dissolving the sugar. "Will you ever forgive me? After the way I talked to you, I wouldn' blame you if you didn't. I didn't like the message, so shot the messenger."

Julie stood up and moved to where Theresa was sitting, the spoon still clutched in her fingers. Bending down, she gave her friend a hug. "I had no right interfering in your life. I'm the one who should be apologizing."

"Rather than arguing about who was wrong and who was right, let's gorge on cheesecake. I baked one this evening," Theresa said.

Julie felt her smile vanish and saw Theresa look at her quizzically.

"So tell me all about it," her friend suggested.

"It all started over a piece of pie," Julie began, then told Theresa exactly what they had overheard in the restaurant.

"Poor Kevin," Theresa commented. "He must be feeling miserable about George."

"And I feel helpless. I wish there was something I could do to make it easier for him, but I can't think of anything."

"Just love him." Theresa sighed and stretched her arms over her head, wiggling her fingers. "Love can work miracles."

Something glinting on Theresa's finger caught Julie's attention. She grabbed her friend's hand. "You're engaged? When? How?"

"It's about time. I was beginning to think you were blind," Theresa told her. "Carlos took Mark out on Sunday afternoon and the two of them settled their differences. When Carlos asked Mark's permission to marry me, the rest was a downhill slide. Or so Carlos says. Mark claims he made Carlos squirm a bit before he agreed."

"It's like a fairy tale!" Julie exclaimed. "And you deserve the happy ending. But I don't think I'm ever going to speak to you again for not telling me."

"Hey, I just found out last night. The two guys planned this without telling me."

"Seems a little strange that the bride-to-be didn't know she was engaged."

"Have I ever been the traditional type?"

"I'd ask you if you're sure about this," Julie said and tapped the diamond, "but I can tell you've made up your mind."

"The past ten years have been a learning experience, a training session, so I would recognize Carlos when I met him. He's reserved, and other people might not notice what a wonderful man he is, but believe me, there beats the heart of a Latin lover underneath that cool, calm exterior."

"Aren't you curious about what Carlos could have said to Mark to make such a difference?" Julie inquired.

"I have a remarkable young man for a son and I'm going to marry a fantastic man. I don't question fate when it's on my side."

Julie was still curious about the reason behind Mark's transformation. "Mind if I check with Mark?"

"Ask away, but he won't answer you. I tried."

Julie found him stretched out on the couch, one hand dangling over the edge, resting on his dog's head.

"May I interrupt?" she asked.

"Mom told you that she's getting married, didn't she?"

"She sure did. I'm really happy for her. How do you feel about it?"

"Great. Carlos treats her pretty good."

Julie pushed aside his feet and sat down on the end of the sofa. "That's it? Are you a Stepford child? Has your brain been replaced by a microchip?"

Mark grinned. "It's me. Busy trying to drag my grades out of the gutter."

"Do you like Carlos?"

"He's all right. I respect what he's done with his life and I want someone around to take care of Mom after I leave home. You know, Julie, I'll only be here for two more years. After that she'll be alone, and we both know how much trouble she'll get into if there's no one to look after her."

The idea that Mark was worried about his mother was amusing, but Julie didn't laugh. He was taking his responsibility seriously, and she wouldn't say a word to undermine him.

"You're right."

"If Carlos didn't marry her, she might go for one of those other creeps when I wasn't around to chase them off," Mark went on. "That's a nauseating thought."

"I appreciate your concern for your mother, but that doesn't explain your about-face. Off the record, what happened?" Julie pulled on his toes and studied his face for unspoken signals. He seemed more relaxed and confident than she'd ever known him to be.

"Just between you and me?" Mark inquired, pulling free and sitting up. "You can't tell Mom. Carlos needs to be the one to break the news."

Julie was even more mystified. "Promise," she said.

"I've been seeing my father. He's living in Seattle."

Julie tried to mask her shock, but knew Mark could tell how surprised she was.

He rushed to explain. "He's changed, Julie. He really has. But I knew Mom would have a conniption fi
if I told her about our visits."

"And you told Carlos about it?"

"Yes."

"What did he say?"

"That I deserved to form my own opinion about my
father. Right or wrong, he's still my father. Carlos said
he would help me tell Mom, but we had to wait for the
right time."

"How did that make things better?" Julie wanted
to know, still puzzled.

"I don't have to get kicked out of the house to see
him. Dad said I could come live with him if I wanted
to, but I don't. Not really. I just want to see him
sometimes. He's not such a bad person, Julie."

"No," Theresa said, "he isn't." Mark and Julie
looked up in shock. "Sorry, but I thought eavesdrop-
ping was excusable, considering the circumstances."

"I'll leave you two alone," Julie said quickly.

"Don't go," Theresa begged her. "I'm not upset."

"You're not mad?" Mark said softly.

"Only at myself. If I had done my job as a mother
you'd have been able to come to me. You almost ruined your life because of my prejudice toward your
father. I've known for nearly two years that he was
living in Seattle. When he contacted me, I refused to
let him see you. Can you forgive me, Mark?"

Julie heard Theresa's pain. She willed Mark to understand that his mother, afraid of losing him, had
acted out of love. *Please, Mark, please,* she thought.

"I haven't forgotten how rotten he was to you, and
neither has he. He always says nice things about you

Mom. Dad said he's been in therapy and told me why he walked out on us."

"He did?" Theresa whispered.

"He was an immature jerk. He's married again and has two little kids. His wife is nice. I think you'd like her."

Theresa started to cry and held her arms wide. Julie watched Mark rush into them. She marveled at the simple conclusion of years of turmoil and upheaval. Theresa was free to marry the man she loved, free to trust the growing independence of her son and free to forgive the father of her child. Mark could love both of his parents without being coerced into making a choice between them. He could pursue his life without the burden of being forced to sneak around in order to build a relationship with his father. One burst of honesty, and years of fear and misunderstanding had been put behind them.

Julie smiled at Theresa's happiness, but the enthusiasm was difficult to maintain, preoccupied as she was with her concern for Kevin.

Kevin and Carlos returned some time later. Kevin wasted no time socializing, and Julie didn't object. She could see that he was depressed. She put a hand upon his arm, trying to communicate her sympathy.

"I have to go home tonight, Julie," Kevin said as they were driving back to her apartment. "I have some things to tend to at my place."

She didn't question his decision, didn't even find his manner odd when he perfunctorily kissed her goodnight. But when she looked at him and saw him avoid her eyes, turning his head away, she ached with his pain. She undressed for bed and tried to fall asleep, but couldn't shake the wintry feeling of dread.

"Are you going to survive?" she asked when she
called him the next morning.

"The jury's still out."

"What's on your agenda for this evening?"

"I'd like to come by about seven."

His tension almost made the telephone wires
crackle. "We'll have Chinese food in bed," Julie sug
gested. "Sound good?"

"Don't bother. I won't be able to stay."

"I love you, Kevin," she told him.

He hung up without answering her.

The vision of his brother being arrested appeared
like a hologram every time Kevin closed his eyes. He
could see the streetlights glinting off the handcuffs on
George's wrists, hear the static of the radios in the car
surrounding his brother and almost smell the fear, the
terror of a man who knew he was trapped with no
chance of escape. Kevin lay awake all night and knew
by morning what he had to do.

All day long, the memory of her brief conversation
with Kevin exaggerated Julie's feelings of foreboding.
She tried to shrug them aside, but couldn't. It was the
longest day she could ever remember, and by the time
she made it home, she felt as if everything inside her
had turned to ice. She sat down in the rocking chair,
not even bothering to turn on any lights, and waited
for him.

Normally Kevin knocked three times in rapid suc
cession and walked in, too anxious to see her to wait
outside until she answered the door. Tonight he
waited, and when Julie looked into his eyes, she knew.

"I'm going away, Julie. I don't expect you to un
derstand, because I'm not sure I do." How could
Kevin explain that if he stayed in Tolt he would de

stroy both Julie and Carlos? A little town like Tolt
didn't forgive or forget.

He wanted to beg her to come with him, but it
wasn't fair to ask her to abandon everything she'd
worked so hard to build, just because she'd had the
bad luck to fall in love with him. She already despised
George, and Kevin suspected that if she agreed to leave
Tolt it would only be a matter of time before she despised him, too. He had thought they could conquer
all the obstacles; it was amazing how blind you could
be when you were in love.

"Where are you going?" What did it matter
whether his destination lay one hundred or one thousand miles away? He was walking out the door and
she'd be alone again.

"I'll be at Nickerson on Friday night, and George
will be arrested right after that. Then I'm gone. It's
back to my old life."

"What about Denise? Who will look after her?"

"She has a large family," he said.

"Carlos? Are you going to bail out on him?" Julie
persisted, unwilling to surrender.

"I'll have legal documents drawn up. Maximum
Security Systems will be his. If I stick around, it'll put
him into bankruptcy. No sense ruining his career. We
both worked too hard to flush it all away."

Kevin spoke coolly, busy recording every detail
about Julie he could. He didn't have a single photograph of her and would have to rely on his memories
of this beautiful, loving woman who had almost become his wife.

"And me? What about me?"

''It's been fun.'' He had planned this curt speech carefully, wanting to hurt her, make her angry. Anger would help her to forget him.

''Fun? You call this fun?''

''Goodbye, J.B.,'' he said.

She watched him turn around and open the door. ''Get back here, Kevin Royce. I'm not finished with you yet.''

''That's just it, Julie. We were finished before we ever began. You were right all along. All Royces are alike.'' Kevin closed the door behind him.

Julie couldn't find the strength to stop him. Sliding to the floor, she drew her knees up to her chest and sat curled in a tight little ball. She knew she should hate him, call him every foul name in the dictionary, but didn't have the energy. Stumbling into her bedroom, she crawled into bed and pulled the covers to her chin. Maybe she could think about it tomorrow. Right now all she wanted to do was sleep.

In the morning she woke long before the time her alarm usually sounded. She lay in bed waiting, waiting for calm. And it came. All through the day it protected her, guided her, never allowing her to cry, to think, to feel.

Kevin was gone and she could accept it. She had always been able to accept life's ups and downs. Someday, one day, she would look back and see that this had been just a minor setback. But for now she would just stay numb. It was the only way to maintain her sanity.

Kevin raged through the next two days.

''Get off my case! I didn't ask for your advice.'' He had been arguing with Carlos for over an hour about signing over his share of the business, knowing Carlos couldn't afford to buy him out and not wanting to burden his ex-partner with a crippling debt.

"I can't believe you're running away," Carlos said calmly.

"George is a crook, and we wouldn't survive in this town once the story hits the newspapers. At least you stand a chance without me."

"What are you going to do?"

"Reenlist. The Marine Corps misses me," Kevin said sardonically. "I made a few phone calls and there's no problem getting back in, though I can't leave until people decide whether they'll need my testimony at the trial. Hopefully a sworn statement will do, then I'll hit the bricks."

Carlos took the papers Kevin had been hounding him to sign and stuffed them into a desk drawer. "I won't sign them."

"I have an appointment with Edwards in ten minutes. We'll talk about this later," Kevin said curtly.

"What are you going to do? Forge my signature?" Carlos inquired.

Kevin stormed out of the office without answering and cut across town to the park where he was meeting Frank Edwards.

"No way," Edwards said when Kevin made his proposal. "You stay as far away from that plant as you can get. If I see you, I'll have you arrested."

"You owe me," Kevin insisted. "I handed you time, place and players. I even helped stage this damn thing, and all I'm asking is to observe. That's it."

The federal agent stubbed out his cigarette. "You'll have a man guarding you with orders to arrest you if you make one peep. Is that clear?"

Kevin nodded.

"Got a call from your former employer this morning," Edwards went on. "You like wearing fatigues, huh?"

"Women are crazy for a man in uniform," Kevin said and walked to his truck.

Although he only had another day and a half left in Tolt it seemed like a lifetime. The temptation to call Julie and beg her to come with him was nearly irresistible but, by setting the deadline of Friday night to have his desk clear, his apartment packed and the details of his life in Tolt wrapped up, Kevin survived.

HE HAD HIDDEN in his office all Friday afternoon, willing the hands of the clock to march faster, but there were still nearly five hours until Olsen and Butler would meet. He had nothing to do until nine o'clock, when they would take up their positions outside Nickerson Electronics. Kevin said goodbye to the secretary, then wandered to his van. There wasn't a soul he wanted to see except Julie.

He finally decided to drive back to the restaurant where they'd shared their last meal. Maybe if the pain was fierce enough, it would burn itself out. Anything was better than this empty, dead feeling.

"Glad to see you like our boysenberry pie," the waitress said, clearly recognizing him. She poured him a cup of coffee, while Kevin tried to absorb the pain. This wasn't going to work.

"Do you have any paper plates, so I can take it with me?" he asked as she was cutting a piece of pie.

"Sure thing."

Back at his apartment, Kevin called Carlos. "How about dinner? Call it a farewell party for the Royce brothers. My treat."

"I'm not going to make it that easy for you, Kevin. That lame excuse about saving the business stinks worse than a compost pile. You're sneaking out the back door and leaving me to face the music because you're embarrassed."

"A simple no would have been sufficient. I didn't call you for another lecture."

"Bye, Kevin."

"Don't want to change your mind and join me tonight?"

"Not a chance," Carlos said firmly. "Make sure you let me know where you're stationed. About tax time I might need to get in touch with you."

"Good luck, Carlos."

Kevin had never felt so alone. Even the death of his parents hadn't been this devastating. People had sympathized with him, coddled him with affection. And there had always been George, standing in the background, his strong shoulders ready to share the burden. Now he had no one.

He managed to waste the next few hours, then drove to the hospital parking lot where the agents were meeting. In Tolt it was nearly impossible to find enough vacant spots to hide six empty cars without arousing the suspicion of the police, and the last thing they needed was to tip off George. Kevin had been the one to suggest the hospital. Cars coming and going at odd hours were no novelty there.

His van was conspicuous, and Edwards had Kevin move it to the clinic's secluded lot just down the road. Kevin wanted to tell him that he couldn't do that, but he couldn't think up a logical excuse. Julie would most likely be gone by now, he told himself. He prayed all the way down the curving private road that he wouldn't see a beige sedan.

He spotted her car and shook his head at his unrelenting bad luck. Her car was still here and the light in her office was burning.

"Let's go," Kevin said, jumping into the surveillance van that had followed him. He wanted out of here. Now.

"You take Royce straight over to the plant," Frank Edwards's voice instructed over the radio. "You know your spot. I'll be just a few minutes behind you."

"Your name is Royce, too?" the driver wanted to know.

"Yep."

"Any connection to Chief Royce?"

"No," Kevin said, not lying. He didn't know the man he used to call his brother.

The driver carefully turned the corner, his eyes darting back and forth in the rearview mirror. "Crooked cops make me sick."

Kevin couldn't answer.

CHAPTER SEVENTEEN

KEVIN REVIEWED the planned chain of events and felt his stomach lurch. As soon as Butler and Olsen had the boxes loaded, the troops would converge, blocking the road and any chance of escape. One team had been assigned to Olsen, the fellows behind the fences would handle Butler, and a third team was across town, waiting for the signal to apprehend George. It had all been neatly plotted and rehearsed, like an elaborate stage play.

The six men crammed into the back of the van were all nervous, peering through the darkened glass windows for the signal to move. There was no joking, no raillery; each one was intent on the task at hand.

The moment he saw headlights approaching, Kevin could feel a trickle of perspiration cut loose down his cheek. It was like a sauna inside the vehicle, but the windows remained rolled up to hide them from view. From their spot in front of a gas station the van looked deserted, a deflated tire adding to the authenticity of the scene.

"Good morning, sunshine," someone in the back whispered as the pickup stopped in front of the side gate.

The driver switched off the lights, left the truck idling and opened the door. Kevin saw a man obscured by shadows step out of the vehicle and Butler

pushed the gate open from the inside, his arms filled
with the first carton. Kevin's senses went on alert, recording every detail.

The instant the gate opened, the contact points
should have been disturbed, setting the alarms wailing, but the night was deathly still, the only noise that
of quickened breathing inside the van. Then the sirens on the other side of the compound began to
scream.

Olsen had plainly fixed things so that the main
gate's alarms would trigger at a preset time; while attention was directed toward the point of the assumed
break-in, they would be loading the neatly boxed
computer terminals into the waiting pickup. Their extra insurance had been obtained from George. He
would delay the response time long enough to ensure
that no one noticed the flutter of activity at the smaller
gate behind the main plant.

Let me see you, Kevin wished fervently. He had a
grudging admiration for Brent Olsen's mind and
wanted to match the photograph in the personnel
folder to the real man. He had distinctive white-blond
hair that would be easily visible even at this distance.
The man accepting the boxes from Butler was finally
illuminated for just an instant, and Kevin broke the
silence with a small whoop of satisfaction as a head of
nearly white hair gleamed in the moonlight.

He heard the men in the van begin to move, poised
to leap out. He could almost feel every muscle in their
bodies rippling in anticipation. This time they were
going to catch the bad guys. It was the moment they'd
trained for, sweet compensation for all the bitterness
of other losses.

"It's show time," the fellow behind Kevin said.

But Kevin barely heard the man's remark. In a burst of blaring sirens and flashing lights, three police cruisers pinned Butler and Olsen against the fence.

"Edwards is going to have a cow," the driver of the van groaned as the federal agents burst out the side door and started running across the deserted street.

"Shut up!" Kevin exclaimed and unrolled his window, poking his head out for a better view.

He watched George leap out of his car; Butler and Olsen were spreadeagled across the hood before any of Edwards's men could intervene. Kevin knew the agent guarding him probably thought he was crazy, but he couldn't help chuckling at the scene before them. George was flailing his arms in righteous indignation as federal agents surrounded him. Meanwhile the Tolt sheriffs staunchly guarded their prisoners, though their federal counterparts tried to muscle them aside.

"Do you still have Kevin Royce?" Edwards barked over the radio.

"Yes, sir," the young man replied.

"See that he doesn't move. I want to talk to him." Edwards was plainly furious.

"Yes, sir."

Kevin immediately realized what Edwards was thinking. The irony of the situation was tragic. Kevin had assumed George was guilty, had set George up, and now everyone would accuse him of warning his brother. Add to that the devastation he had wreaked on his own life, and the toll of Kevin's lack of trust in his brother was astronomical. But still, a part of him was elated. George was innocent!

"Get Royce over here!" Edwards screamed over the radio.

"Yes, sir," Kevin's watchdog responded.

"Don't want to keep the man waiting," Kevin said, trying to sound as lighthearted as if he were going for an early-evening walk. He took his time, steeling himself first for George's tirade.

"Kevin!" George exclaimed. "What in the hell are you doing here?"

Edwards fired off a volley of instructions, stunning George into silence. Then he said, "Chief, could we please step aside and let my men do their job? Then I can fill in the details."

Taking a drag of night air the way Edwards drew on his cigarette, Kevin looked at his brother. "Julie and I were in the booth the night you met Butler and Olsen. We thought you were in on the theft. We didn't realize you were setting up Butler and Olsen."

The effect of his words rendered George speechless. "Why didn't you return my telephone calls?" he finally said to Edwards. "I waited until the last minute and tended to the job myself when I didn't get any response."

"Excuse me, Chief Royce," Edwards said in a newly calm tone. "Before I can answer that I need to check on something." He moved away.

Alone, George looked at Kevin and sighed. "Did you really think I'd take the money?"

"Yes." He couldn't lie.

"Why, Kev?"

"What else was I supposed to assume? You owe a fortune to anybody who will give you credit. I tried to talk to you and you shut me out. The evidence seemed undeniable when I listened to you agree to go along with the plan."

George didn't say a word and Kevin looked up at the dark sky. They were within arm's reach, but neither seemed prepared to bridge the gap.

"Kevin," Edwards said when he returned, "you can go. Thank you for your invaluable assistance."

"Like hell I will. You're not shutting me out like this. What's going on?"

"I just talked to my main office. Seems like Chief Royce did contact us, but the only message I received was that Royce had called. In all of the last-minute confusion, I assumed it was Kevin Royce, not George Royce. The records show that there were three calls. In other words, we goofed."

"You're not the only one who goofed, Mr. Edwards," George said angrily.

"I'm very sorry about all of this. Kevin, want a lift back to your van?"

Kevin couldn't think straight; the enormity of the error and Edwards's bland dismissal were beyond comprehension. "Sure."

"Come on over to my car, Chief," Edwards directed. "One of my men can see that Kevin gets back to his truck."

George and Edwards walked away without another word, leaving Kevin standing alone. All the way back to his truck, Kevin felt numb. He couldn't decide how to even begin rectifying the devastation. But he knew that he'd never be able to live with himself if he didn't face his mistakes and try to put them right. He'd acted like a stubborn dunce, and it was time to plot out his next move—very carefully.

Pacing back and forth in the clinic parking lot, Kevin considered his options. He kept circling back to the same conclusion. He had only two choices: stay in

Tolt and apologize to every person he knew or leave. In his heart he had never wanted to leave. He knew that Carlos would be a breeze. George just might forgive him with enough time and patience. But what about Julie? How would Julie ever trust him again?

"Please," he said, looking up at the star-filled sky, "help me."

Before he lost his courage, Kevin drove to the all-night supermarket and bought every little packet of fresh flowers they had sitting at the checkout stands. Some were wilted, some were fresh, but he didn't take time to sort through them. He simply cleaned out every container until his arms were filled with tiny bouquets of cellophane-wrapped roses and carnations.

THE MOMENT HE ARRIVED at her apartment, he switched off his engine and considered the next step. He could stand outside her door and bang away until she finally answered. Or, he could also call her from his van.

"Julie," he said when her sleepy voice answered, "I know it's late and I have no right to ask, but I have to see you."

"Kevin! Where are you?"

"Outside your apartment."

She sat up in bed and turned on the lamp, glancing at the clock. "Do you realize what time it is?"

"Seems like we've been down this road before, doesn't it?" He remembered the first time he'd asked her on a date, calling early in the morning. "This couldn't wait. I have to talk to you."

"Why? We'll just hurt each other."

His fingers curled tightly around the plastic receiver. "Please. I want to explain what happened tonight."

"It won't change anything."

"I love you, Julie. Give me ten minutes. Then if you want me to leave, I will."

"I'm setting the timer."

Kevin had heard how attorneys pleading before the Supreme Court were given a limited amount of time to convince the justices that their cases deserved the opportunity of a retrial, and he was as nervous as any young lawyer facing the last court of appeal. He gathered the flowers into his arms and slowly walked to her door. The next few minutes would decide the remainder of his life.

Julie grabbed a billowing cotton robe and madly began to brush through her hair. Why did she care what she looked like? she wondered. It was finished between them. But even while her mind was warning her not to read more into this midnight visit than Kevin intended, her heart was pounding and her palms were damp.

"Hello," she said as she opened the door.

Kevin was standing in the shadows and Julie could only see a vague blur, but she was overwhelmed by a fragrant aroma.

"These are for you," he said and stepped into the light.

It was the largest bouquet she had ever seen, and it was successfully hiding Kevin's face. Not knowing what to say, she reached across and pulled out one single pink blossom. At least he had style. Most men would have settled for a single bouquet, but Kevin had stripped the local grocery store.

"Out with it," she said.

"You'll let me stay?" Kevin couldn't believe she was giving in so easily.

"For ten minutes. Just like I said."

He walked into the living room and set down the flowers. He could feel Julie watching him and considered her concentration to be a good sign. At least she'd be interested in what he had to say.

"I love you, Julie. If you'll give me the chance, I want to prove it."

"You already did that. By walking out my door."

"I felt I had no choice. George was destroying himself and I couldn't drag you down, too. I thought anyone associated with the name Royce was going to be blackballed."

She sat down on the couch and tucked her feet under the hem of her robe. Kevin sounded as if things had changed, but George was still his brother. "Is that a big surprise? At least I loved you enough to be willing to challenge my prejudice."

"And destroy everything you've worked so hard to build? Would that be fair?"

"Maybe not, but I never assumed everything was fair. What I did assume was that you were being honest with me."

Kevin sat down on the sofa at a safe distance. He knew if he came too close he wouldn't be able to resist reaching out to her. Much as he wanted to kiss her fears away, erase the hurt look from her eyes, he couldn't. Not yet, anyway.

"They caught the guys who have been causing the trouble at Nickerson. It was quite a surprise," Kevin began.

"Anyone I know?" She couldn't resist the sarcasm and yet she was confused. She'd expected Kevin to be more distraught after his brother's arrest.

"Butler and the strange telephone voice, Brent Olsen. He works for Nickerson. George arrested them at the gate." Kevin hoped his simple statement would have more impact than an elaborate explanation. He watched Julie's face go blank, then saw shock widen her eyes.

"George arrested them?"

"Sure did. Seems like we all misjudged him. It's his turn to think the worst of me."

"What right does he have to judge you? He's the one who's been cheating. He probably spotted us that night in the café and decided to play the part of a hero."

Kevin shook his head. "No. He's completely innocent."

"Then explain all those debts!"

"I can't. And frankly, I don't give a spotted owl's hoot about George right now. I came here to talk about us."

"There is no 'us.' You made that quite clear."

"Julie, I don't want to leave Tolt. I love you and I want to stay here and marry you."

She began to shake. It started as just a tiny quiver in her legs, a reaction she always had when she was extremely frightened or nervous, but if she didn't control it, her teeth would soon be chattering, too. "I can't think, Kevin. I..."

He heard the wobble in her voice and saw her hands jerkily rub up and down her legs. Grabbing the quilt from the back of the sofa, he wrapped it around her shoulders. "Come here," he said softly. "Let me hold you."

Julie allowed him to bundle her up and snuggled into his arms. It didn't make good sense; she had vowed to never, ever let him touch her again, but it felt right. She had been numb under an invisible layer of ice ever since he had left her, and it was as if she were finally thawing. The tears that had been frozen burst forth in a torrent, and Kevin didn't try to stop them. He just rubbed her back and kept softly crooning his love.

"I was a fool," Kevin said once Julie grew calmer. "You're the best thing that ever happened to me."

"Nothing's changed," she whispered. "We'll always argue about George. You two are tied together as closely as if you were identical twins."

She knew how painful a permanent rift with his brother would be for him, yet, unless the two men resolved their differences, her own relationship with Kevin would never be complete, either. Putting aside the agony of the past two days, she knew that more than anything else, she loved Kevin. Right or wrong, she loved him. He had become a tightly woven part of the tapestry of her life, and she couldn't let him go.

The prospect of living without him was much more frightening than that of leaving her insecurities behind. She had been hiding from the truth; nearly losing Kevin had brought it all into sharp focus now. Things would never be the same. She needed Kevin Royce.

"I think it's time for a meeting with George. The three of us," she said, her voice firm with new resolve. "Maybe the shock of an invitation to breakfast this morning will jolt the truth out of him."

"No. I don't want him hurting you."

"Only people you care about have that power," Julie said, staring into his deep brown eyes.

"Never again. I won't ever hurt you."

"Kevin, don't make promises that are impossible to keep. Just love me."

Kevin wrapped his arms around her even more tightly and kissed the top of her head. Julie was letting him come back home. She had given him a second chance.

"Call George," she told him.

The last person in the world he wanted to face was his brother, but Kevin knew she was right. He wouldn't be able to concentrate on building a life with Julie until he had confronted George. Win or lose, it would be over, and then they could move forward.

"Are you certain you want to do this?"

"Absolutely," she said firmly. "I won't live with this cloud hanging over us."

"I love you," Kevin told her and closed his eyes in a moment of thanks.

MOST SANE PEOPLE would still be sleeping, but Kevin knew that George would be at the station, filling out the reams of reports generated by tonight's events. He dialed the number and was promptly connected with his brother's extension. Surprisingly, George didn't hang up the phone, scream at him or even question Kevin. The conversation was short and precise.

"Edwards and I will be finished in about an hour," George said. "Let Julie make the coffee."

Kevin was astounded by his brother's reaction.

"Is he coming?" Julie finally asked when her small reserve of patience was depleted.

"In an hour. He asked you to make the coffee. He's always complaining that I make it too strong."

Secretly Julie admitted that she hadn't really expected George would have the courage to come to her apartment; after all, he hadn't even been able to look at her. Had George suffered an uncharacteristic attack of conscience, or was he setting Kevin up so he could launch his assault in private? Either way she would be ready.

When he did arrive, George politely took off his hat, nodded to Julie and followed Kevin into the dining room, but remained standing. Julie smoothed her hands across the slacks she had changed into and waited for one of the two men to speak. After their perfunctory greetings, neither one of them had said a word, and the tension was menacing.

"It looks like it's going to be another lovely day," she said. She glowered at Kevin, prompting him to say something, anything, but all he did was circle the rim of his cup with one finger.

"Do you mind leaving us alone?" George asked her. "My brother and I have some family business to discuss."

"I mind," Kevin said firmly. "I want her to stay."

"This is family business," George repeated doggedly.

"She's family."

George eyed Julie and shrugged in acceptance "What you hear is not for public knowledge?"

Julie clenched her hands and swallowed a dozen acid responses.

"If she had wanted to ruin your reputation, it woul have been very easy," Kevin told his brother. "All Ju lie had to do was tell the truth—something a bit di

erent from the lies you passed around town about
uer."

"I guess I'm not a very good judge of character,"
George conceded. His shoulders sagged, and he nearly
collapsed onto a dining-room chair. "I'm sorry, Julie. I believed my officer without examining the facts.
Good cops don't make that kind of mistake."

Hearing George Royce use her name was surprising, but hearing him apologize was miraculous. Julie
recognized the sincerity in his voice. "Everyone makes
mistakes."

"Lately I seem to botch everything I touch,"
George said and rubbed his forehead.

"You caught Butler and Olsen," Kevin reminded
him.

"Zeus, but you're dense as a slab of marble!"
George exclaimed. "The man tried to bribe me! It
doesn't take much of a brain to nab someone who ad-
mits to the crime before it's committed. There's not a
lot of skill involved in showing up on the right night.
And my own brother thought I would accept a bribe.
What's that say about the faith everyone has in me?"

"Why, George? Where's the money going?" Kevin
asked. "I don't believe any of the stories you've tried
to feed me."

Julie forced herself to take a small gulp of air. She'd
been standing so still, not wanting to distract Kevin or
George, that she had forgotten to breathe.

"It doesn't concern you," George said.

She could feel Kevin tense and rubbed his arm, si-
ently pleading with him not to say anything foolish.
"George," Julie said, "it does concern Kevin. He
didn't want to believe that you were dishonest, but

what choice did he have? You earn enough money t
support yourself and Denise, but you're not wealthy.'

"Support myself and Denise? Have you price
sports cars lately, Julie? Do you know how much a si
dress costs? Hell, I write a check out to the fingerna
lady for over a hundred dollars a month. Then ther
are visits to the tanning parlor, the hair stylist and th
health club."

Finally Kevin recognized the truth. He knew Georg
wasn't exaggerating and turned to look at Julie. Sh
was shocked but not suspicious.

"How long has this been going on?" she inquired

"A couple of years. At first it wasn't too bad
Lately she spends more money in a week than I mak
all month."

"Why didn't you tell me the truth?" Kevin de
manded. "I might have been able to help."

"How would you do that? Denise won't talk t
anybody. She doesn't see anything wrong in what she
doing. She tells me to go to a counselor if I want, bu
she's just fine."

"She can't spend the money if you don't give it t
her," Julie pointed out.

"If I don't, I'll lose her," George said woodenly.

"You've already lost your wife," Kevin said an
caught his brother in an intense stare. "That's not th
woman you married, George."

"Denise needs help," Julie said.

George stood up and slammed his fist against th
wall. "Fine. You make the appointment and get h
there. I'll pay for it and I promise the check will b
good."

Neither Julie nor Kevin said a word.

"News flash, people," George said sarcastically. "Denise doesn't want to change. She likes things just the way they are. Don't you think I've tried to get her to talk to someone? She says I'm the only one with the problem."

No wonder George was angry and hostile, Julie thought. "I hope you don't believe her," she said.

"I don't know what to believe anymore," George mumbled.

"I do," Kevin said. "We need to figure out a way to pay off your debts and put an end to Denise's ridiculous spending. It seems pretty clear."

"I've been trying," George said. "I've been pulling extra duty on the docks in Everett."

Kevin reached for his wallet and pulled out a shiny black business card. "Is this the company you're working for?"

"Yeah. Where'd you get that?" George asked in amazement.

"You dropped it on the floor of my office one day."

"I switched nights with another fellow and didn't want to forget."

Kevin handed George the card and watched his brother look at the hastily scrawled date and time.

"I would have been suspicious, too, Kev," George said. "Don't be too hard on yourself."

"I should have trusted you," Kevin said.

"And I could have been honest with you. It would have eliminated the entire confusion right from the beginning. Put the blame where it belongs—in my lap."

Julie refilled their cups and took her place behind Kevin, her hands back on his shoulders. She was relieved that the two men had settled their differences, and her opinion of George was beginning to change. Before this conversation she would have bet a year's salary that he would never forgive Kevin. Maybe she'd been as wrong about George as he'd been about her.

"Would you like a woman's opinion about Denise?" she asked him. "I have an idea."

"I won't file for divorce," George said defensively.

"Of course not," Julie replied. "It's obvious you're in love with your wife, and I'm sure she loves you. She's very proud of you."

"She is?"

"When she visited my office, she bragged about you." Julie saw a smile replace George's scowl and realized Kevin had been right all along. George was gruff, but hidden underneath his ready bite was a tender man. "Have you ever considered the possibility that subconsciously Denise might be asking you to put the brakes on? Kind of like a small child that throws a tantrum because any attention from mom and dad is better than being ignored?"

"You do work long hours, and Denise is stuck in that big old house all by herself," Kevin added. "Does she ever mention getting a job?"

"Of course not," George said. "My wife doesn't work."

"Maybe she's bored," Julie suggested. "Besides, what's wrong with your wife working? Suppose she came to work for me?"

"You'd do that after everything that's happened?" George asked quietly.

"That's what families are for," Julie told her future brother-in-law.

Kevin jerked back so hard that he nearly tipped the chair over; regaining his balance, he jumped to his feet. He cupped Julie's face in his hands and stared into her eyes. "Are you sure? Because once you make this commitment, I'm never going to let you go."

"Promises, promises, promises," Julie said gently.

She wished they were alone to discuss the matter in private, but she could tell from the dangerous twinkle in his eyes that Kevin didn't have any type of conversation in mind once George left. *Why do I want to object?* she asked herself and grinned jubilantly. Kevin always did communicate better with his body.

"Did I miss something?" George inquired.

"Julie and I are getting married."

They both saw the perplexed look on George's face and smiled at one another.

"I think it's about time for me to leave," George said, adjusting his uniform belt and service revolver as he stood. "Are you certain you want Denise working for you?"

"Only if she agrees," Julie said. "Have her call me."

"We're not through discussing this yet, Kev," George went on, "but I'm ready to fall asleep. After Denise and I have a chance to talk, I'll call you."

Kevin nodded.

"Julie," George said and reached for her hand, "I don't know why you would even consider speaking to me, much less helping me, but I'm grateful you're not as mule-headed as the rest of the Royces. Thank you and welcome to the family. If he doesn't treat you right, come down to the station. This time I'll listen."

She leaned forward and gave George a quick hug. "It'll work out. You're not alone anymore."

There was silence, and Julie watched George slowly walk across the room. He stopped, plucked a rose from one of the vases she had filled and turned around, holding the flower in the air. "Think they'd work for me as well as they did for you, Kev?" he inquired and winked.

Tears were choking her, and Julie spotted a sheen in George's eyes, too. As soon as the front door closed, she turned back to Kevin and nestled her head upon his chest.

"I love you, J.B.," Kevin said and buried his face in her hair.

"Again," she whispered. "Say it again."

"I love you, Julie Bennett." He slipped his hands underneath the loose blouse she was wearing and stroked her narrow back.

"Aren't you tired?" she asked and playfully nipped his earlobe.

Her lips sent an electrifying message through his body, banishing every trace of fatigue. Kevin scooted his fingers past the waistband of her slacks and touched silky fabric beneath, sliding his fingers back and forth while his mouth voraciously covered hers.

Julie accepted the expression of urgency. He needed her as much as she needed him, and Kevin would never let her go. She was safe. She was finally home.

"Let's go to bed," she suggested.

He saw that her cheeks were flushed and heard the huskiness in her voice. "You're addictive."

"I hope so," Julie murmured and started to pull him down the hallway. "All my life I've wondered what love really means. You're my answer."

She stared at him, storing the way he looked in her special cache of memories. He stared back at her.

Finally she asked, "Why are you looking at me like that?"

"I was waiting for you to disappear. This has to be a dream."

"Then don't ever wake me," Julie said and stepped into his arms.

"GET AWAY FROM IT ALL" SWEEPSTAKES

HERE'S HOW THE SWEEPSTAKES WORKS

NO PURCHASE NECESSARY

To enter each drawing, complete the appropriate Official Entry Form or a 3" by 5" index card by hand-printing your name, address and phone number and the trip destination that the entry is being submitted for (i.e., Caneel Bay, Canyon Ranch or London and the English Countryside) and mailing it to: Get Away From It All Sweepstakes, P.O. Box 1397, Buffalo, New York 14269-1397.

No responsibility is assumed for lost, late or misdirected mail. Entries must be sent separately with first class postage affixed, and be received by: 4/15/92 for the Caneel Bay Vacation Drawing, 5/15/92 for the Canyon Ranch Vacation Drawing and 6/15/92 for the London and the English Countryside Vacation Drawing. Sweepstakes is open to residents of the U.S. (except Puerto Rico) and Canada, 21 years of age or older as of 5/31/92.

For complete rules send a self-addressed, stamped (WA residents need not affix return postage) envelope to: Get Away From It All Sweepstakes, P.O. Box 4892, Blair, NE 68009.

© 1992 HARLEQUIN ENTERPRISES LTD.   SWP-RLS

"GET AWAY FROM IT ALL" SWEEPSTAKES

HERE'S HOW THE SWEEPSTAKES WORKS

NO PURCHASE NECESSARY

To enter each drawing, complete the appropriate Official Entry Form or a 3" by 5" index card by hand-printing your name, address and phone number and the trip destination that the entry is being submitted for (i.e., Caneel Bay, Canyon Ranch or London and the English Countryside) and mailing it to: Get Away From It All Sweepstakes, P.O. Box 1397, Buffalo, New York 14269-1397.

No responsibility is assumed for lost, late or misdirected mail. Entries must be sent separately with first class postage affixed, and be received by: 4/15/92 for the Caneel Bay Vacation Drawing, 5/15/92 for the Canyon Ranch Vacation Drawing and 6/15/92 for the London and the English Countryside Vacation Drawing. Sweepstakes is open to residents of the U.S. (except Puerto Rico) and Canada, 21 years of age or older as of 5/31/92.

For complete rules send a self-addressed, stamped (WA residents need not affix return postage) envelope to: Get Away From It All Sweepstakes, P.O. Box 4892, Blair, NE 68009.

© 1992 HARLEQUIN ENTERPRISES LTD.   SWP-RLS

"GET AWAY FROM IT ALL"

Brand-new Subscribers-Only Sweepstakes

OFFICIAL ENTRY FORM

This entry must be received by: May 15, 1992
This month's winner will be notified by: May 31, 1992
Trip must be taken between: June 30, 1992—June 30, 1993

YES, I want to win the Canyon Ranch vacation for two. I understand the prize includes round-trip airfare and the two additional prizes revealed in the BONUS PRIZES insert.

Name _____

Address _____

City _____

State/Prov._____ Zip/Postal Code_____

Daytime phone number _____
(Area Code)

Return entries with invoice in envelope provided. Each book in this shipment has two entry coupons — and the more coupons you enter, the better your chances of winning!
© 1992 HARLEQUIN ENTERPRISES LTD.   2M-CPN

"GET AWAY FROM IT ALL"

Brand-new Subscribers-Only Sweepstakes

OFFICIAL ENTRY FORM

This entry must be received by: May 15, 1992
This month's winner will be notified by: May 31, 1992
Trip must be taken between: June 30, 1992—June 30, 1993

YES, I want to win the Canyon Ranch vacation for two. I understand the prize includes round-trip airfare and the two additional prizes revealed in the BONUS PRIZES insert.

Name _____

Address _____

City _____

State/Prov._____ Zip/Postal Code_____

Daytime phone number _____
(Area Code)

Return entries with invoice in envelope provided. Each book in this shipment has two entry coupons — and the more coupons you enter, the better your chances of winning!
© 1992 HARLEQUIN ENTERPRISES LTD.   2M-CPN